The Best of Gival Press Short Stories

Edited by Robert L. Giron

Arlington, Virginia

Published by Gival Press, an imprint of Gival Press, LLC.

For information please write:
Gival Press, LLC
P. O. Box 3812
Arlington, VA 22203
www.givalpress.com

First edition
ISBN: 978-1-928589-95-2
eISBN: 978-1-928589-96-9
Library of Congress Control Number: 2015908260

Cover art: © Paul Maguire | Dreamstime.com.
Design by Ken Schellenberg.

Acknowledgments

Each story was previously published on the Gival Press website.

Progressive Linkage Copyright © 2015 by Steven J. Cahill.
For All the Obvious Reasons Copyright © 2014 by Lynn Stegner.
Void Copyright © 2013 by Karenmary Penn.
The Music She Will Never Hear Copyright © 2012 by Kristin FitzPatrick.
Fat Tails Copyright © 2011 by Daniel Degnan.
I-95, Southbound Copyright © 2010 by Perry Glasser.
Water Copyright © 2009 by Tim Johnston.
Better Terms Copyright © 2008 by Mark Wisniewski.
Harvest Cycle Copyright © 2007 by Marie Holmes.
On the Verge Copyright © 2006 by Tim Mullaney.
Legacy Copyright © 2005 by Iqbal Pittalwala.

Contents

Introduction

This anthology of award-winning stories represents eleven years of fiction written by eleven excellent writers who have won the Gival Press Short Story Award since it was established in 2004. In keeping with our tradition at Gival Press, the previous winner of the contest in turn chose the next winner from a collection of stories that were read anonymously, as I have always believed that the text needs to stand on its own merit and these stories do that with a skill that seems easy at first read.

As you this read these award-wining stories, we begin with Tim Johnston's story "Water" which takes us on a journey of stories that deal with the complexities in one's everyday life which in this case can lead to tragedy.

"Water" was much the best of the ten entries I read, and it is one of the most developed and loaded short stories I have read period. There is complexity here—of character, emotion, plot, history, and overall vision—and, yes, such complexity might challenge some readers, but in this story it pays off with that grand sense of having experienced the upshot of a stranger's fully lived life. Motherhood, guilt, sweetness, crime, marital love, denial, friendship, hope, brotherhood, death, rejuvenation, legality, and the claustrophobia many folks must suffer after dogged endurance in a small town: how can all of this fit into a single piece of short fiction? Yet all of it does, threatening to sweep even the cynical reader into this victorious narrative, which by turns flows as tenderly and powerfully—and as naturally toward tragedy—as can water itself.

—Mark Wisniewski

Next, we move on to a revelation of the moment that can stun in Perry Glasser's "I-95, Southbound."

In a field of strong contenders, "I-95, Southbound" prevailed because in addition to its incredible fineness of language, its mastery of point-of-view, and its pitch-perfect voice, it simply knocked me out of my chair with a great wallop of surprise. I don't mean a surprise twist in plot or any kind of artificial trick; I mean the story delivers a moment of revelation, of truth, so exquisitely timed and rendered that it plunges the reader into deepest empathy and sends him reeling back through the story, back through time, along with the protagonist. There are, as one would expect in fiction of this caliber, signposts to this powerful moment along the route, but they are embedded so artfully in the narrative as to only seem like signposts on a second trip—which "I-95, Southbound," beautiful and hilarious and terrifying, certainly merits, and rewards.

—Tim Johnston

Life would not be life without betrayal as eloquently portrayed by Karen-mary Penn in "Void."

Iris's husband, Cropper, has just come home with a grenade. He enters their bedroom each night followed by a 'company of ghosts' since he returned from war, and he talks to them more in his sleep than he talks to Iris all day. His keen sensitivity for betrayal tells him she's having an affair just as she's working up the nerve to betray him with Frank, a man who can make her eyes absorb light (as an iris should) rather than just reflecting it.

As a funeral home aesthetician, it's fitting that with so much death weighing Iris down at work and at home, she'll do anything to bring out all the beauty and light she can find around her. She begins the story 'sure that the body [has] its own wisdom,' and yet, she's become rather unsure about Cropper, whose chest is covered by a 'mystery scar' he won't explain. Iris prefers the lighthearted 'company of sunnier emotions,' but the dark grenade's heft and its 'big, unholy bang' are hard to resist. By her third run-in with Frank, he is grieving his brother's death and Iris is 'a flame atop a moving candle,' ready to resort to bodily wisdom in order to lighten up both of them.

"Void" is a luminous and nuanced portrait of a wife's loneliness in the wake of a husband's experience that she knows she will never understand. Iris also wrestles with her inability to help solve the heaviest, darkest troubles of the world, but it's hard to find a ray of light in these faraway wars and tragedies when she sees evidence of them in Cropper's eyes, which are 'eddies of despair.' Although she enjoys working in the funeral home, she's run out of ways to talk survivors like Cropper and Frank through their losses. Now Iris faces the temptation to cross into the darkness and destroy everything— Cropper, Frank, and the pain they absorb or reflect, as well as her marriage and herself—by pulling her own kind of pin. The story's use of light and darkness—especially in subtle moments when Iris stargazes with Cropper, when she powders up the discolored hands of a corpse with cotton under his eyelids, and when soft lighting does not calm her fear of explosions—provides a contrast of hope and despair, with Iris on the line between them.

—Kristin FitzPatrick

Marie Holmes' story "Harvest Cycle" entices us into the mysterious and ambiguous motivations that drive our impulses.

Meticulously observed, deftly constructed, lucidly written, "Harvest Cycle" is a story whose merits cannot easily be summed up or pinned down. It is that rare kind of story which does not itself sum up or pin down its subject matter, but artfully charts the territory of ambiguous emotions, mysterious motivations, and contradictory impulses. In beautifully calibrated prose, Marie Holmes crafts characters both recognizable and idiosyncratic, and spins a compelling plot which unfolds gracefully. "Harvest Cycle" is about, among other things, the power of a good story. Holmes has written a powerfully good one, which illuminates as well as entertains.

—Tim Mullaney

From ambiguous motivations and hidden lives we travel to the secrets of one's family in Iqbal Pittalwala's "Legacy." Certainly the June 26, 2015 Supreme Court decision granting marital rights to all regardless of one's orientation would have had an effect on these characters but our deep secrets may still go on in light of strong cultural and religious traditions.

Relationships always present a challenge and "The Music She Will Never Hear" by Kristin FitzPatrick takes us into the psyche of Jace as he rustles with is partner who can't feel the music that liberates.

Dr. Sims, a history professor and expert in the mining era, employs Jace, a geology student, drummer, and Grateful Dead and Phish aficionado, as his guide on a trip to an abandoned mineshaft.

As the pair descends into the mine, into distant history, Jace explores his more recent past. He wrestles with his relationships, the 'complex bonds' of his life: reflections on his absent father, memories of his dead mother, and recognition that the situation with his Uncle Brad and Brad's girlfriend, Keiko, has reached a critical juncture.

When their excursion takes an unexpected turn, Jace realizes he can no longer hide behind his music. Brad is returning, Keiko has not been well—life is on the line.

"The Music She Will Never Hear" is a tightly composed, original exploration of a young man's experience of death, life, love, and the liberating power of music. Imprints of pressure and time— the ponderous formation of white mountains and moonstones, thunderous strikes on a drum, arduous pumps to restart a heart— provide the story's rhythm, enhance its specific gravity, infusing it with a musicality that is a pleasure to hear.

—Daniel Degnan

In "On the Verge" by Tim Mullaney we enter the world of a young man as he deals with aspirations and the frustrations of loneliness.

In fluid and inviting prose, "On the Verge" quietly captures a young man's desires and loneliness, and records with honesty his observations of, and engagement with, a world just slightly out of his reach. The author's artful attempt at translating experience into words, his efficient and evocative use of language, the success with which he portrays young people, and the sound architecture of his fiction ensure that "On the Verge" stays alive in the mind long after the reader has emerged from the text—the mark of strong and beautiful writing.

— Iqbal Pittalwala

In "Progressive Linkage" Steven J. Cahill carries us through a modern sibling rivalry which many of us might relate to with echoes of Cain and Abel.

The characters in "Progressive Linkage" may know their way around a souped-up Chevy but Steve Cahill, the story's author, knows his way around the terra infirma of the human heart. What begins as a reasonably healthy sibling rivalry takes a dark turn fueled by misunderstanding, casual intent, and the small, almost-sins of carelessness. Cahill plays the language like the instrument it is meant to be, with a driving intensity and exuberance. The extended metaphor that indirectly celebrates the internal combustion engine never once falters, even while on another level it transports the characters into the landscape of callow passion and its unanticipated consequences.

—Lynn Stegner

As we read on, Daniel Degnan leads us into the lives of Billy and Meg in "Fat Tails" and as we delve in we can reflect on how one calculates decisions and lives a difficult life.

In this long short story, the reader is exposed to what at first seems like bewildering accumulating details about local color. The details are in fact meaningful images. As the story progresses, those details become resonant with meaning and offer us insight into the lives of the characters as well as ourselves. None of it is random details. All go toward a central thematic question: How well can we calculate the odds for the decisions of our lives?

Billy, a doctoral candidate with special expertise in game theory and decision-making, is in love with Meg. Meg is the center of a small family that makes its living as salmon fishermen in Alaska.

But Alaska is far from the soft sand and beaches of Santa Cruz, California. What Billy imagined was to have been a romantic summer of fishing and meeting Meg's family turns into a time that engages him, and us, in ongoing uncertainty and drama. Meg's family is dysfunctional in ways that make her father and brother codependent. Whether she will be able to break free of family entanglements to make a life of her own with Billy is at issue.

Removing salmon entangled in barbed nets is dangerous, bloody business; fat tail salmons in nets look like bell curves on graph paper; flesh of all sorts get gutted in the wilderness; poker is a pastime of mathematical calculations; romance for Billy and Meg is quick, furtive and always colored by a twinge of guilt in the close quarters of her family's isolated Alaskan camp.

The threads of these rich images become more tightly tangled with each page. The skilled hand of an artist moves subtly behind the rendered details that seem at once to be 'merely' about the lives of the characters, but plainly are threaded, complex metaphors for difficult human relationships. The story draws us to a powerfully surprising, yet inevitable, ending, achieved as much by plot as by intertwined images. When there are Jokers in the deck, all the mathematical certainties of decision-making expertise are insufficient to calculate matters of the heart.

—Perry Glasser

Mark Wisniewski a compelling author has the ability to limn how we struggle to connect with others and "Better Terms" delivers.

"Better Terms" is propelled by the strength of its narrator's voice: contradictory, confused, and entirely believable. With a poignant and compelling mix of self-pity, disillusionment, self-deprecation and disbelief, the narrator takes the reader through what begins as a seemingly regular day in his life. The story earns the emotional impact of its final, kaleidoscopic scenes through a series of interactions between characters who refuse to deny their complexities. In the end, it is not the eccentricity of these characters that keeps the reader invested in their story—it is their beautifully depicted and very human struggle to connect with one another.

—Marie Holmes

The final story in this collection is "For All the Obvious Reasons" by Lynn Stegner. While we have been intrigued by the characters in these stories, in this story Stegner shows us the complexities we search for in fiction as a means to better understand ourselves. Because as we know too well, what relationship doesn't have complexness at its core?

Early on in "For All the Obvious Reasons," you realize you're in a very capable writer's hands. There is wit and wisdom, and plenty of beautiful language in Lynn Stegner's story.

Not long into the protagonist Charlotte's trip into the 'veined interior of British Columbia' with her seemingly perfect husband Harry, and their Indian guide, you get the creeping sense that her newlywed life with him— in which every day is a 'holiday morning surprise' —has some cracks.

There are ominous hints that something terrible has come to pass for young Charlotte. Stegner skillfully and patiently layers in glimpses of darkness and pain, giving the reader a deeper understanding of Charlotte. The strong narrative pulls the reader into a marriage in trouble, and deeper down into an inner bleakness at this story's center.

A good short story should leave you wanting more, and Lynn Stegner's story certainly does that.

—Karenmary Penn

In short, these stories will hold your attention because they are vividly cast and the characters are so real you are bound to identify with them on different levels, even if you may not be walking in their footsteps.

Read for your pleasure and diversion or read as one who is learning the craft of writing stories that will stick to readers like tar on the soles of their shoes during a hot summer day, as the characters in these stories will inhabit your imagination for weeks to come. In either case, you will not be disappointed.

—RLG

Water

by Tim Johnston

WINNER OF THE 2008 GIVAL PRESS SHORT STORY AWARD

She was a good sleeper, a dependable sleeper, but that night Charlotte woke up with her heart whumping, like a young mother. There had been something.

She lay there in the dark, not breathing. At one window the drapes were shaped by faint light from the street, but at the other there was nothing, no light from the neighbors, no moonlight, and the effect was briefly frightening, as if the wall had fallen away into space, or a black sea.

She drew the alarm clock into focus: 1:36. She had a son who would stay out late, but when he came home he was like a cat, and if she heard him at all it was because she had gotten up to use the washroom, pausing by his door just long enough to hear him clicking at the computer in there, or humming to the iPod, or shhshing Ginny Simms, his girl.

She heard none of this now, nothing at all but the heat pumping invisibly, bloodlike, in the walls of the house. This was late October, two nights before Halloween, the first truly cold night of the season.

She closed her eyes and the dream she'd been having eddied back to center—a dream of hands, the feel of them, the smell of them; muscle and tendon, palm and finger. Her body, under the bedding, still hummed. She breathed, she slowed, she drifted down.

And heard it: Water.

Water was running in the pipes somewhere. Not the shower, or the toilet, or the kitchen sink: this was the distinctive 1-inch-pipe gush you heard when the boys were washing the truck, or the dog, or filling the plastic pool for the neighbor kids. She had been married to a plumber and she knew about pipes.

She got into her robe and went down the hall, past the boys' rooms— John's door open, no John; Dukie's door shut but him in there, a mound of sleep she could feel like a pulse—and down the stairs to the kitchen, where the noise was loudest.

John's truck was in the window over the sink, lit up by the worklight he used at night, a light usually manned by Dukie but now positioned somewhere out of view, like John. Two yellow smiley faces stared in at her, plastic hoods for the foglights, or whatever they were, he'd mounted on the cab. Her comment on the hoods—A bit cheesy, John—was still amusing him, apparently, when he and Dukie carved the identical inane faces into their pumpkins. She'd rolled her eyes but was secretly moved: they'd never done twins before.

Charlotte held her robe to her chest and leaned over the sink. She saw the truck's fender, the tire, a thin disk of water leaching into the gravel, and just then the spigot gave a squeal and the water stopped running and a face popped up before her so suddenly her hands flew up. John saw the movement, then saw her, and Charlotte's heart surged, as if he were hurt, as if he were washing out some great wound she couldn't see. In the next moment she heard the dog, Wyatt, shaking his hide, rattling his tags, and she understood: John would let the dog out in the park, and it would find some other animal's filth, or carcass, to roll in, and later it would stand there grinning under the hose.

The worklight snapped off and in they came, Wyatt shoving past to dive face-first into her carpet, driving his upper body along with his hind legs, first one side, then the other, grunting in ecstasy.

"Wonderful," Charlotte said, and John said, "I'll get a towel," but then just stood there.

"Did you get it all off?" she asked, and he flinched, as if she'd shouted.

"—What?" he said.

Charlotte gestured at the dog. "Did you get it all off?"

John looked at the dog but he wasn't really looking, she could tell; he was thinking of something else altogether. A year out of high school and there were bars he could get into, him and Mike Simms, and some mornings she'd smell the smoke on him like he'd slept in an ashtray. Other mornings she'd smell strawberries and know that Ginny Simms, Mike's younger sister, had been in the house. Charlotte did not approve of such things, of course—but the next thing you knew John was under the sink with his tools, or throwing the football to his brother, or fixing some neighbor kid's bike. A good boy, at the end of the day. A good son.

"I got it all," John said at last, and he turned for the stairs.

Charlotte switched off the lamp and followed.

"Now what are you doing?" she asked, at his door.

He went on shoving clothes into his duffle.

"Gonna go see Cousin Jer for the weekend," he said. "Shoot some birds."

"John," she said. "It's almost two in the morning."

He didn't reply.

"Does he even know you're coming?"

Of course he did, he told her—it was all set up: he'd be at Jer's in an hour, they'd sleep late and then head up to Uncle Martin's cabin. Back Sunday night.

Charlotte was confused and strangely heated, as if she'd done something humiliating.

"And all this is fine with—your boss?" she said, and John paused, they both did, as the idea of Bud Steadman came into the room: his smell of earth and copper, a certain kind of deodorant. His big good face. His hands.

Charlotte saw something on the switch plate, a dark fingerprint, and began to rub it. There'd been a few men over the years but there had been none for several years, and at forty-three, with two grown sons, she'd been ready to believe that all of that was over for her. But it wasn't, not quite. Bud had a nineteen-year-old daughter at home, Caroline, who didn't get along with her mother—or any older woman, so far as Charlotte could see—and the going was slow. But it was going. When the phone rang these days Charlotte's heart jumped. New bras and panties bloomed in her bureau. She'd lost weight.

The only reason John was out late tonight, with work in the morning, was because she and Bud had made plans for tomorrow night—Friday night, a date—and John had agreed to stay home with his brother.

"I'll call Bud in the morning," he now said. "Mike will cover for me."

"And me?" Charlotte all but yelped, swatting him lightly. "We had a deal!"

He shrank from her.

"You can still go out, Ma. I'll take Big Man with me."

"Oh, you will, will you? Hunting?" She stared at him, waiting for one of the Duke's howls to fill his head; most recently, it had been the torn heap of rabbit at Wyatt's feet. A smashed jack-o'-lantern could do the job.

"You got a point," John said.

A moment passed. The dog was on the bed, on its back, twisting and snorting as if in agony.

Charlotte shook her head. Uff da! her grandmother would say, venting the woe from her old Norwegian heart. The same pressure would build in Charlotte but she resisted, remembering the farm in Minnesota: Granddad pulling her off some piece of machinery with a swat; Grammy Moore whacking the neck of a chicken—the jetting blood, the headless, frantic life that didn't want to end. Nothing in this life comes easy, Charlotte had been told, and though it turned out to be true, she'd never said the same to her own children, in case it was the saying so that made it so.

She shook her head, she sighed. She would see Bud Steadman in the morning, at the Plumbing & Supply. A change of plans, she'd say. Home-cooked dinner instead. She'd get Dukie to turn in early. Like her, that boy was a sleeper.

But Bud Steadman wasn't at the Plumbing & Supply in the morning, his van wasn't there, and Charlotte followed the sullen Dukie into the store with something childish, something ridiculous and acute jabbing at her heart.

"Big Man!" Mike Simms called as they came in, and the Duke raised his hand for a gustoless high-five, then disappeared into the back, stranding Charlotte with no good-bye. It was her fault John had gone off to the cabin without him, was the message.

She stood there a moment amongst the pipes and fittings. The smell of the place was a smell she loved: pipe dope and PVC glue and sweated copper and men. She remembered the summer when Bud and Raymond had bought the building and began fixing it up. Sawdust in the nostrils, freckles of paint on all their faces. Charlotte and Meredith had fallen for each other like schoolgirls, the kind of gushy, overnight friendship men don't even try to understand. They both got pregnant the same month, and then, five months later, when Charlotte and Raymond learned there was trouble with the twins—one healthy, one not; they could terminate one to save one, or risk losing both—it was Meredith and Bud who loaned them money for more tests, a second opinion, the monitoring that saved John's life. He had his heart murmur, but he'd grown strong as a lion. And the Duke, well, the Duke was the Duke... No one had seen that coming.

Six years later, Raymond was dead. The cancer they'd been fighting in one lung had jumped to the other like a clever rat. Charlotte had to give up the business to keep the house. She and Meredith's friendship began to falter, and she realized that after all it was the men, not the women, who kept the two families close. She heard through other friends about Meredith's miscarries, but only called after the first. Both had been boys, she heard.

Then, when her own sons were sixteen, here came Bud again, with jobs: custodial duties for Dukie and the secrets of the trade for John. Bud had never gotten around to changing the Steadman-Moore sign on the side of the building, and a hyphen that had once said family to Charlotte, then loss (a minus sign), then another lifetime, suddenly said family again.

Now Charlotte asked Mike Simms if he knew when Bud would be back, and the boy replied cheerfully, "Can't say, Mizz Moore. He ain't been in yet."

"Oh," she said, puzzled—actually bothered by this answer.

"Anything I can help you with, Mizz Moore?"

And there it was: Mike Simms had opened up the store. Bud had given him keys.

She'd thought John was the only one.

***

In her car again, driving across town to the mall where she works. A brilliant, stunning blue day in October. Cars moving along in their lanes, catching the light. On the radio two women are talking in quiet tones: one has written a book about her childhood, her abusive drunken father, but it's the women's voices, more than the subject, that takes Charlotte back in time, to a night when she felt friendship land on her like a blow. They had all been working on the store and now she and Meredith sat alone on the deck with the wine. If they were pregnant, they didn't yet know it. The bellies of insects pulsed green in the dusk. Bud had taken Raymond to the basement to talk about turning it into something called a game room. The women could hear the low, manly voices down there.

When she was sixteen, Meredith said, refilling Charlotte's glass, then her own, she had slept with a teacher at her high school.

Charlotte picked up her glass. Took a sip. In her stomach she felt as if a notorious man had just grinned at her.

What kind? she asked. Of teacher.

Art. Mr. Beckman. Mr. B. He thought Meredith had talent. She thought he was a fairy. Everyone did. He passed her one day in his car, an Oldsmobile. She was wearing her best skirt.

Meredith was quite a bit smaller than Charlotte, tiny in fact, with the most extraordinary skin. At sixteen, Charlotte could not even imagine.

They talked about Dali, Meredith said. They parked. He had a mustache that tickled. He wanted to see her again. He stood behind her in class, as she drew. He began slipping her these little drawings—very good, very dirty. He was in an artistic fever, he said into her ear. She showed the drawings to just one person, her best friend, but that was enough. A substitute teacher came to Mr. B.'s art room one day, and stayed. The school was talking. Meredith's father heard it at the plant from some other kid's father, came home and slapped the living crap out of her.

My God, Meredith. Charlotte put her fingers on her friend's cool forearm.

Her dad had these brothers, Meredith continued after a moment in the same quiet, factual tone. Five of them. One, Uncle Donny, was a piece of work. In and out of jail, drunk at Christmas, fuck this and fuck that. About a month after the Mr. B. scandal, Uncle Donny came by the house. He was there just a minute, barely said hello, and two days later they found Mr. B. walking along the interstate. His head was cracked. His teeth were gone. All his fingers were broken.

Laughter came to them from the house, from the basement, making them both turn to stare. Meredith raised her glass again and Charlotte heard it clink lightly against her teeth.

She waited for the cops to come, Meredith said. She stopped eating. She typed a letter at school and sent it anonymously. No one ever came. No one ever did. Mr. B. was in the hospital a long time but he couldn't recognize you, they said, so what was the point of going up there? His parents came and took him away, finally, like a child.

My God, Meredith, Charlotte said again. She could barely see her friend in the dark. Her heart was beating with pity and love. After a while she said, What do you do with that?

There was no reply, a long, unnatural soundlessness, a black well of listening. Fireflies like little bombs going off at a great distance. Men coming up the stairs, loud and huge. Meredith's eyes flashed and she said, You bury it, Charlotte.

***

The morning passed. Charlotte in the back room tagging sweaters amidst tinny bursts of ring tone from the jackets and purses of the salesgirls. At ten o'clock she walked to the far end of the mall, all the way to the restrooms and the building's—maybe the world's—last payphone. (The little cellphone John and Dukie had given her for her birthday—"Look, it takes pictures!"—sat dead in a kitchen drawer, next to the dead camera.) She intended to call Bud, tell him the new plan, but at the last moment she dialed John's cellphone instead, got his voicemail.

"John, here. You know what to do."

She asked him to leave her a message at home, just to say he arrived at Cousin Jer's OK, then she hung up and began the long walk back to work. She would call Bud later, at her lunch break. It was Friday, and they had a date.

Back at the store, something had happened. Alicia stood alone on the sales floor, thin arms folded over her thin stomach. Ten years younger than Charlotte, she would talk about things like chakras and third eyes and orgasms.

Now she came from behind the register as if Charlotte were some girl with an Anne Klein blouse stuffed up her shirt. In the door of the back room Charlotte saw two salesgirls with phones to their ears, one listening, open-mouthed, the other moving her lips in a ceaseless rapid-fire.

"There's been an accident," said her boss, and the store rolled and Charlotte pitched backwards, sickly, into a scene on the highway, John's truck inverted on the shoulder, wheels to the sky, black smoke spiraling—

"No, no," Alicia said quickly, "not that, not one of yours. It's Caroline," she said. "Bud Steadman's girl," she said. "They found her this morning in the river."

***

The story was going around, cellphone to cellphone: Caroline had been walking home from her boyfriend's. No, she was walking home from the bars. She was alone; she was not alone. She'd been drinking. She was high. The girl had problems—she'd lost her license to a DUI the year before, that much was a fact. She was cutting through the park, along the river, and had fallen in. Jumped in. Been pushed in. She'd been there all night. Someone crossing the bridge had seen her, wallowing against the concrete piling below like drift-wood.

Charlotte was in her car again, driving across town. A brilliant, cold blue day. On the sidewalk a young woman with long black hair drew a kite-tail of small children behind her. A man in tights ran by them, smiling. The sun, the blazing trees, the silvered bend of river, all exactly as it should be on a day in October, a pristine day. She tried to picture it: Caroline Steadman, this girl she'd known since birth, floating in the water with the branches. But all Charlotte saw clearly was the blouse, the one she'd given the girl on her nineteenth birthday, Bud looking on uneasily: a smart, semi-sheer blouse she had spent too much on, even with her discount, all night in the river under the black sky, the fabric wetted to skin except where air slipped in, raising white, tremulous welts on the water.

***

"Charlotte—"

He was startled, confused to see her. His pale face, the bruised unfocus-sing eyes, swept away anything she might've been ready to say.

"I'm sorry," she said, "I tried to call first..." Three times, from the store—three times got his service, three times hung up. What was the message you left for this? Go, Alicia said finally. He's going to need you.

But he was not asking her in, or even letting go of the storm door so she could put her arms around him. She wasn't surprised, she told herself, certainly not hurt—it had nothing to do with her. He had to handle things his own way, in his own time.

"I'm so sorry, Bud," she said into those eyes.

"They took me to her," he said. "The police. To make sure."

"Oh, Bud. By yourself?"

He didn't answer, he seemed to be listening, and she listened too: someone else was in the house, on the phone. A voice of calm, male authority. She glanced at the extra car in the drive, a black gleaming Lexus.

"Someone's with you?"

"Duncan."

"That's good. That's good, Bud." His brother Duncan, she remembered, was some kind of lawyer for the state. She'd met him once and had been struck by the cleanliness of his fingernails.

"Can I do anything, Bud, is there anything I can do?"

He caught her eyes, fleetingly, possibly by accident. He said, "Meredith's on her way. Her sister's driving her down. I thought it was them when you knocked."

Charlotte nodded, but couldn't speak. She hadn't seen Meredith in years, not since before the divorce. She remembered that night on the deck, with the wine, when her heart had filled with pity and love. They were going to be friends forever, old ladies, arm in arm in Mexico, Europe, after the husbands were gone. When the first crack in their friendship appeared, not long after Raymond's death, it was that story again, that secret—Mr. B.—that somehow widened the crack and made it permanent.

"They think now maybe she didn't just drown," Bud said abruptly.

"They—?" said Charlotte.

"The police." He dug at the black and gray whiskers on his face. "They think someone hit her with a car."

"My God." Charlotte had the sensation of dropping through space, her stomach rising.

"They think this person didn't see her maybe," Bud said. "Then tried to cover it up by pushing her in the river. Can't be sure," Bud said, "but it looks like she was still alive, then. When they pushed her in. Looks like she was still breathing."

***

"Mama," Dukie said when she came in, "the police men was here. One man and one girl police man." He was at the plate glass window, spritzing away smears and fingerprints. Mike Simms sat behind the counter, unsmiling. Charlotte looked at him and he nodded.

"They're going around talking to people," he said. "Anyone who mighta seen her last night."

Charlotte nodded, too. She thought a moment. She tried to think. She had meant to ask Mike about John, if they'd been together last night, but now she didn't want to look at him again. She couldn't seem to breathe.

"Dukie, get your jacket," she said, lifting her purse to dig in it, though her keys were already in her hand.

"Gotta do windows, Mama."

"Tomorrow, Dukie. Today's a short day."

At home she was barely in the door, had barely glanced at the answering machine—no blinking red light, nothing—before she saw the car outside, in the street. A plain blue sedan parked as if it had been there all day, when she knew it hadn't been there just seconds ago. Two men in ties and jackets were coming toward the house. She met them at the door, and the taller of the two, calling himself Detective Carson, watched her face as he made sure Charlotte was aware of the unfortunate news regarding...while the other man, Detective Something, brushed past her with his eyes and began tearing the house apart.

They were trying to learn as much as they could about the night before, this Carson was explaining. They understood that her son John had been at the bar where Caroline was last seen alive.

Charlotte wasn't sure if this was a question, but she said she couldn't say about that, she didn't know where he'd been.

The other man, chewing gum, looked and sounded as if his mouth had been invaded by some small creature.

After a moment—after Carson asked—she let them in.

*

There wasn't much she could tell them, as there wasn't much she knew, and just a few minutes after they left she had trouble remembering their names, their faces, trouble believing they were ever there at all. She tried to call John again. Kept trying until she heard, from her brother Martin, calling her, that he was in custody. They'd found him up at the cabin, and there was no trouble.

"In custody—?" Charlotte heard herself say.

"Not arrested," her brother said quickly. "Not charged."

"But in custody," Charlotte said.

There's a gray area, he told her—and he went on reassuring her, but Charlotte's mind was tumbling. She was at the kitchen window, as she had been the night before. Two yellow eyes looking in the window, the twin smiley-faces. Water, she remembered. The dog had rolled in something. She saw her son's face, the gust of white breath when he saw her in the window.

There was nothing out there now. No truck. No son.

In custody.

***

It's dark when tires crunch in the drive, and she quickly turns off the TV. A car door slams, the tires crunch the gravel again, and in walks John. Charlotte is up from the sofa but everything about him says Stop, don't touch me. Dukie comes in and lifts him in a bear hug until John says "Put me down, idiot."

"John," Charlotte says.

He ignores her, going for the stairs.

"Hey, where's Wyatt?" Dukie bellows.

"I had to leave him up there, with Jer."

"Oh, no!" cries Dukie.

"Who brought you home?" Charlotte asks, afraid to hear the answer—

that it was those men, the detectives—and John stops on the stairs.

"Why are you even here, Ma?"

Charlotte stares at him.

"Why aren't you on your date?"

"John——" she says again, with purpose, but then falters. She has a feeling of choking, of drowning. His eyes burn into her a moment, then he turns again, and the two of them, her boys, disappear over the rise of the stairs.

She locks the doors and closes drapes. It crosses her mind to pull the phone line from the wall, and in that instant the phone rings.

It's Martin again, her brother. There's nothing for her to worry about, he says, he's been talking to the lawyer. He spends some time telling her things she hardly hears, something about physical evidence, the phrase "erratic, troubled girl," and Charlotte mechanically takes down the number of the lawyer.

There's a silence, and she asks, "Do you think he knows?"

"Who?" Martin says.

"Bud Steadman. Do you think he knows...about John?"

"You haven't talked to him?"

"Yes, earlier. Briefly. He wasn't—he..." She doesn't finish.

"He's a good man, Char," Martin says. "And he's been good to those boys. But what he's going through right now... Hell, I don't even want to imagine."

***

She waits for the detectives to return, but they don't—not that night, not all day Saturday.

She waits for Bud to call, although she knows that won't happen either, not as long as those cars are parked in his drive—the black Lexus, and now a white Volvo she knows is the car Meredith came down in.

And then it's Sunday night, Halloween. John emerges from his room at last, on his way to Mike Simms' waiting truck, and off they go. Charlotte sits home with the Duke, who sits in his Packers helmet and jersey, ready to dish out candy for kids if any come. None do; not one. It's a bad night for it, a bitter wind blowing, so no wonder.

Later, after Dukie's gone to bed, something sails through the living room window and lands on the carpet. A small stone out of the sky. It's surprising what a clean, small hole it makes, with only a few slender shards to pick up. The pieces are still in her hand when the phone rings.

"Hello?" she says. "Hello—?"

"Hello? Mrs. Moore?"

Mrs. Moore! The blood goes out of her, she steadies herself on the counter. But it isn't him, it isn't Bud. It's his brother, Duncan.

Charlotte manages to give her sympathies, then listens while Duncan explains that Bud isn't going to open the store tomorrow, so the boys should plan on staying home.

"Of course," Charlotte says. She sees the scene over there, at Bud's house: Duncan at the phone and Bud beyond him, heaped in a chair, staring into coffee, Meredith on the sofa, their daughter, their only child, dead.

"But I wonder," she says, "is there any chance—"

"In fact," says the brother, "they should probably plan on staying home until further notice, Mrs. Moore."

After he hangs up, Charlotte keeps the phone to her ear, listening to the strange, enormous silence there, a sound from the windy blacks of space. She stands frozen in it, her chest emptied. There was a day, years ago, when something happened, or nearly happened, between her and Bud Steadman. A gray afternoon, the window panes ticking with bits of ice. She had come out of a bath and felt weak and had sat down on the bed. Before her was the cheval glass that had belonged to her grandmother, her mother, now her. Who would she give the mirror to, this girly keepsake?

Charlotte—?

A man in the house, downstairs. Her heart gave a kick.

His footfall across the living room, and then her name again, lobbed up the stairs. A stair tread creaked and she reached for her robe, but stopped.

Two days ago they had buried Raymond. This afternoon, Bud had picked up the boys and taken them to a movie so Charlotte could sleep. Now they were back.

Charlotte—? he said from around the corner.

Yes, she answered. That was all. He came anyway, into the frame of the door.

Oh— His big face filled with the shock of her there, on the bed. I'm sorry, he said.

She heard kids in the yard, boys and girls, already into some kind of contest. Caroline could be mean but John would keep things fair and good for the Duke.

Brought the boys back, Bud said, not looking away, looking her in the eye. He reached up and worked the flesh under his jaw with a coarse, sandpaper sound. He was a man who was sure before he acted, who didn't operate by guesswork or even intuition, but who held in his head all the hard facts of mechanical things. Over the years there had been moments, yes, when she'd wondered what it would be like to be with him instead of Raymond, to simply switch. Innocent, helpless thoughts such as every woman must have...

He took a step, then came certainly toward her. In the wash of movement she smelled the outdoors, the steely clouds and the wet, moldering leaves. Green buttons rode the flannel wave of his stomach down to his belt. The buckle was a little brass mouth with a little brass tongue. Her heart beat in her breast. She turned to the mirror and the picture there was incredible: this naked, wet-haired woman, this man beside her dressed for cold—the forward cant of his body, the emptiness of his hands.

Charlotte— he said, and in the next instant Caroline's voice, shrill and imperious, penetrated the room like a wind.

Hands off, retard!

Out there, in the cold, John said something low, and silence followed.

Bud's face was crimson. His jaw muscle jumped.

She knows better, by God.

It's all right, Charlotte said.

Nothing else happened. The day was going dark. In the mirror she saw Bud's arm drift toward her shoulder, then beyond it. She saw her robe rise up like a spirit, felt it brush her shuddering skin. In the mirror, as in the flesh, he got the robe over her shoulders and over her breasts without quite touching her.

There is glass in her hand, Charlotte notices, standing at the sink. Slender fragments pressed into her palm, and after a moment she remembers the broken window, the strange little stone. She dumps the glass in the trash and rinses her hand under the faucet. She had wanted to tell him something, that day—something true and unafraid, such as how she'd often felt, her secret thoughts. Caroline's voice had stopped her.

And if it hadn't? If everything had gone just a little bit differently? Meteors, they said, were on the way, right now, crossing billions of years of chance. If Caroline had not spoken and Charlotte had—would things be different? Would Caroline be alive?

It's late, almost midnight. Wind is moaning in a gap somewhere. She begins going around the rooms locking doors, switching off lights. She's halfway up the stairs before she remembers John is still out, but she doesn't go back down to turn on the lamp. In a few weeks, he'll be gone. He'll take off one day while she's at work, leaving just a note saying he's gone down to St. Louis, to work construction with a friend of his. The lawyer will call a few days later looking for him—John's cellphone number no longer works—but it's a social call, mainly, just checking in. John's a good kid, the lawyer will say before hanging up. Charlotte raised a good boy.

Not long after that she will see that Bud Steadman has finally changed the sign on the side of the building—white-washing out the hyphen and everything after—and that's when she'll decide to go, too. Her father still has the farm in Minnesota, where as a girl she learned nothing comes easy. It's a place, a life, she had left behind. But you never do. There's room for her and Dukie and the dog, Wyatt, which John has left behind. The first time she cooks for him, at the old stove, her father weeps.

John will come up for Thanksgiving and Christmas that first year, then just Christmas, then not even that. One day Charlotte will get a card in the mail, two photos inside. Here is her new daughter-in-law, Cheryl; here is her grandson, Grant—the very image of John and Dukie when they were born. But "healthy," John writes, "and normal."

When the dog finally dies—of cancer, like Raymond—Charlotte decides to call her son. She's remembering the day he found the dog, just this bag of bones down by the tracks. He'd fed it some licorice and when he turned to go it latched its jaw onto his calf muscle. Seeing the teeth marks in his skin—the skin unbroken, thank God—Charlotte got up to call the pound, the Board of Health, the police. But John had looked at her, and then at Dukie, who was studiously petting the animal's skull.

This was late November, maybe December. Raymond had not been dead very long.

John kneeled next to his brother and began stroking the dog's ragged spine. You know what they'll do to him, he said quietly, as if to himself.

What? said the Duke. What will they do to him?

Don't, Charlotte said. John, don't...

Well. He had been a good dog, after all. Smart, happy, devoted to John as if he'd never forgotten that piece of licorice, that sudden change of fortune. After John left, leaving him behind with Charlotte and Dukie, he was not the same animal. His heart was broken. Sickness saw an opening.

"What do you want me to do with him, John?" she now asks on the phone, her voice under control. It was the water, she remembers—the sound of water in the pipes. If he had never turned it on she would never have come downstairs. She would never have seen him out there with the hose in his hand, would never have seen the look on his face the moment he knew she was there, the moment he knew he'd been seen.

Of course, if she had not had a date with Bud Steadman—if she had never had feelings for Bud Steadman—John would not have been out at all that night. This is Charlotte's final thought on the matter, again and again, up there in Minnesota.

"What else can you do?" John says at last on the phone, in the voice of an older man, a husband, a father. "You bury him, Ma."

I-95, Southbound

by Perry Glasser

WINNER OF THE 2009 GIVAL PRESS SHORT STORY AWARD

The day starts bad, then gets worse.

Who should be surprised?

Not yet 7:00 AM, too far from home, Geist sets his sole piece of luggage into the trunk of his red Toyota. The pink valise and a son are all that remain of his marriage to Linda. Geist travels too little to warrant buying anything new; besides, the silver duct tape holding closed the vinyl wound that an airline baggage handler "accidentally" slashed gives it a masculine look. Geist closes the motel door, and almost as an accident he glances at his front tires.

They are low.

Now what the hell is that about? They were repaired only yesterday.

Geist is one careful man. He plans. He plans a lot. Geist owns two of everything that matters. In his basement, on industrial strength metal racks well off the floor, he stocks toothpaste, tomato sauce, trash bags and a shopping cart's worth of other nonperishables. He stores gallons of water against the day the mains go to hell. Geist pays his bills as they arrive. His dishes never soak in the sink.

Look, alone, there is no other way to live. There is no rest; you plan. You stay on top of things. You do for yourself, because if you don't, who will?

Just look at those tires.

Yesterday after a breakfast of one scrambled egg with dill, a toasted

Thomas' English Muffin, black coffee, and his newspaper, Geist packed the pink bag. He'd planned to set out by noon, but the tires bulged like a middle-aged man's waistline. No need to bend and measure pressure. A person could see the problem.

He'd been rolling on them for a year. Plenty of tread remained. Geist had purchased road hazard insurance and a free rotation every 5,000 miles. It's a religion with him. Do unto others as you would have them do unto you, eat fiber, rotate your tires. Cripes, his appearances at the tire shop were so regular that Hector, the manager, sometimes offers Geist a powdered donut right out of the very same bag he and the shop workmen use.

Loyalty ought to count for something, but it counts for crap. Yesterday, instead of heading south on I-95 by noon, though he needed to drive all those miles from coastal Maine to North Carolina where Dennis, his son, was making his life, Geist sat like a schmuck brooding for two hours on a shabby, green vinyl-covered chair in the tire store office. The only heat in the cinder block building was an electric space heater with cherry red coils glowing behind a clunky fan. He kept his hands in his pockets, his jacket collar up.

"Your tires are OK. We didn't see nothing." Hector wiped his hands on a rag.

"Nothing?"

"Nothing. We'll grind your rims; make sure the tires fit. Maybe you parked against the curb, you know?"

Geist drove away, but his confidence had evaporated.

At one time, Geist would have planned the trip to be accomplished in one sitting, but now he must pace himself. He hates being tentative. Reflexes slowing, it is not inconceivable that his mind fails to process information fast enough. So he plans to avoid fatigue. Jesus, what would Geist be if his mind went? Oh, sure, he forgets things, but who doesn't? Everyone over 50 has CRS—Can't Remember Shit. So what? Still, Geist worries. If his mind goes, how would his mind know it was gone?

That's how it is with Geist, like roads lead to more roads, thoughts lead to more thoughts. It's the cascade effect, the doctor told him. He can choose to stop it. This is 21st century American Feelgood bullshit, but Geist knows no better alternative. He is about as much in charge as a man trapped on an elevator with a severed cable. He can stab at buttons, but the descent accelerates.

Knowledge of the coming crash doesn't mean you get off the elevator. Geist has low tires; next thing his mind plunges him into grim visions of senility, incontinence, and lonely death.

He flushed the Happy Pills years ago. Geist already takes enough medications, thank you, all preventative. His heart, brain, kidneys, stomach, and lungs are just peachy. Counting out pills is a morning ritual, like the coffee his GP urges him to give up. The small yellow diuretic has him pissing like a racehorse. The blue vasorelaxant keeps his pressure low enough that blood does not spout from his ears. The sand-colored pill pumps his liver—or is it his pancreas?—to delay his inevitable diabetes, the disease that killed his mother. The food supplements for his eyes and joints do nothing at all. The children's aspirin thins his blood and may prevent a stroke, but the aspirin also gives him an occasional nosebleed. Forget the Church of Tire Rotation; Geist is an acolyte to the Church of Perpetual Life through Preventative Medication. At monthly, quarterly, semi-annual and annual intervals, he pays his tithe to druggists, an endocrinologist, a GP, an ophthalmologist, a dermatologist, a podiatrist, a dentist, a periodontist, and the odd specialist. They take his blood, cluck at the results, and tell him to change his ways. But for what? Geist sees, pees and shits, the definition of health.

By plan, he should have awaked in southern New Jersey, close to Camden, but he crouches with his silver tire gauge in hand on a dank December morning before sunup, in a mist-enshrouded motel parking lot in central Connecticut.

He confirms what his heart already knew. Unless he's run over a tank trap, there was no reason two tires would develop leaks at the same time.

The tires are defective. End of story.

Geist spits on his fingers and wipes grit from his fingertips on the seat of his jeans. He is near Lyme, the town that gave its name to a disease spread by bloodsucking deer tics.

Geist stamps his feet, two blocks of ice in sweatsocks and running shoes. The opalescent sky drips like an infected sinus. Geist wants breakfast. Geist needs coffee. But instead of waffles or eggs or oatmeal or any traditional road food, in the morning gloom of central Connecticut, Geist will play "Find the Air Pump."

A few hundred yards down the two lane blacktop, back beyond the interstate, on the northbound side of the highway, he finds a Mobil to his left, a Shell to his right.

The ancient Greeks believed in inescapable Fate; we, on the other hand, believe we are the sum of our choices. Different cultures, different illusions.

Geist chooses the right.

Geist often marvels at the number of television personalities and moronic books that reinforce this lie of choice. Oedipus brains a stranger on the road with a rock, solves a riddle, and winds up a king who sleeps with his mother. Dr. Phil leans forward to inquire, "So tell us, Oed, what were you thinking when you picked up that rock?" Oprah herself might interview Jocasta. What studio audience eye would be dry as the Queen of Thebes tearfully confessed that she had been a victim of a fool and brute, her husband, who should never, ever, have sent away their infant son.

Had Geist chosen to turn left, everything might have been different. A grinning Hispanic guy with a hose and nozzle in hand leans into his window. The Shell is full service, so, no, Geist cannot pump his own gas. He asks the guy if they have an air pump, and the guy nods and smiles and says, *jess, jess, jess*. Geist fishes out a credit card and the gas pump nozzle rattles into the Corolla's side. Geist stands in the too warm December morning, but no air pump is in sight. Tires are stacked against the whitewashed wall of a dim garage bay.

"Where is the air pump?"

"*Jess, jess, jess.*" The gas station attendant gestures at the office.

The office guy is a bantam in a jumpsuit, but at least he speaks English.

"Air pump?" Geist asks.

"No."

"Your guy said you have an air pump." The station owner shrugs. His breast pocket's red embroidery reads *Richie*. "How do you fill all those tires you sell?"

"A tire machine." Richie blows across his steaming coffee and delicately bites what might be a cheese Danish. His chin is covered by whiskers like steel wool.

"Open the garage door and let me pull up to it."

"The hose is three feet long. It would not do you any good."

"You could change the hose, right?" Richie shrugs and turns his back. "Thanks a lot," Geist says. "I appreciate your help."

"Go fuck yourself."

Nice, Geist thinks. *Nice*. He's been told to fuck himself before breakfast, a sentiment he has not heard since his third wife left him for a failed actor.

In the Mobil station across the street, the air compressor requires 75 cents to operate for three minutes. A yellow metal tag on the machine reads, *Air free to our customers. Inquire in office*. Had he turned left, he'd have a full tank, free air, and not have to deal with Nazi bastards eating cheese Danish.

But Geist chose the right.

His knees pop when Geist squats to unscrew the tire valve caps. He slides three quarters into the slot and the compressor chugs into life. Not only does the chuck fit, but the hose gauge works. He is able to inflate two crappy, defective tires in less than the rationed three minutes.

Pulling out of the Mobil station, Geist flips Richie the Nazi Bastard the bird. With luck, Richie saw him. Maybe the little prick will choke to death on his cheese Danish. Maybe Geist will hit the lottery, too, but he does not count on it.

Thirty minutes later, southbound, Geist abandons any hope of finding a half decent eatery. What does he expect? A blue roadside sign that reads, *Decent food. Not the usual crap. Next exit. Easy access?*

So the Corolla delivers him to what is either an official Connecticut rest stop or the last stop on the railway station for the Hellbound Express. People of every age and nationality enter and exit. Babes in arms and the elderly, unsteady on canes. Boys on rattling skateboards with their hats on backwards, and men in rumpled suits. Women in muumuus and quilted jackets walk tiny dogs on a grassless strip behind a cyclone fence. Intense teenage girls text into cellphones. Geist hears what might be French. He hears what is certainly German. The tumult in God's waiting room will be no different from the traveler's plaza on the Connecticut Turnpike.

The Men's Room smells of piss. He was not expecting Chanel No. 9, but couldn't a man hope to relieve himself where no stuffed auto-flush toilet ran ceaselessly, creating a not-so-clear flowing moat between him and every urinal? Geist does not wash his hands. Be serious. There are no paper towels, and the allegedly sanitary air dryer blasts only frigid air if you are crazy enough to press your palm to the metal plate already slapped by the wet palms of 5 million disease-ridden travelers.

The food court line snakes back to the entry doors, but after two garages and the Great Air Hose Hunt, Geist is too hungry to leave. Against the lessons of his own experience, Geist orders the egg, sausage and cheese sandwich, and given the options of medium, large and extra-large coffee, he chooses the large. Had no other travelers been queued up behind him, he'd have asked for a small just to see the high school kid grapple with the stupid old fart ignorant of the self-evident fact that the tiniest size was a medium.

Behind the wheel of his car, Geist unwraps his breakfast and makes a lap tray of the paper bag. When will they develop edible paper? What are they waiting for? His ration of grease, salt, swine, dehydrated egg, starch, and a goopy dome of hydrolyzed fat, a near-food called "American Cheese food product," is totally satisfying. Scalding coffee chases the medications down his throat. Because he has no newspaper to distract him, he wonders how an arrogant, petulant, cheese Danish-eating Nazi fuck asshole who owns something called a *service* station can tell a distressed traveler *fuck yourself*. On the American frontier or in the Middle Ages, times and places where justice was not determined by advocacy but by action, if Richie had run an inn and slit the throats of wayfarers, one glorious day a hero would have caught him at it, gutted the son-of-a-bitch, and while buggering his wife before his still living eyes would have fed Richie's entrails to livestock.

Southbound again, Geist plans his choices.

Who'd need a GPS for this ride? What the Mississippi had been to timber and water, I-95 is to rubber, glass, steel, oil and concrete. Yes, a driver could choose the 3-digit bypass routes around cities, but those roads once through cornfields had become the central arteries of character-free suburbs, a pallid landscape of malls and car dealerships, the soul-sucking invented locations that bred teenage boys whose only vision of escape was to tote Dad's armor piercing automatic weapons in a book bag, slaughter classmates, and then spatter their own deficient brains onto a pale blue cafeteria wall.

Geist cannot play the radio loud enough. The elevator is falling, and he's trapped within it.

You had Portland, Portsmouth, Boston, Providence, New Haven, New York City, New Jersey—which was not so much a place as the space between places, an entire state halved by petroleum cracking plants, a place whose residents located themselves in space and status by exit numbers. What was the collective psyche of people who knew themselves and each other only by where they left the road? Manhattan at your left, eyes tearing from toxic fumes, you might notice Newark, but you'd never notice Patterson, cradle to poets. You sidled past Philadelphia before Baltimore, the murder capital of America. A mere 40 miles more and there was Washington DC, Mecca to America's addled homeless. A few hours further south to Richmond, Virginia, capitol of Dixie, where the war to defend slavery was commemorated on Monument Avenue by alabaster statues of men who strove to overthrow the Federal government. Lee, Jeb Stuart, Stonewall Jackson, all on horse save the newest addition, Arthur Ashe. Geist would have paid to be present at the debate that approved the addition of a black tennis player to the pride of the Confederacy. No revision of history was too grotesque to make a world safe for children in America, the Theme Park. No smoking, no drinking, no fornication, fleshless, sinless, pure of heart, nothing in America allowed an adult to know he was an adult. Shiloh, Gettysburg, Chickamauga, Spotsylvania, and center court at the US Open in Forest Hills, equivalent moments of high valor, all suitable subjects for any seventh grader's book report.

I-95 plunged further south to Miami, but Geist's mind follows the Corolla's intended path off that line as if the Corolla was a radioactive isotope in search of heart blockage. He would depart arteries and veer west into lesser vessels, eventually lodging like a clot at Dennis's home in the Piedmont, now called the Research Triangle. *Piedmont*, from the French for *foothills*, but *Research Triangle* sprang from the lips of necessary revisionism. Come now, who could live happily ever after where the oldest and richest names were associated with fortunes build upon slave labor and tobacco? Poison and blood built Winston, Salem, Raleigh, and Duke, all once cigarette brand names.

Geist was clueless as to what his boy did for a living; it involved the Internet and was very, very complicated.

East of New Haven, muttering more of what he should have said to the Nazi sadist prick Richie, Geist, preoccupied, misses his easiest chance to avoid the heart of darkness, New York City. Geist's stunning ripostes designed to leave little bastard mute and humiliated, distract him from the Merritt Parkway and the easiest route across Westchester to the Tappan Zee Bridge where Geist planned to cross the Hudson far north of the Bronx.

Any man who did not pay total attention to details loses his way.

Geist considers correcting course. It is still an option. How much net time would be gained or lost returning to Milford? Geist, a native New Yorker, the genuine article, not some Johnny-come-lately transplant from the toolies of Ohio or Kansas or West Bumfuck asserting that claim after a few seasons stomping roaches in a Greenpoint walkup, has a healthy respect for New York traffic. So though he knows other, direct routes, he also knows they are likely to be difficult. He'd lived in New York City his first thirty years. Geist knows his way around.

Dr. Phil leans forward to ask, "So, Geist, when you *chose* not to turn around, and you then came to that total dead stop in Bridgeport, you *knew* all along you'd risked that path?"

Let's be clear. Traffic does not slow. It stops. Stone fucking dead.

Years ago, Bridgeport actually declared bankruptcy and left widows and orphans gumming worthless paper. Bridges and roads crumbled. Trapped atop a highway bridge, Geist gazes at the gray ocean. Fog makes the sky and sea one.

At the last chance to escape westward across Westchester, they crawl past the problem—nothing less than two trucks and three cars piled up at the Cross County exit. The highway lanes are clear, but idiot rubberneckers look for blood. The Sawmill to the Henry Hudson and onto the GW is no longer an option. To cross the Hudson River, Geist will require not only the George Washington Bridge but the Cross Bronx Expressway.

Should a ruddy imp ever appear before you and offer riches, fame, love, a bigger dick, and perpetual youth in an extended life if you agree to spend ten thousand years in Satan's anus or one afternoon on the Cross Bronx Expressway, take your time in the Devil's asshole. Your suffering will be less.

Maybe if Geist had that morning turned left instead of right, he might have been alert instead of being trapped on his plummeting psychic elevator. Blame Hector for cutting the elevator cable by selling defective; blame Richie, the Nazi Bastard who ate cheese danish and conflated "service" with "persecution."

"Stop it," Geist says aloud to no one, stabbing at elevator buttons. *Just stop it.*

Where the road forks right from the Bruckner to the Cross Bronx and then the George Washington Bridge, a route on which traffic moves at glacial speeds, at the last second, Geist impulsively pulls the Toyota to the left. The Throgs Neck Bridge beckons to him. It went nowhere he needs to go, but at least he would move.

Geist evolves some vague plan to slice across Queens on the Van Wyck, circle Brooklyn on the Belt, and then slide under and up a ramp onto the Verrazano, the bridge known to locals as "The Guinea Plank." After that, he'd dart across Staten Island to the swamps of New Jersey on the other side of the Outerbridge Crossing. The route is not impossible; looking at a map, a stranger might thing Geist clever.

That would be a stranger.

Idling in a queue of cars, Geist burns gasoline awaiting his turn to put a mere five dollars into the hands of a toll collector. His "Thanks" is unanswered. The toll collector's hand is in a surgical glove. Rectal exams and money—all the same to her.

But as the Corolla descends onto the Cross Island and then the Grand Central Parkways, Geist no longer can kid himself. The Corolla is taking him to Susan's old neighborhood.

She might still be there. It's not impossible. Decades might pass, but Susan and her husband and her two kids were as constant as WINS, the all-news, all-the-time radio station now recapping the same stories for the fourth time.

A Puerto Rican guy saw the fire that almost killed the old lady. She's nice, *jew know. No trouble.* This may be news; an old lady in New York City is not Ma Barker. Then there is the fourteen-year-old stabbed to death in Astoria, like any fourteen-year-old stabbed to death in Astoria out for a stroll at four in the morning had been destined to cure cancer and start an orphanage for blind children, had he only lived after gathering tuition for medical school by selling crack cocaine.

The traffic report that informs Geist there is no road in a twenty-five-mile radius of Manhattan not more clogged than his arteries. Geist's index finger stabs the radio mute. He sings aloud:

> *There's a hold-up in the Bronx*
> *Brooklyn's broken out in fights*
> *There's a traffic jam in Harlem*
> *That's backed up to Jackson Heights*

There's a scout troop short a child
Krushchev's due at Idlewild...
"Car 54, where are you?"

Arguably the stupidest TV show ever. Arguably the worst theme song to the stupidest TV show ever. "Gilligan's Island" is Puccini by fucking comparison. Geist sings the ditty three times. He bounces on his seat with enthusiasm, yodeling on *Idelwild*. Does anyone younger than forty know who Krushchev was? Is there another stanza? Is anyone in America, this great nation of 300 million souls, singing the same tune as he? Cluttered with whatever has been discarded, useless, and embarrassing, Geist's mind is the cluttered attic of American culture. Geist, the poster-boy for CRS, is cursed to remember only the useless and inane.

Irene undeniably knew about Susan. He practically told her all about it. Martin could not have been two, and Dennis was to be born to a wife in the future. Lifetimes pass, but as soon as Geist gets a whiff of New York City air, the DNA of his body revitalizes with the intense memories of those six months with Susan. His cells remember. Her name was a word he might utter on his deathbed, like "Rosebud," an opaque mystery laden with meaning.

So screw the Van Wyck and the Belt. The Toyota navigates the Brooklyn-Queens Expressway, ripping past East River crossings fast as flip cards. The Fifty-Ninth Street Bridge, the Queens Midtown Tunnel, the Williamsburg Bridge, Manhattan Bridge, Brooklyn Bridge. Geist could do this drive with his eyes closed, though the lanes seem more narrow than they did in his day. Where once he wove through traffic like Mario Andretti closing on the finish line at the Indie 500, Geist now drives like a frightened old lady who lost her spectacles.

At the Prospect Expressway, as if his car was a lost mutt returning home to sigh and die after twenty years, he finds the street. He finds the block. This is Park Slope.

Brooklyn—life is on the street. If there were a Spenser Gifts, someone would steal the lava lamp. Not an escalator or fountain in sight, just black-specked New York snow, and not much of it, either.

Look, when Geist sees a space broad enough for him to pull in nose first, how could he not do it? The space is a few doors down from where Susan lived.

The time is only just past two o'clock, but Geist is not eating any lunch after that breakfast. He has time to spare.

So parked before four-story brownstones with vaulting windows, Geist rolls down his window, releases his seatback, and inhales the city. Even in leafless December, Geist smells Prospect Park—the Olmstead miracle more impressive than the more famous Central Park. Why don't people know all he knows?

An Hispanic kid dribbles a basketball, his cap on sideways. So the kid wears his cap like an idiot. So what? Live and let live, that's what Geist always says.

An older woman — she has to be Italian — pulls a squeaky two-wheeled wire frame cart. It's filled with brown grocery bags. Geist sees celery. His mother had such a cart. This woman's white wispy hair is under a black scarf tied beneath her chin. Her coat is black; her shoes are like cheese boxes. Where do these women come from? Why don't they die out? Generations come and go, but there is an endless supply of old women who cannot be five feet tall, bent like question marks, tugging loaded two-wheeled carts up and over curbstones. When she makes her way around a puddle—can you believe it? — the basketball player yields space on the narrow sidewalk. Civility sends Geist into a nostalgic reverie.

Susan and he had walked across the Brooklyn Bridge. A freezing night so long ago that the Trade Center behind was almost new, a scandal of sorts because the Port Authority could not rent all that office space, but the windows twinkled like diamonds on black velvet as they moved and their perspective changed. They were lovers by then. Cold, the night, the wind, the moon, the city, it was a conspiracy of perfection. They were lovers. They'd lain damp and sated in each other's arms only an hour earlier. Their gloved hands clasped, hers in red wool, his in black leather. He would for a lifetime carry that moment, a treasure. What woman before or after could match her? He'd damaged the souls of three wives who could not displace his memory of another woman. They must have found the dark truth lurking in his heart. His memory transformed and grew beyond mere history; no woman could ever have been the Susan he created in his soul. Memory was false. The heart births its own truth. If women suspected what men made of them, what woman would dare lower her eyes or undo her hair? Who would draw close, caress, breathe, yield up her lips? What woman could open to a man? But Susan had. Susan had opened to him, to him, to Geist. The only certainty Geist had of women was that eventually they left. They smiled, but they forgave nothing, and then they left. Susan had smelled of Tea Rose, the skin at her throat skin tasted of copper. In passion that day she bit his lower lip until he bled. On the bridge it was not midnight, though it should have been. They walked from Manhattan, arcing over the river on the bridge's elevated wooden walkway, as if they walked on a great black cat's back, their steps hollow on the wood, clouds of silver breath before them, full of each other, but unwilling to end their time together, the touch of their hands enough, the wind too strong to allow them the speech they did not need, an impossible moon above, its light rippling on onyx water below, water black as Susan's eyes, her striped long scarf tight over her lips, the ends whipping the air before them, the wind a thousand knives slicing through their pea coats, a night when he was young and filled by confidence, strength, his self-evident immortality, and endless hope. What could end? What could he not achieve? Time was infinite. They were lovers. A million such moments would be theirs, indelible, irreplaceable, endless, an army of triumphant moments that could never have become that vagrant mob of ragtag broken promises, betrayals, and self-induced lies that became his life.

Then he sees her. He's out of the car instantly. Susan. His Susan. She looks just as she always did. He is not ten feet from the stranger when he realizes this is impossible. His mind, out of control and growing more feeble every day, now plays him dead false. The woman's black eyes blink quizzically at him, an oncoming stranger. Could she be Susan's daughter? She looks like her, a figure like a Hindu carving on a temple with a knowing smile. Geist begins to open his mouth to speak, but no word escapes his lips, and a good thing, too, as speech might have been fatal. The young man beside her already clenches a fist, and who knows what weapon he carries in his coat pocket?

Geist's propensity to live in the past has once more propelled him into the dangerous pursuit of an illusion in the present. He pulls up, slaps his forehead like a cartoon character who has stepped off a cliff and hangs in the air, an anvil in his hands, suspended over nothing.

His heart palpitations and overwhelming shame do not subside until he is well over the Outerbridge Crossing, free of New York and its alluring memories, however false, engulfed in the toxic twilight of the New Jersey Turnpike,

I-95, where Geist is back on course. He'd have been on course all day, except for that prick, Richie, Hector's two shitty tires, and Geist's impossible series of evil choices.

Geist cannot recall the drive across Staten Island. The space in his mind is like a gap left by a lost tooth. Flames atop the smokestacks that rise from mid-Jersey oil cracking plants paint the sky pink and red. His self-indulgent delays, his absurd daydreaming, Geist is all business now, struggling south in rush hour traffic until he escapes the mob south of Cherry Hill.

Geist has been sliding down the east coast for eight hours, he has skipped lunch, and he has accomplished no more than 200 miles. He could walk at that speed. He has 400 miles more to go. He resolves to drive all night. He has no choices: fuck you, Doctor Phil.

Geist pushes.

He eats something in Maryland—or was it Delaware?—and tanks up. Why stop again? His tires seem all right, but Geist is a cautious man, so to be certain he pumps air, deliberately over-inflating to 38 pounds. No tailgating, he tells himself. Less rubber on the road.

South of Washington DC, Geist is plunged into unequivocal night. Civil War armies marched for weeks over terrain Geist covers in hours. He has never seen Fredericksburg. Where is Spotsylvania? A river of red taillights recedes endlessly before him; flowing at him is a river of white.

No one defeats physics. Rate, time, and distance do not yield to sudden acceleration, shortcuts, or compulsive glances at his watch. At 60 miles per hour, in one hour, the Toyota will cover 60 miles. At 65, it will take cover 65 miles. If he dares 80, he will accomplish 80, but at such speeds Geist cannot trust his reflexes to guide the car in any emergency, so he hopes for 70 and settles for 65. Lunatics pass him; idiots crawl before him. Time compresses and expands like the chest of a weary marathoner. Released felons summarize even forty years as near nothing. They call it *doing time*.

So when the Toyota's defective tires quietly crunch up the gravel of Dennis's driveway at the end of the *cul de sac* off a street like a dozen others in the development, though his ass hurts, though Geist has an annoying twitch in his left arm, though his back feels like a column of cracked glass, and though the blue digital auto clock reads 1:07, Geist can hardly remember the trip. He has been on the journey for an instant that started long, long ago.

Geist thinks of taking a room nearby and presenting himself in the morning, but, dammit, this is his boy. He's made the effort. He's done what needed to be done, and he's done it heroically, overcoming a day that started bad and just got worse. Nobility and courage deserve reward.

Dennis' house is dark. When in hell did the boy put in hedges? Geist stumbles over an exposed root beside the flagstone path, but rights himself before he falls. That would be the perfect end. He'd shatter a hip or something.

Dennis' place is a generic McMansion, two floors, two wings, gleaming hardwood floors that shine like the lifeless marble eyes of a carousel pony. All the houses in the *cul de sac* have white columns and a portico. You'd think right after designing Monticello, Jefferson had handed his blueprints to some developer in the Research Triangle.

Dennis' door chimes sound like church bells. Geist leans on the button three times. He has to pee. He slaps the brass knocker onto the red door. A yellow light within ignites.

The woman who swings open the door is backlit in her diaphanous aqua nightgown. What's with these kids? No shame. Couldn't she put on a house dress? She's older than Geist thought she would be. His future daughter-in-law should be more modest. A single index finger moves the blonde bangs from her sleepy eyes, and then they open in recognition. Her dry lips part.

She turns and shouts up the winding staircase, "Bob, it's that man again. Bob! You hear me? That man is here again!"

Pushing his head through a t-shirt, Bob in sweatpants and slippers hurries down the maple stairs. "I'll take care of it," he says, and touches his wife's shoulder. "Calm down, Cheryl. I'll take care of it. I think he woke the kids."

"Bob, you're calling the police this time. I don't care who he reminds you of. Call the police. If you don't, I will. I swear to God I will."

Bob steps out into the night, and half shuts the paneled door behind him.

"Where's Dennis?"

"There is no Dennis here, partner. He moved three years ago, remember? Dennis left no address. Try to remember."

"But where is Dennis?"

As Bob tries to slide an arm around Geist's shoulders, Geist twists away like a football runner. All right. Yes. The truth is that he sometimes becomes confused, but why strong arm him? Geist is bewildered. This Bob should know where his Dennis is. Geist's stomach knots and he feels himself leak urine. Acid rises in his gullet. *If a man were to lose his mind, how would he know it?* Dr. Phil sits back in judgment. *Oh, come on, Geist, you knew. You knew all the time. You had to have known. Come on, Geist, what could you have been you thinking?*

Geist doesn't want to wet himself; he fights nausea. He shakes. He asks again, this time with bewildered hope, his voice cracking, "But, please, just tell me. Where is my Dennis?"

From inside, Cheryl shouts, "I'm calling! Bob, tell him I am calling!" A small child cries. Dennis is not yet married and so he could not have children. All right. But where is his Dennis?

Bob stands squarely in the door. Geist tries to look past him. The house appears comfortable. "Look, partner, you need help. Let me help you get help. But you have to stop showing up here whenever you feel like it. It scares the kids. Tell me this time, okay? Where do you live? Where are you from? Can I help you get back?"

Get back? Geist would like nothing better than to get back. What's wrong with this guy? There is no getting back. People should know that. "What happened to Dennis?"

"I don't know any Dennis."

"Go fuck yourself," Geist mutters.

Bob sighs, steps back, and the red door quietly clicks shut. Geist's bladder voids. The warm mess quickly grows cold. He hears Cheryl, but can make out no words. The house's windows darken to black. The baby cries for a while, but then is still.

Beneath the cloudless crystal canopy of a winter sky, Geist lifts his chin high. The stars blur when his eyes fill. He points a single finger heavenward. There's Orion's belt, the Hunter, red Betelgeuse glowering nearby. Geist is a man who knows things, what stars shine where, the stories of the constellations, the figures of the zodiac in eternal pursuit, and how each cold pin of light wheeling about Polaris is in truth a nuclear furnace.

"Go fuck yourself," he repeats.

Void

by Karenmary Penn

WINNER OF THE 2012 GIVAL PRESS SHORT STORY AWARD

Iris returned from work to discover her husband Cropper, still dressed in his brown uniform, sitting in the recliner, holding a grenade. It was round and muddy green in color, with a metal loop hanging from the pin.

"Bad day?" Iris said, keeping her voice light.

He lifted an eyebrow.

Iris sat on the sofa. "Where did you even get that?" She straightened her dress and looked around the room, for what, she couldn't have said. Bare walls. Secondhand furniture. "So I had this client today, this little old lady named Millicent. She died at the dinner table. Her sister said she looked over and there was Millicent, fork in hand, staring off into eternity."

Cropper leaned forward to put two fingers on top of the grenade, like a man deciding where to move a chess piece. Iris imagined picture frames and cushion stuffing and stereo components all exploding in a big unholy bang. Pieces of their life together, blown to kingdom come.

Iris said, "The sister brought in this raggedy red fox stole for Millicent to be buried in."

She'd always been grateful he didn't own a gun. Guns created a lot of work for funeral home aestheticians. Suicide was such an unsightly way out of life. The body tried to rid itself of whatever poison a person put into it—gas, pills, poison, lead. It shoved foaming, reeking pollutants out of every available opening. If people only knew that, maybe they'd reconsider their exit strategies. (Mr. Schmidt, while suturing the jaw of a decedent one day, had told her about bacterial decay and cells despoiled by enzymes to explain that type of "purge", but she felt sure the body had its own wisdom and did not care to spend eternity full of toxins.)

Of course, old age was no picnic either: bodies rotted from within, brains eaten by dementia moths, bones transformed into chalk. If she could, she'd choose incineration, be one of those who vanished in the World Trade Center; everything about them reduced to blowing ash, to be vacuumed off untold carpets and bookshelves. Or perhaps she'd be one of those women in India who threw themselves on their husbands' funeral pyres, disposing of both sorrow and carcass so efficiently, the embers of their lives becoming tiny orange stars, floating heavenward.

Cropper's cheek twitched. He stared at the dark television screen.

"Did you watch something that upset you, sweetie?" Iris said. He was so exquisitely sensitive to betrayal that he couldn't watch a movie in which one person deceived another. To him, it was the most cardinal of all sins, punishable by death, his own if necessary. His eyes were just this side of murderous when he looked up at her. She knew the look.

"Perhaps you'd rather be alone." Iris thought she might have walked into an invisible storm of explosions and tracers, bleeding bodies and moaning. A company of ghosts followed Cropper into the bedroom every night. She occasionally awakened to see him sitting on the corner of the bed, slump shouldered, speaking with one of the phantoms who lived on his side of the room: Souza, Wartowski, Beaner, Old Man, Hassan, and Jojo. (Her side of the bedroom housed only one ghost. He wore starchy blue jeans and smelled of sawdust.)

"Drop your cocks and grab your socks!" Cropper would growl.

"I swear to fucking God I just swallowed some of the Wart's brains." He'd spit.

"Put that fucking cigarette out," he'd hiss.

"Stand up!" "Lie down!" "Arms up!" he'd bark.

"Shh," he'd whisper.

When he was fully awake, like now, she could look in his face and know he'd gone away, back to someplace hot and dry, a place filled with booby traps and death. She understood because she disappeared inside herself sometimes, crossed a frozen river to a place filled with squawking chickens. Fleas. A secret as big as a barn.

When Iris took his free hand between two of hers, she felt the burden of him, the sucking weight of his despair dragging her down, pulling her apart. She imagined herself skidding away from him, like a bug in a toilet, trying not to get flushed.

What she knew of his history amounted to stories that occasionally rose up out of him, unbidden. Just recently, as he squatted on the lawn digging up dandelions with a steak knife, he told her about the James Souza, how he hopped off the back of a Humvee and landed on a mine buried in the dirt. "His mom used to send him Playboys that she'd stapled Road & Track covers over," Cropper said. Then: "He landed right on my boot print. Pow." And then James Souza, like some dark Leviathan, sunk down again. Iris knew some of his stories and he knew some of hers but they seldom pressed one another to fill the empty spaces in between. And yet they understood each other better than most married couples.

"Are you having an affair?" he said, pulling his hand free.

She sighed. "Why would you ask me something like that?"

He said he'd seen her car, three Wednesday nights in a row now, in the parking lot of Mackenzie's Wine Bar, late at night, when she claimed to have been at home. She told him her sister Rose asked her to go to MacKenzie's, which was technically true. Iris asked, without emotion or indignation or even surprise, if he'd been following her. He didn't reply. She wondered how she'd driven so far, on three occasions, oblivious to a boxy brown van lumbering along behind her. She pictured his pale face peering through a window, watching her sitting at the bar.

He asked questions and she answered them truthfully. She wasn't in love with another man; she swore on her parents' Ohio graves that she'd not made love to another man since the day they met; she loved him as much today as she did on their wedding night.

She knew Cropper wanted to believe her. At times like this, she resented the burden of being the one reliably decent person in his life. Eventually, he wrapped the grenade in a beach towel, and put the bundle in a Justin boot box on a high shelf in the linen closet. Iris felt tired watching him. Lately, her bones did not seem up to the task of carrying her through each day. They seemed more like balsa wood.

"I think I might need a bone marrow transplant," she said.

He gave her a puzzled look, then smiled his sad smile and said he loved her. She knew it was true, even though what he called love was not the fragile, tender, eternal stuff that people wrote about in poems. Cropper's version wasn't so much eternal as it was bottomless and icy in places, with barbed, stinging things winging past.

They spent the evening on the roof, gazing through his telescope at the stars above. Cropper explained neutrinos and proton accelerators to her. He pointed out constellations and she pretended to see them, enjoying the feel of his rough cheek against hers. He could be so tender when he broke free of his own gloominess. As he put the telescope back in its case, he told her that sometimes a star couldn't stand the pressure of its own gravity. It didn't have enough energy to continue, and eventually it would collapse, crushed by its own weight.

"The end," Iris said.

Cropper shrugged. "Not really. That's how black holes are born."

She shut her eyes to try and imagine the size of a billion galaxies but he interrupted her thoughts by saying something about a quasar having a "huge black hole spurting infinite streams of matter", making them both laugh. Cropper could squeeze a sexual joke out of any topic. Sailing. Economics. He could have been one of those morning disc jockeys, if he had a more natural inclination toward lightness.

***

Iris avoided Mackenzie's Wine Bar after that. She discovered a quieter place, a three block walk from work, called the Blackhawk Lounge. There she sat on a stool near the curved end of a grand piano, nursing a Perrier, listening to black man in tuxedo play jazz. A group of men wearing suits stared at a baseball game on a muted TV hung high in a corner. Two couples sat talking and nuzzling in leather booths. She treasured this small, secret life away from her husband.

Iris had long, wavy black hair and blue eyes. On this night, she wore a satiny, crimson dress that felt like breath on her fair skin.

A man stood on the other side of the piano, looking at the backs of his hands, which lay flat against the piano. He was thick-bodied and rugged in a fireman kind of way, with chapped skin and thick, graying hair. Iris loved men. She loved their musky scents and rough faces. She loved the way their broad shoulders tapered down into small waists and narrow, round buttocks. Most of the time, she admired the way men held emotion dammed up behind their skin. They were so much tidier than women that way.

After making love with a man, she used to love to lie with her head on his chest, so she could listen to the burbling stew of his insides and wonder about the gurgles and thrums as she drifted off to sleep. (Cropper kept everything locked up so tight he sounded like a snare drum.)

The day she married Cropper—nearly six years ago, before a justice of the peace—she resolved to end any flirtation at the first display of lust. As time wore on, though, she felt herself opening up to strange men, almost involuntarily, in the manner of a flower unfurling under a store-bought grow light.

The man caught her looking at him and smiled. He had a hangdog face, and eyes the color of bourbon. "I'm Frank." His deep voice caught in his throat. He moved his gaze to his drink.

"I'm married," she said.

"Join the club."

"I didn't come here to pick up men," Iris said.

"That makes two of us."

After a minute, he said, "You look like that actress who played that blind gal in the movie with what's his name. The dude who's in rehab all the time. Did you see that one?"

Iris gave him an exasperated look. He held up both hands, as if in surrender, but he moved closer. She felt him probing behind her eyes, feeling for something to hold onto. She let him. Her eyes were colored glass, reflecting everything, absorbing nothing. When loneliness swelled up inside her and threatened to spill out, she looked away. He got on the subject of football helmets and then moved on to dog racing and polar ice caps and fuel made from corn and finally some soccer stadium in Afghanistan. He seemed lonely.

"You get this little vein that pops up on your temple." Frank touched his finger to her temple, traced a lazy S. Iris felt a pleasant ruffling of nerve endings beside her left eye.

She pulled her head away and looked up at the television in the corner.

Lately, Iris experienced surges of resentment toward her mother, and her sister, for not letting her in on the substance of marriage, its relentless routines and mutated truths. They never told her that she'd wake up day after day for weeks with a certainty like a pile rammed through her that she could not live one more day as somebody's wife, not even Cropper, who loved her, albeit in a way that bordered on frightening.

Frank reached up, pushed a lock of hair up behind Iris's ear, then lowered his hand slowly, running his thumb along her jaw line. He tilted her head back and she closed her eyes, savoring the sugary anticipation of a come-on. Something frayed in his voice when he said, "Great dress."

He said nothing for a while. She stared at the television without really watching it. When he spoke to her again, he put his hand on her knee to get her attention, and then left it there, lifting it away when he got himself worked up about Iraq, or maybe Afghanistan; one of the war countries. She kept her expression bland when she removed his hand and placed it on his own knee. She sat quietly beside him, listening to the music and to his chatter, until her watch beeped in her purse. Cropper would be home soon.

"I have to go," she said.

Frank trailed her to the parking lot. She stood in the cool air, unable to recall where she'd left her car. "Do you need a ride?" he said. She told him she'd left her car up the street. He unlocked a dark sedan and opened the back door. His face looked suddenly and desperately needy. He might as well have led her to his bed and pulled back the covers. She felt like a person rushing to a plane knowing that she'd forgotten something.

"Do you love your wife?" she said.

"Can't imagine being married to anybody else."

"I'm not really this person. This dressy" She looked down, shook her head. "I'm..."

His voice sunk low and uneven. "I know what you are."

She didn't stick around to hear what she was. She was lonely, but she was not a whore.

***

That night, Iris sat on the couch next to Cropper, watching a nature program about a drying- up Botswana watering hole. A baby elephant trapped in mud up to its shoulders thrashed and struggled. His mother and aunts tried to pull him free with their trunks but the mud wouldn't let go. Iris thought she wouldn't fight it if she stopped at a drinking fountain one day and Mother Earth decided to reclaim her, to fold her up in great gray arms for a never-ending hug.

When that narrator mentioned the great herds that once roamed those over-baked savannas, and how they'd been whittled down to nothing by poachers and farmers and war, Iris unmoored her consciousness. The grander problems of the world, their causes and solutions, were all too unmanageable, too far beyond her ability to help. Occasionally a news story blew untidily into her awareness, like dirt under the door. She usually swept it back out again with a check made out to some outfit that could help. She wrote checks to Oxfam any time she saw photos of fly-covered people starving somewhere, to the Red Cross whenever earthquakes rattled a city into rubble. She helped other people do things about cancer, AIDS, muscular dystrophy, cystic fibrosis, homeless pets, cleft palates, Bengal tigers. In return, she got a lot of personalized address labels. They were currency, buying her freedom from deeper involvement.

She said, "Why doesn't the cameraman quit filming and dig that little elephant out?"

Cropper just lay there on the couch with tears shining in his eyes. The nature shows really got to him sometimes. Not that he was particularly protective of God's creatures. He was as likely as anyone else she knew to smash a moth with the bottom of his slipper.

She tried to stroke his cheek, but he turned his head. Cropper's face was more interesting than handsome. He had slightly hooded eyes, a strong jaw, and big, white teeth.

He was kind to her, almost always. Occasionally, the best parts of him burrowed deep inside, and she'd find herself sharing a bed with a person who hadn't spoken for three days straight. One minute he'd be sitting across the table from her at the Trattoria, going on about internal combustion engines, and the next, he'd go cold, silent as a headstone. Even his skin cooled to the touch. He could have been one of Iris's refrigerated customers. She'd never have guessed marriage could be so lonely.

He switched the channel to Jeopardy. "What is the Holy See," he said. Cropper read book after book, all nonfiction, trying to tire his brain so it would sleep when he did, instead of launching nightmares behind his closed eyelids. He was the only adult she knew who owned a library card. "Who is Andrei Gromykyo," he said. "What is Lapland."

She only got one answer before Cropper: "Who is Madonna."

After Jeopardy, Cropper turned off the TV. He unbuttoned his shirt to reveal the long, shiny, Y-shaped mystery scar that covered his chest. He claimed not to remember how it happened. There were gaps in other areas as well; unseen perforations where bits of his humanity had dropped out altogether. The part that let you get over even unintended slights, no matter how small, for example. Or the part that made you love your brother, even if you didn't like or understand him.

Iris hiked up her skirt, climbed on top of Cropper's legs, pulled her top over her head. He reached behind her to unhook her bra while she fumbled with his belt. They stroked and moaned and kissed until she began to grind against him, slowly. She still thought he was the perfect man for her, fitting inside her like a puzzle piece.

Before long, Cropper pitched her onto her back and began thrusting away. He hung onto her as though she were something solid, like a jetty, and he were a swimmer, trying not to be dragged out to sea. Iris avoided his eyes because she could see every terrible thing that had ever happened to him there, eddies of despair, sucking her in.

***

On the table at Schmidt's Funeral Home lay a middle-aged decedent with thick hair, still damp from washing, and a salt and pepper mustache, freshly trimmed by Iris. He had a crooked nose and a deep dimple in the chin. A pale scar bisected one eyebrow.

He looked a lot better than he did a few hours ago. Mr. Schmidt had pumped pink embalming fluid into the man's carotid artery, cleaned his face with disinfectant, then shaved him, and trimmed his nose hair. He'd packed cotton under his eyelids and in his one dented cheek, to prop everything out where it belonged. The decedent's biggest problems were below the neck, which wasn't Iris's department aside from the hands. Iris wiped them with disinfectant then powdered them. Long ago, Mr. Schmidt had showed her how to arrange them to hide the palms, which were purple and mottled with settled blood.

People left this world with different expressions on their faces. Some looked surprised to have been wrenched out of life; others looked sad or peaceful or indignant. This guy looked tired. The lucky ones, Iris supposed, grew to be withered old apples that dropped off the tree when they couldn't hang on any more. Assuming somebody found them right away, of course.

When she smoothed his tie against his crisp white shirt, she felt the jagged hardness of staples holding his sternum together. One time, Mr. Schmidt let her feel a decedent's heart. It was just larger than a baseball and the color of a Japanese maple, with what looked like globs of chicken fat adhered to its cold skin. She would have thought a heart would be tough as an overcooked roast because it spent its whole life working, but it felt hard and slippery, like a lie.

Iris tossed the gloves. She dusted the decedent's face with powder to match his hands, and then brushed his hair. Squirts of Aramis covered the embalming fluid odor.

Iris heard a knock on the metal door jamb. "They told me I could see my brother, before" It was Frank from the bar, dressed in a blue suit, looking shaky and pale.

"What are you doing here?" Iris said, alarmed and irritated.

Frank's face registered surprise, briefly, before going flat. His eyes flicked to the person on the table.

"Oh." Iris looked down at her hands. "I'm sorry. For your loss."

Frank walked a slow circle around her table. She thought the decedent looked handsome, considering. Bodies bloated and stiffened before loosening up again. Skin stretched. People expected Sleeping Beauties, waiting to be kissed out of their final sleeps. If they saw what some of these bodies did in Mr. Schmidt's prep room, farting and twitching and blinking their eyes open, they wouldn't complain about off-colored skin.

He touched his brother's hand, then recoiled, probably at the coldness. Some men liked to say their goodbyes without a dozen other grievers standing behind them shifting and craning, as though the casket were a concession stand instead of boxed up death.

"I was driving," Frank said.

Iris touched Frank's back and murmured again that she was sorry. He sobbed, noiselessly. She squeezed his shoulder. Unexpectedly, he wrapped an arm around her waist, cinched her tight against him, then pulled her around for a full-on hug. She could have stayed that way for a long while, feeling loved.

She wished there was a way to tell him a person could burn up millions of brain cells wondering why he wasn't the one lying with his muscles loosening from the bone and eye caps holding his lids shut. Why didn't he look right again before pulling out, or leave the house thirty seconds later, after the van had passed.

A person could exhaust herself wondering why she kept clomping across a frozen river and a stubbly field, Saturday after Saturday, returning to that sagging barn with all its clucking, reeking chickens, when she hated the smell of sawdust and the cold on her bare thighs. The barn seemed to have its own gravity. A person could be propelled by something inexplicable, a force beyond the reach of words.

She knew it was inappropriate to be hugging Frank, but comfort, like happiness, was finite, fleeting. A person had to grab hold of it when it came into reach. Judgment was for those who'd never experienced a thousand fleas crawling all over her innocence. Iris chose the company of sunnier emotions. It was easy to do if she surrounded herself each day with people whose misfortunes so clearly outweighed hers.

Frank cleared his throat. "How can you do this job?"

"Money's good. And I like the people that I work with." Iris pulled her hand off the decedent's foot. "Coworkers, I mean."

Frank looked at the tile floor. "People keep saying, 'Give it time.'"

Iris nodded, even though she knew true sorrow never dried up. It could shrink and retreat, but it was always there, ready to reconstitute itself on fresh pain. People said time healed all wounds, but in her experience, time lacked the right tools for the job.

She walked him out to the Oak Room, where the visitation for his brother would take place. It was a muted, pleasant space filled with bland landscape paintings and deep, comfortable couches. The heavy, wooden door closed behind them with a muffled thud. Afternoon sunlight filtered through the drapes, creating a quiet warmth. Two extravagant arrangements of white flowers stood at the front of the room. The cloying scent of lilies hung heavy in the warm air.

"We said no flowers," Frank said.

"People send them anyway." Iris fiddled with a seam on her dress.

"Goodbye then." Frank brushed past Iris on his way to the doors, his hand grazed her hip, leaving a trail of goose bumps in its wake. He paused. Iris waited for his bourbon-colored eyes to be drawn toward her.

Her body seemed at times to have been guided by invisible hands working from within. They pushed hips and breasts out where they'd be noticed, then pinched her waist in and stretched her legs long and her toes straight and pretty. They smoothed her pale skin to where women she didn't know stopped her to ask what products she used. ("Ivory soap," she'd say.)

He stood staring at her, his face unreadable. Iris unzipped her dress, armpit to hip, hearing each metal tooth release its partner with a tiny pop. When the dress hit the carpet, she stood in her black bra and panties, pale and goose pimpled. He stepped toward her, then stopped abruptly, like he'd clanged into something.

"I was just trying to make you feel better," she called, but he was just footsteps by then.

Her dress lay on the floor like something she'd molted.

***

Weeks passed. Iris joined Rose and her husband at a cowboy bar one Friday night. Cropper hated crowds so he stayed home. The walls were covered with rusted spurs and fringy chaps, branding irons and rodeo art.

Iris sat on a cowhide-covered barstool, sipping a wine spritzer. Rose and her husband knew every line dance, sang along to every song. Iris longed to whirl one way and then the other, to knock her heels against the wood floor the way they did, but something solid kept her apart. She imagined all those people with their thumbs through their belt loops, spinning one by one into her invisible shell, crumpling like stunned birds to the floor.

A man dressed in black jeans and a pearl-buttoned shirt moved around the outside of the floor, dancing the two-step with a woman in a flowy, blue dress. Both wore black cowboy hats pulled low on their heads. He had a paunch but somehow glided. When the music stopped he kept right on moving, twirling and dipping his partner, pulling her along as though she had no more heft than a silk scarf. They could have been on skates. When he removed his hat to smooth his hair back, Iris realized it was Frank, looking heavier and older. He'd grown a mustache. He danced with two other women, both of whom he flew like kites around the dance hall.

She should have called Cropper for a ride. She stayed, though, watching Frank dance. Eventually, he strode off the dance floor, sat at the bar and ordered a beer. Iris approached him, walking on wooden feet. He dabbed his damp forehead with a cocktail napkin and ate a peanut from a bowl on the bar without removing the shell.

"I'd like to apologize," Iris said.

He looked at her for a long moment, then raked his eyes over the dance floor. She didn't remember his skin being so red.

Frank said, "Is he here?"

Iris shook her head. She thought of Cropper, sitting in his recliner with his eyes half closed, murmuring, What is hemoglobin? Who is Akihito? He suffered from perpetual restlessness, as well as tiredness. If her heart were intact, it would surely ache for him.

Frank took her by the wrist and led her onto the dance floor. He arranged Iris's arms the way he wanted them and said, "Relax. Look up." At first she felt uncomfortable holding her chin so high and her arms so stiffly in position, but that melted away as he maneuvered her around the dance floor.

Iris watched Frank's face so intently that everything else blurred into color and noise. She felt like a flame atop a moving candle, swaying up and down, side to side, more color and heat than body. He could have put his hand right through her without causing more than a flicker.

She experienced something warm and rich expanding inside her. She squeezed his meaty shoulder and enjoyed the sensation of fullness. When the second song ended and Frank let go of her, though, the feeling collapsed.

Iris tried to call the feeling back but what emerged instead was the image of her mother in a turquoise parka, standing on the bridge that spanned the river near their home. Iris stood below, on the frozen river, watching exhaust curl up from the tailpipe of the station wagon and disappear into the wintry air. Wind lifted and twisted her mother's dark hair. She held it back with one hand and yelled, "If you fall through that ice, they won't find you until spring."

Trudging home after that, Iris believed her mother was more everywhere than God, with an infinitely bigger pull.

After a quick look for Rose and her husband, who were again on the dance floor, Iris took Frank's hand and led him past the restroom and the storeroom, out the metal door into the alley. She didn't wonder why she did what she did. Interior exploration blotted out all the pleasure in life. She was drawn to men, even when she didn't find them particularly attractive, even when they were indifferent to her. Sex never filled her with regret or self-loathing. It made her feel solid. For a little while at least, she wasn't a glass Christmas ornament, a shiny bauble that a careless squeeze could shatter into glittering dust.

Frank kissed her. She enjoyed the unfamiliar mouth and the feel his hands roaming all over her body. Iris unbuttoned her silk top, slowly, with him watching her hungrily. He inched up her long, dark skirt while she unbuckled his belt, unbuttoned his jeans, unzipped his fly, and stroked his waiting hardness. Frank moaned. He reached around her backside and slid a hand down her buttocks and pressed it against the heat gathering between her legs. He rubbed and teased; he kissed and groped and squeezed. Over and over, he told her she was beautiful. Everything in his face gave way to desire. He leaned her up against the front door of a pick-up truck, and pulled her legs up around him. The heels of her red boots knocked together at the small of his back. He pushed himself into her waiting loneliness with a gasp.

The elegance he'd displayed on the dance floor seemed to disappear all at once. She used to find reassurance in sex, a quenching of some unnamable need, but all she could feel right then was cold against her back, and a stranger sawing away at the tenderest part of her.

A few minutes later, he was zipping up, tucking in, kissing her on the mouth, saying, You really are beautiful. She felt wholly drained, infinitely void. The heavy door hissed its way closed, and then shut with a soft click that sounded exactly like a pin coming out of a grenade.

Harvest Cycle

by Marie Holmes

WINNER OF THE 2006 GIVAL PRESS SHORT STORY AWARD

Cassie found her announcement one day on the medical students' board. It was the first flier of hundreds she had read during lunch breaks that could possibly be directed at her. The paper was pale pink, free of distasteful clip-art, the bold text arranged in a simple, double-lined box: *Loving Couple Seeks Openhearted, Caucasian Woman, 21-34.* That was all. There were two num-bers in small type lower down on the page. One was obviously a telephone number—a hospital extension—and the other, while not preceded by a dollar sign and not containing a comma, was, Cassie felt certain, a monetary amount. That figure was five thousand. She removed the pushpin and folded the sheet of paper in half and then again so that it fit inside her palm.

Cassie worked in medical records at the hospital, pushing carts of paper between high metal shelves, hopping up a stepladder to retrieve manila fold-ers neatly labeled with colored stickers. It was not where she had intended to end up, with her bachelor's in sociology. What exactly her intentions were remained a mystery to Cassie, and she dedicated great swaths of time to imag-ining the endless iterations of shape that could be created with her life.

Cassie pulled files, replaced files, silently singing the alphabet all day long. What made her job bearable was the loose paper, transcriptions of dicta-tions telephoned in by doctors and e-mailed to her computer from someplace in India. These she hole-punched and inserted into individual charts. She read every page that she touched, and racked up volumes of anecdotal medical knowledge—fearing aneurysm every time her head ached, stomach cancer when her gut cramped. She became a repository of fascinating hospital gossip—a baby wounded during a caesarian section, an old man who had died of a heart attack while waiting in the emergency room—which nobody would ever ask her about. None of the other clerks read the files. Not like she did. Cassie had asked: her colleagues found the material in the charts indecipherable and dull. But these stories—plain, tragic, typical—were entirely responsible, Cassie believed, for keeping her from losing herself to her own mind in those gray, fireproof basement rooms.

"Gynecology," answered a receptionist when Cassie dialed the extension from her cubicle that afternoon. She scanned the sheet of paper for a name, some other identifying word.

"There was a flier?" she ventured, "posted by the mailroom?"

"You're calling about the donor ad?"

"Yes," said Cassie, disappointed to think that she was not the first.

The woman transferred her call. A male doctor, a reproductive endocrinologist, as he introduced himself, ·said he was just going to ask her a few questions: date of birth, height, weight, skin color—he wanted a very specific description here. Cassie said she tanned easily, and he said, Why don't we say olive. He needed to know how far she had gone in school, her SAT scores, and whether anybody in her family carried a genetic disease—cystic fibrosis, Tay Sach's, Fanconi's anemia, phenylketonuria. Cassie was fascinated—what were those last two? But it wasn't an appropriate moment to ask.

***

College graduation had come like a sudden, sheeting downpour that left her scurrying for shelter. Cassie had done well in school. But between the chalked protest messages and the poetry and the decadent discovery of her sexuality, there had been little time to contemplate her post-college existence.

The town she lived in wasn't far from where she had gone to school. School, however, had been far away from the rest of the world: an overpriced oasis of the liberal arts in the middle of the desert. The job at the hospital had been listed with career services, and although the position was clearly in medical records, the language of description— *oversee, liaison, confidential*—had intrigued her. Her ex-girlfriend, Gwen, was going to be teaching on the nearby reservation, as part of a national service program, and she was looking for another housemate. Their unkempt two-story with the overgrown lawn was a kind of halfway house, a last pit stop before passing into the limits of adulthood. Teachers' salaries were, inexplicably, generous, and Cassie's roommates provided take-out burritos and beer and stories of maladjusted children and monstrous parents and tyrannical administrators that filled long, warm evenings on their peeling porch.

Cassie still cared for Gwen. Their relationship had been brief, but exhaustive, in its way. Gwen was androgynously beautiful. Tall and athletically slender, with the hint of some delicateness about her. Gwen and Cassie had gone together to a summer program in Italy, and when the course in Rome was finished they changed their tickets, squeezed every last cent from their credit cards and caught the ferry at Bari. For two weeks, they caught early morning boats between the least-visited of the Greek islands, where the black sand was so hot that you had to lay on thick straw mats in order to be near the water. They breakfasted on fruit and honey and thick yogurt and their skin crusted with salt from swimming topless in the sea. When the relationship ended— not long after their return to school—they met in Gwen's dorm room to divide the photographs. The only picture that Cassie had really felt she needed was a shot she had taken of Gwen knee-deep in the ocean, walking towards her, her hair and skin glistening in the late afternoon sun. Something about the way Gwen's body held itself up—as though still buoyed by the salty water— struck Cassie with a sense of openness, as though the memory of that moment could expand to fill landscapes past the edge of the picture.

Since becoming housemates, there had been glimpses of the intimacy that they had once shared, and this pleased Cassie. Gwen struggled with the young students foisted upon her in September, and found in Cassie an attentive audience. Their conversations provided Cassie with a focus beyond her own unsettling aimlessness and the incessant difficulties of maintaining her bank account. Cassie's parents did send money, every so often. They were earnest, aged-hippie types who assured her that, with time, she would mark her own path.

***

On the day of the interview, Cassie wore a freshly washed shirt and sensible shoes. It seemed important to project an image of cleanliness. The doctor who she had spoken with on the phone met her, alone, in his office. There was no official egg donation program at the hospital, he explained, but they had the facilities—meaning the doctor himself, Cassie guessed—to perform in-vitro fertilization with a donor egg. If they could find a suitable donor, it would save this couple from having to travel out to one of the big city clinics for as many cycles as it took them to conceive.

He had pages of questions. Somebody brought Cassie a cup of coffee. First they went through her own medical history—sexual, social, psychological. The doctor had big, prickly-looking white eyebrows, which he cocked cartoonishly. He could not suppress his pleasure at Cassie's lesbianism.

"So you've never had intercourse with a man?" He pushed his face forward from the neck, leaning out from his cushioned chair.

Cassie shook her head, wishing that she had dressed a little less conservatively. She was a dyke, not a nun, after all.

"But I have—you know—in high-school—"

"You've performed fellatio."

Cassie nodded.

"Did you develop any sores in your mouth?"

"No."

Cassie was neither especially ashamed nor humored to say such things. She knew that the doctor had seen stories much stranger than hers. She wished, in fact, that her own history were a little more colorful, contained something for them both to ponder in that drab office.

As the interview progressed, the questions grew stranger. Cassie forced herself to pause thoughtfully before each answer. The doctor asked which hand she used to write with, whether she could sing on key, how she rated her athletic abilities. Did she consider herself especially agile, average, or clumsy?

Average, Cassie said. She thought of herself standing on one foot during a yoga class that she had taken at school to fulfill a physical education requirement and pulled her spine straight against the back of her chair.

She became slightly frantic, towards the end, certain that her answers could not have captured all that was genetically desirable about her. The doctor cooperated, duly noting everything that she rattled on about. There would only be one chance. It wasn't a job interview, but rather a cross between a medical visit and some other type of evaluation— she felt the shadow of something beneath each inert question. Cassie was being checked out, by the doctor, on behalf of the infertile couple. The process of selection had been clinicalized, and she was sure that their rejection would come over the telephone like an unhappy test result. She was no med student, no athlete, no artistic genius. These people, Cassie thought, would not pick her, and she would return to her stacks of files, to a bedroom window overlooking a tangle of weeds, without any proof that she had done this, that she had risen to the top of a stack.

The last thing the doctor did was take her picture. It was a Polaroid—the hospital was for some reason full of Polaroids, as Cassie had learned from notices for missing cameras that appeared above the photocopy machine in the basement. The doctor didn't offer to let her watch her picture develop, but as he was showing her to the door, he looked down at the white square in his hand and smiled slightly. After saying goodbye and thank you Cassie paused a moment in hopes that he would say something more, something silly and inappropriate, perhaps tell her she was the cutest one so far. But instead he wished her a pleasant day.

That night, Cassie asked Gwen if she was attractive. *Cute* was what she said. "Do you think I'm cute?"

Gwen was smoking a cigarette, flicking ash into the garbage can as Cassie washed her plate in the sink. "I still find you attractive," Gwen said coolly. She looked to Cassie's face and then held her gaze there. Cassie felt something gooey and warm spreading in her stomach.

***

Two weeks went by. Cassie told herself that she was resigned to rejection, but there was a fluttering in her chest whenever the telephone in her cubicle sounded. She had told no one of her interview, and this allowed her to hope that she had made a good impression on the doctor. When he called to tell her that the infertile couple was indeed interested in harvesting her oocytes, pride rose up and bathed her like a cooling salve.

First, she was to meet with a young psychologist who had been recruited, it appeared, to deem her fit to withstand the cycle and harvest. She went over the process with Cassie, who assured her that she had no ethical qualms about leftover embryos being frozen or discarded. Cassie had done some reading on the Internet, and she worked as much medical terminology as possible into her answers, calling her eggs *oocytes* and mentioning various hormones by name.

After a time, the psychologist put down her pen and closed the folder in which she had been taking notes. Cassie scooted into the front part of her chair, preparing to stand, but then the psychologist sighed, just loudly enough for Cassie to hear.

"I'm just curious, why do you want to do this?"

Cassie had hoped against this particular question, as she could concoct no response that would be both rational and seemly. The obvious incentive was money, and the obvious thing to say was that she wanted to help these people. No words and no reasons, however, explained the way she felt at that moment, clutching her bag to her chest. A strange heat fingered its way towards her face and neck.

"Because I can," she said, willing her tongue to move in a manner that wouldn't betray her. "I'm healthy, I have time, I don't think I have the kinds of problems with all this that some women would."

"And the payment?" The psychologist had tossed her rapport-building mantle. She was asking this one for herself.

"It's nice. But I guess there are easier ways to get money. What I'd like is to make a down payment on a car."

"You don't have a car?" The psychologist seemed genuinely surprised.

Cassie shook her head slowly.

"That sounds perfectly reasonable. I'm sorry. I was just wondering—"

"It's okay," Cassie interrupted. "It's all kind of fascinating—I mean, I think it is."

"Are you a med student?" The psychologist squinted at her.

Cassie gave her best polite laugh.

She was quick to shut the door behind her. Medical school, she thought. Just one of a thousand options she had never contemplated. Yet there was a promise of forward motion. She would not be at this tedious job forever. She had written, she had read, she had traversed far-away waters. And there too was that round weight sinking, with its incessant threat of anchoring here. Cassie found it difficult sometimes to tell whether she was moving along or she was falling. She had a secret wish, nestled like a small, burrowing animal inside her chest, to be a part of something larger, to scratch somewhere and know it would be permanent.

***

She had passed muster with the psychologist, the doctor called to inform her. Cassie's next task was to meet with the lawyer. He met her in the doctor's office with some papers he had drawn up for her to sign, relinquishing her rights to the embryos created with her eggs and any children that resulted.

"They don't want to meet me?" Cassie enquired. "Before?"

"It's standard procedure," said the doctor, who sat behind his desk and tapped on his keyboard while the lawyer unearthed documents from an over-stuffed briefcase.

"Even if the harvest is successful, a pregnancy doesn't always result—it's best if there isn't any contact between the donor and the recipient."

Cassie didn't entirely believe him—surely, some of the people who placed these ads selected their donors themselves.

"Don't I get to know anything about them?" It seemed fair. They knew her entire medical history, had seen the Polaroid picture that she herself had not gotten a look at.

The doctor looked down at his desk, away from Cassie's gaze. "These people want very badly to be parents. They're grateful for your help," he said. The lawyer handed her a pen.

***

Teresa Ankeley was thirty-four years old and her folder was as fat as the ones they sent stacked in carts to the transplant center or psychiatry. After days of carefully negotiated sifting in the files that were called up to the infertility clinic, Cassie had identified Teresa Ankeley and memorized her location: third shelf from the bottom, a few palm's lengths from the back of the row. Every time she went into that gray, cinderblock storage room to pull or replace a cartload of charts, she would slip Mrs. Ankeley's tome on the top of her stack, reading as she looped the shelves. One page per file handled. She longed to take Mrs. Ankeley's story home with her, or to at least slip it away for her lunch hour so as to devour its pages in the privacy of a dark booth in the cafeteria. Cassie had lost the urge to eye other charts with anything more than a passing interest, and the thought of getting caught with her head in this one was too terrible to imagine. Nobody could know, not before she had fingered every page, every lab form, every physician's scrawl.

Eight years earlier, Mrs. Ankeley, then Teresa Martin, came to the hospital for a colonoscopy. She was referred by a doctor at a private clinic across town. *Patient complains of excessive fatigue*, those records read. *Anemia?* The doctor had ordered blood tests and instructed Teresa Martin to provide a stool sample. Cassie envisioned Teresa Martin—just a few years older than Cassie—outside a stucco clinic building, sitting behind the wheel of her car, tired and sad and scared, staring at the plastic cup that she was to return with the next morning.

The doctor's office had sent the hospital a photocopy of some lab results. Certain numbers were highlighted orange. The notes section from Teresa Martin's visit to the GI clinic read, simply, *Chief complaint blood in stool*. Cassie examined the pictures taken inside her lower intestine—grainy images that she could not imagine were of any diagnostic use. Several growths were removed during the procedure. There was writing that Cassie could not decipher, and words she did not comprehend. She recognized, however, the term *malignancy*, which appeared several times. Cassie thought of a doctor in one of the clinics holding the pictures up to the light, circling things with his finger. He would have made the call himself. He would have told Teresa Martin that she needed to come in to discuss her test results.

***

After her period had come and gone, Cassie made the appointment upstairs.

In the exam room, there was a small bowl of smooth, colored agates, and photographs on the wall of newborn infants cradled in enormous flower petals. A lavender gown, which tied across the chest instead of in back, lay neatly folded on the padded exam table. Cassie imagined that this was what a beauty spa would feel like—it was impossible to think that she was still in the hospital. The slim women sitting in the waiting area, with their leather purses and their handle bags from upscale mall stores, were not the hospital's usual clientele. According to the papers she had signed, it was the infertile couple who would be cutting Cassie's check once her eggs were harvested, it was to their home that the bills for her office visits were to be sent. No insurance would cover any of this.

The doctor did an ultrasound to examine Cassie's ovaries. He slicked up some kind of probe with a gel, inserted it, and pressed against her cervix. Her ovaries sat like round sacks on the screen, gray and giant. After, a nurse came and gave her an injection of Lupron. The initial puncture of the needle stung a bit. Cassie exhaled, as the nurse directed, and the pain faded , but as she pushed the fluid into Cassie's thigh, her muscle began to ache and then pulled into a piercing cramp. By the time the nurse withdrew the needle, Cassie's eyes were brimming, and when she wiped at them with her fingers she only spread the water across her skin.

"That's a tough one." The nurse handed her a tissue.

"I didn't think it was going to hurt," Cassie said. "Are they all like that?"

Cassie's skin was bumpy with cold underneath the thin gown, the tissue damp and wadded in one hand. She felt suddenly small and stupid.

"It'll all be over before you know it." The nurse placed the palm of her hand on Cassie's exposed knee and shook it gently.

***

The records from the oncology department begin two weeks after Teresa Martin's colonoscopy. *Patient eager to schedule surgery as soon as possible.*

The brief "social history" section of the preformatted clinic notes pages provided little descriptive information for Cassie to add to the image of Teresa Martin. As Cassie would have guessed, Teresa Martin was a non-smoker who had never injected herself with drugs. She was heterosexual and single. She worked at a gym—a trainer, perhaps? or a masseuse?—and lived alone. It was this last detail that struck Cassie as she read standing between the shelves, pretending to work. She imagined Teresa Martin's clean, quiet apartment—large, unused candles on square side tables and a refrigerator moderately stocked with vegetables and fruit. Who would stay with her while she was sick? Was there a sister?

A portion—it was impossible to ascertain how much, without an anatomy textbook, as the Latinate terms meant little to Cassie—of Teresa Martin's colon had been removed during the operation. Then another phone call. Another office visit. More difficult news. The cancer had not penetrated the colon and spread to other parts of her body, and the surgery was to have been the only treatment. But there had been some complication, some unforeseen quality to the tumors.

Discussed removal of growths and possibility of cancer remaining. Patient requests that chemotherapy begin immediately. Concerned about nausea and hair loss. Says not worried about possible effects on fertility.

Teresa Martin's thoughts about having children made an intuitive sense to Cassie. There was a demarcation, she saw, a line that circumstance could deepen into a chasm, between an obsession with the shape of a future and an obsessive focus on the having of one.

***

On the day that she brought home a paper sack of vials and syringes and dumped its contents onto her bed, Cassie decided to tell Gwen. To keep it secret seemed unnecessarily martyr-like. She thought she would say it that evening on the back porch, where she could watch the horizon as she spoke. She would pop the top off a bottle of beer, raise it to her lips, say, *So I'm going to do this thing*, and take a long, cool sip. But it had rained earlier so the porch furniture was still wet, there was no beer and it was just Cassie and Gwen making sandwiches in the kitchen.

"Guess what I'm doing," Cassie said.

Gwen didn't glance up from the tomato she was slicing. "Tell me," she said. And Cassie wondered if she should. Gwen's voice had a hard quality to it—she was tired, Cassie thought. Her students leeched something from her.

Cassie attempted to change the subject, asking Gwen about her day at school.

"Just say what you're going to say." Gwen tossed the remaining tomato wedge into its wet plastic bag.

Cassie described, as succinctly as possible, how her oocytes were going to be cultivated and monitored and finally harvested.

Gwen grabbed a head of lettuce from the refrigerator and began ripping off the outermost, limpid leaves. "You"—she watched intently as the look in Gwen's eyes traveled and transformed into the words on her lips—"are fucking *weird*."

Cassie eyed the kitchen door. Imagined the sound it would make slamming behind her. She told Gwen it was five thousand dollars.

"That's more than a down payment on a car," she added.

"But *why*?" Gwen's arms hung flaccidly at her sides, the lettuce dangling from her fingers.

"I need the money," Cassie said weakly. "I just need to do this."

***

Teresa Martin's chemotherapy was unique—new, possibly experimental. It required her to be treated in a series of three cycles. *Self-conscious about thinning of hair,* read one note. *Hair loss only noticeable to patient.*

At another visit, Theresa complained to a nurse that her labia had grown so dry that they cracked and bled against the brush of toilet paper. *Personal lubricant recommended.*

A couple of pages later, there was a reference to a baseball cap, beneath a notation that nutritional drinks had been suggested. Cassie flipped back the pages to the first visits, and calculated that by this point Theresa Martin had lost nearly twenty pounds. Cassie imagined her striking, bony face, under the brim of a red cap, whittled to a gangly, teenage shape.

***

The first weeks' worth of injections were relatively simple, the syringes small. But then the doctor gave her a new hormone, which was to be injected deep into the muscle covering her hip. Gwen did not hesitate when Cassie asked for help.

The first couple of mornings, Cassie thought for sure that she would scream before the needle was out. But Gwen quickly grew deft with her angling. Cassie found a prickly sort of comfort in their new, clinical routine. Gwen would enter Cassie's room before seven, expertly pulling the fluid from the vial. She pressed the syringe until a tiny spray shot from the tip of the needle, wiped Cassie's skin with an alcohol swab, pinched a width of her flesh then jabbed the needle straight in. Slowly she pressed the fluid into Cassie's muscle and then a fast exit, with her fingers wiggling the skin as though to shake off the pain. There was no earthly reason for a Band-Aid; nevertheless, Gwen stuck a tiny, beige adhesive strip to the injection site, tapping it into place with the tips of her fingers. What amazed Cassie was that she kept trying so hard to be gentle, after each of her efforts had plumed up into purplish-brown bruises.

For the entire six-week cycle, Cassie took great care when lowering her hips into bus seats and chairs. She was bloated and her breasts swelled slightly, but otherwise didn't feel that the hormones were affecting her. There was one evening when she opened the refrigerator and found the ice cream gone and before she could stop herself her eyes had filled with stupid tears. She was especially tired at night.

Mornings were the best times. Cassie would arrive early at the hospital and make her way to the clinic, where the nurse waved her into the usual exam room. Then the doctor arrived. He left other women waiting for her, Cassie was sure. Hers was a precious load. She would pull off her pants, lay back on the table, and within moments there would be the soft knocking at the door. Then the doctor would perform a quick ultrasound, tell her everything looked good, that at three weeks they'd be ready for harvest.

She came in on Saturdays as well, and by the time she arrived, the doctor would have turned on the lights, opened the window in the stuffy exam room, and set the bottle of ultrasound gel to warm in a sink-full of hot water. It was a longer trip for Cassie, with the buses running on their truncated weekend schedule. The doctor was thoughtful. On Saturdays he brought her coffee with milk and sugar—from the store, not the cafeteria.

***

During her third round of chemotherapy, Teresa Martin made six visits to the emergency room. *Unable to keep down water. Dehydration.* The doctors gave her Compazine, IV fluids, and discharged her the same day.

Once, she arrived with chief complaints *fever and shortness of breath*, and was eventually admitted to the hospital with pneumonia. Her treatment was suspended for a time, so that the third cycle grew into what was practically a fourth.

By the time the chemotherapy was over, and test results pronounced her remission, more than a year had passed since her initial diagnosis. There were few pages left in her file. Some colonoscopy pictures, just as indecipherable as the first. And ink-jet printouts of laboratory results. Finally, the records from the infertility clinic began. They were the first to mark the name change. Between her remission and the search for an oocyte donor, Teresa Martin had become Mrs. Ankeley.

These latest records lacked the oncologist's sense of detail, of language. The current doctor—Cassie's doctor— left no sense of Teresa Ankeley's transformation from a woman unsure she would want a child to a woman who needed a child so much that she went looking for Cassie. There was nothing about the marriage, the return of her health, all the years that had passed. No clue as to when she had changed her mind. Cassie wondered if the idea of the baby had come when there was no need for birth control. If the fact of the impossibility, the blank permanency of no children, had charged Mrs. Ankeley's desires.

Cassie replaced the file in its spot, sorry to have finished it so quickly, with days to go before the harvest and nothing more to discover. She tried reading the files that passed across her metal cart, but there was no comparison to the story of Teresa Martin's cancer and remission, and Cassie returned to the shelf each day to re-read a few pages. Her appreciation grew upon second and third readings. No other chart was so brimming with information, so *complete*.

The oncologist was, it seemed, a man after Cassie's own heart, a literary type prone to full sentences and evocative descriptions in place of doctor shorthand. He had once written that Teresa Martin was *crestfallen* upon hearing test results. It would go on like this for pages, and Cassie came to see that something other than writerly instinct, something beyond clinical concern, moved the doctor's hand. Even before Cassie finally deciphered the signature at the bottom of a lined page, she knew that what she had been reading was some kind of romance. Dr. Ankeley had stopped by Teresa's bedside every day that she was hospitalized, not for the perfunctory task of examining her but to ask how she felt, to discuss the long course of her treatment. He wrote about the sound of her breath. He noted that she seemed *revived, animated.* Teresa Martin was bone-thin, balding, and seriously ill, and Dr. Ankeley wrote of her not in idealizations—she was *clammy* and *depressed* and *coughing productively*—but with a singularity of observation that could only be art, or love.

***

Dr. Ankeley's first name was Clarence. Cassie looked him up in the staff directory on-line. His offices were on the fourth floor. Department of Oncology. The clinic hours were posted.

The next Tuesday, after her morning ultrasound, she looped the hospital corridors, passing through sets of swinging, windowed doors, until she finally spotted a sign for Oncology. As in most of the clinics, the waiting area spilled out into the hallway, where some chairs and tables and old magazines had been set. There was an elderly man with an oxygen tank, an old lady in a wheelchair, a teenager playing a handheld videogame. He was tan and full-bodied, and it took Cassie a moment to notice that, in addition to being bald, he had no eyebrows or lashes. There were a couple of women wearing head-coverings— a floppy red fishing hat and a scarf with purple flowers.

Cassie approached the reception desk and took hold of a clipboard, as though she had done this before. It was a sign-in sheet: name, physician, appointment time. There were two doctors listed, Ankeley and Miller.

"Need a pen?" offered the woman behind the desk. She eyed Cassie curiously.

"No," Cassie mumbled, reading the sheet before her. "Here's one."

She picked up the blue ballpoint tucked into the top of the clipboard, and with the slow, deliberate motions of a first-grader, traced the neat cursive of Esperanza Sanchez, the last patient to have signed-in to see Dr. Ankeley. Then she sat, unsure for what it was she waited. For Dr. Ankeley to introduce himself? To emerge, name neatly stitched to his white coat, calling Esperanza's name?

The next patient was summoned by a nurse. Fifteen minutes passed, then twenty, and Cassie thought that she might have to wait until Dr. Ankeley left for lunch to get a look at him. But then she heard a man's voice inquiring, "Sanchez?" The woman with the purple-flowered headscarf stood and stepped away from her seat. Cassie stared into her lap, breathing hard, and then she looked up.

To say that he was not who she had been expecting wouldn't be accurate. Cassie did not so much have a vision of Dr. Ankeley as an idea. For weeks she had imagined how it felt to look at Theresa Martin from his privileged, clini-cal vantage—and Mrs. Ankeley she could see. She had a height, a (recovered) weight. Cassie had selected for her a hair color (light brown) and eye color (blue). She had a birthday. Dr. Ankeley, until that moment, had functioned simply as her eyes and hands, observing and recounting his wife's story. To look up and see anything other than a mirror image of herself was its own kind of shock.

He wasn't wearing a white coat but a shirt and tie, with a stethoscope coiled around the back of his neck. He was of average height, and his belly hung softly over his belt, wrapped snugly in the fabric of the salmon-colored dress shirt. Wiry tufts of white hair seemed to have been stuck haphazardly around his crown, behind his ears. The skin of his face hung in creased folds, as if weather-beaten. Sixty, Cassie thought. He looked to be at least in his six-ties. She stared, and he caught her gaze, staring right back at her for a long mo-ment, longer than he should have been comfortable looking, as though it were a kind of pleasure, an entitlement. Cassie felt her blood swishing frantically in her veins, pumping up something inside her that would soon burst.

Dr. Ankeley motioned for Mrs. Sanchez to go on ahead back towards his office, the exam room, whatever it was they had hiding back there. When she stepped in front of him, he drew a hand to her back and ran it delicately down her spine, tapping his fingers against her tailbone. Cassie heard a strange sound, like a sneeze and a gagging. There were breaths coming fast, and she realized that they were her own.

She stood, steadied herself, and walked with long, swinging strides to-wards the set of double doors that led to the elevator. When she turned to glance back, Dr. Ankeley and Esperanza Sanchez were gone. The other pa-tients had returned to their magazines. Forgotten the girl in the waiting room, her strange sound absorbed in the peripheral din of bodily malfunction and bizarre behavior.

***

The next morning, Cassie bit her lip and held her breath during the injection. When Gwen left, she lay a while on her mattress, lingering with her image of Dr. Ankeley and a trembling uneasiness in her gut. She felt as though she had been the one to cast him as the father, and now, finding him unfit for the role, she had only herself to blame.

She could back out at any time, Cassie reminded herself. The lawyer's papers allowed for it. And she knew that she wouldn't. It was for Mrs. Ankeley that she was going through with the harvest. She needed her.

***

Gwen surprised Cassie by taking a day off so that she could accompany her to the final appointment. She was supposed to have someone escort her home, lest she fall down the stairs or walk out into traffic in her anesthetized haze. In the softly lit waiting area, Gwen looked sleek and androgynous—perfectly out of place—and Cassie was sorry that she had come all this way.

It was a different room, on the day of the procedure—there were more tubes strung about, more bottles, brighter lights. Cassie changed into the requisite lavender gown. The doctor came in, accompanied by another young doctor, who would be administering the anesthesia.

"This is it," the doctor said, with some measure of pride. Everybody—the two doctors and the nurse—had been reduced to heads hovering above her, and she felt suddenly exposed.

Cassie tried not to think about the forest of floating follicles blooming with round oocytes that she had watched growing on the ultrasound pictures, which was about to be snipped, or deracinated—she didn't attempt to recall the details of the procedure, not while supine on the table. It would hurt, when she woke, in some way that she had never felt before. The nurse told her she might be sore for a day or so, and that she might be nauseated and dizzy from the anesthesia. Cassie felt her fingers begin to shake, and she looked up at the nurse, who was already reaching down for her hand.

"Whiskey," said the anesthesiologist. His voice sounded like he was trying to take a picture of a kid.

"Here comes the whiskey." There was a pinching at her arm, and his smooth pate was floating over her, his words soft and dulcet like thick liquor over ice.

"What do you like to drink?"

And Cassie remembered thinking: *beer*, but before she could push the sound from her lips her mind slipped into blankness.

***

It didn't hurt, when she woke up. She was in the same room, her legs removed from the stirrups and tucked under a blanket. Sunlight shone in directly through the windows, reflecting off the glistening floor. Cassie struggled to form a thought through the haze enveloping her brain, and all she could come up with was, Time has passed. Her mouth tasted filmy and strange, and she remembered that she had not had anything to eat or drink since the night before. She felt the same down there, she didn't even feel numb.

At one point, the nurse came in and asked if she would like help getting up, or if she wanted to sleep some more, and Cassie said, Sleep.

The light coming in through the windows became so bright that she couldn't keep her eyes open, and the taste in her mouth grew more bothersome. A trail of bubbles passed ferociously through her stomach. She didn't trust her legs to hold her up, and she hung onto the edge of the table as she stood.

When the nurse returned, Cassie was standing at the window. There was a white-haired lady bent over her walker inching towards the entrance below, making her slow, slow way to an appointment.

"You're up," the nurse said, with a note of congratulation. "How are you feeling?"

Cassie turned to face her, to tell her that she was fine, she was ready to leave. She looked to the stirrups, the steel sink by the wall, the glass jar of cotton gauze, the nurse's face. She pulled the thin gown tight across her chest, and as she exhaled the tears came tumbling thickly down her cheeks.

"It's over." Her voice scraped against her throat.

"It's all over now."

The nurse was accommodating. She helped Cassie back into her clothes, handed her tissues, caught her shoulder when she stooped low into a sob. By the time she was dressed, she had regained enough of her composure. The borders of her world—the invisible measurements that held together a moment—had reconstructed themselves into something recognizable.

Gwen sat anxiously, waiting in the same chair Cassie had left her in. Not so much time had passed as she had thought. Cassie said that she didn't feel sick. She said she wanted to get home and get something to eat. Gwen slipped her arm through Cassie's elbow, fastening her there, as though she might shatter were she to fall.

***

Cassie followed Mrs. Ankeley's medical record carefully, waiting for new documentation, for the implantation, for the pregnancy, to appear. But it often took days for charts to make their way from one department to another, or for copies of clinic papers to be sent down to the basement—sometimes these would arrive a month after an appointment—and there were as of yet no new additions to Mrs. Ankeley's file. The doctor, however, was unexpectedly generous with information during Cassie's follow-up visits: Seventeen eggs had been harvested and subsequently fertilized, he explained. After five days, there were left six robust-looking embryos, two of which were transferred into Mrs. Ankeley's womb, and the remaining four cryogenically frozen.

When the lab results proving the fact of her pregnancy finally appeared in her chart, Cassie made herself a photocopy, which she folded into quarters and tucked in her back pocket. For weeks after, there was no more news. Nobody even called up her file. Cassie wondered if she had miscarried early, never bothering to return to the hospital.

She imagined fiercely and she believed that Mrs. Ankeley was still pregnant, that one of the fetuses had sloughed away and left the strongest to grow—a girl. She would survive this, too, and one day she would take her child and drive away. She would leave town and head off in some direction. Cassie knew she would keep going.

Legacy

by Iqbal Pittalwala

WINNER OF THE 2004 GIVAL PRESS SHORT STORY AWARD

Thirteen years after he became a widower, the father decided, at age sixty-eight, to remarry. The wedding in San Francisco was a simple, bland affair. Along with hundreds of couples, the father and his partner of four years, Jerry, stood patiently in line outside San Francisco City Hall to receive the certificate they'd been denied for centuries. It rained incessantly in the city that February weekend. Televisions poured wet images into homes all over the world so that, by the end of the weekend, viewers, young and old, had watched gay couples huddled beneath a meadow of rainbow-colored umbrellas. The downpour and gloomy skies over San Francisco weren't what deterred Sameer, the son, and Nila, the daughter, from showing up at City Hall. Sameer—unable to locate the logic behind a same-sex marriage despite much support for his father—decided to abstain from the ceremony, writing it off at the last minute as a made-for-TV gimmick. Nila, the older of the two by six years, had never planned to go, having taken poorly to the father's coming out gay.

Within days of the marriage, inheritance matters usurped conversations in Sameer's apartment in Queen Anne, Seattle, driven by an emotional email the father shot off to his two children. In Jerry, the father declared candidly, he had found the soul mate he'd been seeking all his life. "Financially, he is not in good shape—he lost everything in his divorce and the stock market crash," the father inserted in the middle of the eighth paragraph. "I am going to help him in every way I can." Rosa, Sameer's wife, whose staunch Catholicism could be traced back to her Mexican and Colombian ancestry, hung on to those sentences. She insisted the father ought at least to draw up a will and list Sameer and Nila as beneficiaries of his new four-bedroom house in Laguna Beach, California, before he proceeded to help "whoever showed up in his bed."

"Why should this Jerry guy get anything?" she said, curling her lips as she readied herself for bed one night in early April. Her wavy dark hair, tied into a high ponytail during the day, fell heavily on her shoulders. Once a literary agent for upcoming ethnic writers, she was now the managing editor of a Latino magazine in Seattle. Thin, she believed she was not thin enough. An hour ago, she had returned bubbling with energy from a turbo kick-boxing session at the gym. She sat on the edge of the bed and, as she bent to apply a moisturizing cream between her toes, the crucifix around her neck flickered with reflected light. She glanced at the window, distracted by a pitter-patter sound. A drizzle painted silvery streaks on the pane through which, on the occasional rainless day in Seattle, one could view the shimmering cityscape and, looming in the distance, Mount Rainier. "This marriage isn't really a marriage no matter what their certificate says," she said, returning her attention to her toes. "It's not legal, not worth the paper it's printed on. You and Nila are his children. That relationship is legal. He ought to keep your mother in mind before he turns over everything to this Jerry guy."

Sameer, shirtless and already in bed, stared at the ceiling, his hands locked behind his head. His belly rose gently and fell. A software engineer at Microsoft, he'd reached a point in his life where he wished he were free to do something different from what he was accustomed to—something rash, something radical. Five years of living in the northwest had left no impression on him worth noting. Unable to say where he'd like to be five years down the line, he toyed in his mind during his most rebellious moments with taking up carpentry, or volunteering in a strife-torn country to provide food relief or, best of all, renouncing everything, becoming Buddhist and fighting for Tibetan freedom. "It's only a matter of time before gay marriages become legal," he said, still staring at the ceiling. His brows were gathered as though he were still at work, debugging dense computer code. "If he'd married a woman, would we be having this discussion?"

"What kind of question is that?" Rosa said, getting beneath the covers and snuggling up to him. "If your parents hadn't emigrated from India, or if you and Nila had been born there and not in the U.S., would we be having this discussion? See what I mean, honey? Such questions are irrelevant." She kissed Sameer on the shoulder and settled her cheek against his upper arm. "I tell you it's amazing the kind of bold and bizarre actions some immigrants take after they get here. Things they would never dream of doing back in their home countries they'll push ahead with like fools in America. I mean it's one thing to blur your identity by wearing a baseball cap, shorts and a t-shirt, and avoiding Indian grocery stores. It's another for an immigrant guy to marry a guy. ¡Dios mio! The man is a retired math professor. He is well respected in the community. He needs to think of what he is doing, what ramifications his self-serving actions are having on us all. But what can you do with people who can't think beyond themselves?" She took Sameer's hand in hers and massaged it lightly. "One day we'll be having children and could use his help—financially and otherwise. Has he thought of that?"

Sameer turned on his side, showing his back to her. "He got tired of living all by himself. You said you didn't want him to live with us. So he did what he had to do. In the end, we do what makes us happy, and us only."

Rosa let go of his hand. He thought of the conversation he'd had with Nila earlier that day. She'd called, as she usually did, when he was about to leave the office, her living in New Jersey, three hours ahead, making it convenient for her to reach him at work on weekdays to discuss matters in which she had no desire to include Rosa. She suggested he visit the father soon to sort out inheritance issues. She couldn't afford to fly out from the East coast, she said, being nearly broke, and wouldn't go even if she could because, unless he secured his children's future, she didn't want to see the father's face again.

Nila believed the father had been seeing men even when their mother was alive. Throughout their childhood years in Orange County's Garden Grove, he had desecrated their family bonds by leading a double life. "Remember that Latino guy, Adolfo, he used to hang out with? That was no ordinary friendship," she has said in the past. "And then that Armenian or Persian fellow—whatever his name was. Something about him never seemed right to me." "To think that we were born of a gay man—*tchha!*—and that, if he could help it, he wouldn't have had us at all," she has said more recently. "Trust me, this freeloader Jerry hasn't landed recently from the skies to dock onto his crotch," she said vulgarly today on the telephone. "He's probably been bouncing on Dad's lap for decades. You know how it is with Dad. You never get the full story from him. What's really going on in his head or in his life, we never know."

Years before their mother had died from liver cancer, Nila had posited that a significant fraction of the father's life remained permanently in the dark from them. 'The family moon,' she labeled him. One side forever hidden from view, he orbited his children's lives—always present, yet forever distant. For much of his married life he had schemed and juggled stories in his mind, she believed. "Imagine the energy he has had to invest in keeping his sick lies together," she'd say, "in making sure his intricate stories didn't collide."

Today, Sameer explained to her that what was done was done. Their father had remarried and, whether they liked it or not, it was what they had to work with. He had every right to remarry, he pointed out. He may live twenty or thirty years—who could say? Why should anyone live even a handful of years in solitude? If there is promise of joy for even a few years, why shouldn't the father go for it? He was bored, miserable and lonely, he had written in the email to his children. Like everyone else, he was entitled to happiness, to companionship, to a future with whomever he wanted to share his life.

"Well, let him shack up then with whomever he wants—who the hell's stopping him?" Nila retorted. "Why does he have to marry and create a mess for us to clear?"

"Well, he has done it," Sameer said. "Whether gay marriages become legal or not, we have to bring Jerry into the equation. Look, I've said before I don't get the need for gay people to marry, but Dad has gone ahead with it and at least we, his children, have to accept that. Much of the world won't support him."

"I won't acknowledge, accept or support," Nila said. "It's not legal. It's not yet sanctioned by the world, thank God. You know what I dreamed the other day? Mama was lying in her bed, in a fetal position, and crying. She was in a plain red sari that was too short for her. You and I were very young and we were clutching her ankles, imploring her not to remove her wedding ring, which she was struggling to do. Please—let's not forget: the man is a liar. He lied to Mama and to us all these years. Now you listen to me, Sameer, and quit arguing. Go down to Laguna Beach and put some sense into his head."

Sameer and Rosa met Jerry once, one late afternoon three years ago. The father and Jerry were driving to Vancouver from San Francisco and stopped in Queen Anne on the way. The meeting went without incident, with not a voice raised, with a minimum of words exchanged. Jerry—a short, boyish-looking Asian-American architect in his forties and introduced nervously as the 'boyfriend'—handed a box of Godiva chocolates to Sameer, a porcelain vase from the Kwang Hsu period to Rosa. They stayed for less than half an hour, not even finishing the jasmine tea that Rosa served. They needed to get to Vancouver in time, the father said. For dinner with friends, Jerry added. The sooner they left, the better it would be. For us, too, Rosa was tempted to say but held her tongue.

Three years later, now in bed with Sameer, she rubbed his chest with her hand, then gently pulled at the graying hairs, twirling them around a finger-nail. "Why don't you fly down to chat with him face-to-face some weekend?" she said. "Emails and phone calls won't work. Better we settle this matter once and for all."

"You're right," Sameer said, and reached for the bedside lamp to switch it off. "Nila has been saying the same thing all week. Sweetheart, why don't you come with me? We could make it a weekend holiday."

Rosa pulled away from him and faced the ceiling as well. "Don't be silly. This is a matter between you, Nila and your father. I shouldn't come across as having designs on your inheritance."

Sameer responded with silence. He sank his head further into the pillow and pulled the covers to his neck. One corner of the ceiling was partially con-cealed behind a cobweb, he noticed. He turned to face Rosa and threw an arm around her to lightly massage her shoulder. He didn't think it was a good idea to go to the father to discuss inheritance, he wanted to say. How would he bring up the topic, especially in Jerry's presence? You're a disappointment to me, the father might say, as he used to say years ago when Sameer's grades were poor. You can't fend for yourself, so you come to me like some beggar.

Sameer turned away from Rosa and returned his gaze to the cobweb. He should forget about flying down to southern California. Nila could go if she was so concerned about inheritance. It wasn't his fault she was an unhappy high-school science teacher in Carteret, New Jersey, that she'd chosen to live her life as a childfree single woman. It surely wasn't his fault she'd made lousy financial investments in life and lost much of her money. So she would never be able to afford a home on her own. Big deal. Let her fritter money away on sky-high rent. Why should he care?

If he went to the father, however, the father could help her in a way he, Sameer, could never. Moreover, with the father's help on its way one day, Sameer would never have to help Nila financially. It wouldn't hurt to ask. Asking the father in person would be appropriate, more effective, he thought. Nila needs your help, he'd say and leave it at that. All right then: he'd go for a short time. He'd fly out on Saturday afternoon and return Sunday morning. He'd stay in a hotel near John Wayne Airport in Orange County. He'd take a taxi all the way to Laguna Beach. He'd travel light so there'd be no luggage to check in, no baggage claim headaches to battle.

He was about to consider the logistics of the trip back to Queen Anne when sleep took over and drew him in.

***

On Saturday evening, within moments of stepping out of the terminal at John Wayne Airport, he retreats to the time of his boyhood in southern California. He has never left, it feels to him. As he takes the escalator down toward ground transportation, he wonders if he has erred by coming. He shouldn't have come. Orange County—its surfer-friendly beaches with strands for endless inline-skating, its overwrought web of freeways, its proximity to Little India in Artesia—held too many memories of his childhood, of his mother, of the close-knit family he thought he'd had as a boy. Moreover, he was not going to go up to his father today, or any other day, to ask for what is not yet his and Nila's and may never be. He shouldn't have listened to Rosa. It was time Nila stopped bossing over him as well, a carry-over from their childhood days. He should have told them to fight this battle on their own. How did he become the spokesperson for the triad?

He considers taking a taxi. He rents a car instead and heads toward the South Coast Plaza, the sprawling mall in the heart of Costa Mesa. He'll lose himself in that city-within-a-city, he decides, kill some time away in the crowds until his mind clears. Orange County is busier than he can remember—ethnic knots of people at every bus stop, the streets chockfull of gleaming cars. His cell phone rings. He scans the number, notes it is his father calling him, and ignores the call. The cell phone rings again and stops. Moments later, it beeps to indicate a message received.

At the mall, which is bursting with shoppers and music and splashed liberally with bright lights and colors, he walks past a glittery Godiva store, then a Gucci one and finds himself eventually in the futuristic electronics section of Sears. A slender saleswoman, whose ethnicity he cannot determine, comes up to him to ask if he needs assistance. Her mannerism strikes him as so rehearsed, her voice so theatrical, that he imagines she has emerged from one of the plasma TVs quilting a nearby wall.

He shrugs. "Just looking," he says above the noise saturating the store. "I'm looking to buy a refrigerator actually. I've gotten tired of renting one. Where are they?"

She directs him toward the appliance section where he finds a bank of upscale refrigerators. He opens and closes the doors of a few, impressed and intrigued by their soundlessness. Surprised that some of them cost as much as a small car, he leans into the inside of one to take a closer look. Three of him and a little more could fit inside, he thinks. Gently, he closes the door and stares at it for a while. A young fake-blond salesman with a flawless shiny complexion comes up to him to ask if he has questions. "Just looking," Sameer says, reading the salesman's badge. "No questions, Mr. Papathanasopoulos." The salesman smiles and tells him to give a holler if he wants more information on an item. Sameer nods. He doesn't avert his eyes until the salesman feels awkward and walks away.

He leaves the mall feeling annoyed with himself. He heads back for the car. He jumps into it and drives down Bristol Street toward the roar of the 405. He feels relieved to be stopped by the traffic lights. He needs to slow down, rein in his mind and put his thoughts in order. He is amazed by the changes in Costa Mesa—also by its familiarity. Street names come back to him. It takes only seconds for the city's geography to re-crystallize in his mind. Surprised by how much he can recall, he watches several Hispanic families with strollers and oversized shopping bags crossing the street before him.

Just as the traffic lights turn green, he spots a strip mall to his right. Between two palm trees, just behind a neon sign listing the strip mall's stores, he sees a realty. He swings the car in its direction to pay a brief visit. What *is* a four-bedroom house in Laguna Beach worth these days? He enters the low-ceilinged office just as his cell phone rings again. He ignores it and makes his way to the front desk. He is asked by an effeminate dark-skinned man to proceed toward a stocky woman, seemingly of Japanese or Korean descent, seated behind a desk. "Hello, I am Audra Tokoyoda-Pfotenhauer," she says without rising, her eyes measuring him from above narrow tinted eyeglasses. "How may I help you?" Her chunkiness suggests a tough solidity to him, her body a toughness that one associates with rubber-like density. Though small in stature, she must weigh a ton, Sameer thinks. An orange-blossom fragrance yanks him out of his reverie. He's not sure if it's from one of the perfumes with which Tokoyoda-Pfotenhauer has doused herself or if it's the office streaming the sweet odor isotropically in some effort to lull clients toward a sale.

He considers turning around and leaving. "Oops, wrong office—I wanted the store next door," he could say over his shoulder, and step out. He decides to stay. Tokoyoda-Pfotenhauer has time to spare, he surmises from her polished, paper-free desk. He tells her he is looking for a two-bedroom condo close to the South Coast Plaza. He won't go over $250,000, he says. She raises an eyebrow, laughs in a way that resembles a cough, and informs him that he'd find no listings for such a low price. He tells her that's what he can afford and to pro-ceed anyways, moving in her computer-search as close to South Coast Plaza as 250K would allow. He adds that the monthly home association fees must not exceed $150, that, if there is a garden to attend to, it should be no larger than a doormat.

"I hated having to mow our lawn as a kid—right here, in Garden Grove," he explains. He leans towards her and rests his palms on her desk. "I'll be back in 30 minutes," he says, rising from his chair. "I'm going to get a bite."

"Why don't you call first?" Tokoyoda-Pfotenhauer says, rising as well. "In case, you know, nothing is available in your range. It will spare you the trouble of returning. Here, please, take my card."

He shakes his head. "It's no trouble at all," he tells her, not accepting the card that has emerged, magically, like a blade between her fingers. He bows, Japanese-style, and proceeds to leave the office. In the car, the cell phone rings again. Absently, he answers it.

"Sameer, oh thank god, where *are* you?" his father yells. "We've been waiting. I even left two messages on your—"

"Hor-horrendous traffic," Sameer says, wishing he were in Seattle. He can feel a headache growing in his mind. "I'm on my way."

***

The bottom line was that the father was happy, the way he'd never been with their mother. Sameer came to this conclusion when he stepped into the father's two-level house perched halfway up a hill in Laguna Beach, overlooking from three sides the Pacific Ocean's blue expanse. The father greeted him with a hug, made awkward by weight he had gathered around the waist. His hair, combed back, had thinned. His forehead seemed broader to Sameer, the lines on his face deeper. His thick moustache concealed his upper lip. Bushy eyebrows, pushed forward by permanent furrows in his brow, darkened his eyes. Sameer was noting how leathery the father's cheeks were when Jerry emerged from behind the father. Awkwardly, Jerry wrapped his arms around Sameer in a light embrace.

"What took you so long?" Jerry asked, standing beside the father.

"Come, sit," the father said.

"I drove north from the airport by mistake," Sameer lied.

"Forgotten Orange County already?" the father said.

"Where are your bags?" Jerry asked, rubbing the father's back with his hand.

A black leather couch marked the center of the room, its back facing the front door. Sameer approached it. "My bag is still in the car," he said. "I won't be staying overnight here though—"

"What nonsense," the father interjected. "You're staying with us overnight."

Sameer sank into the couch. He found himself in the center of a geometrically pristine living room. The walls were painted soft peach with white trim on the molding. Fabrics from Asia and Africa punctuated the wall facing the couch. To his left, an open, glassy exposure revealed the Pacific Ocean glistening below. The fireplace stood to his right, clean and unused. Two framed photographs on the mantelpiece caught his eye. In one, the father and Jerry stood cheek to cheek before the Hearst Castle in San Simeon. In the other—taken, Sameer guessed, in Palm Springs at least twenty years ago—the father, Nila, he and their mother posed inside the city's aerial tramway. Sameer turned back to the wall facing him. A Chinese floral painting had been placed too high, inadvertently leading the eye to the vaulted ceiling where a skylight, admitting natural light, brightened the hardwood floors. None of this was his father's creation, Sameer knew. His eyes fell on Jerry who was approaching him.

"What can I get you to drink?"

Sameer opted for cold water, which he gulped down rapidly. He needed to leave. Though the house was inviting and though Jerry and his father were cordial, a sharp uneasiness stirred inside him, combating the soft tranquility the house induced.

"I'm working on a project—a meditation center in Yorba Linda—that I need to return to," Jerry said. "The deadline for the renderings is tomorrow unfortunately. Please excuse me." It was only as he watched him leave the room that Sameer remembered that Jerry was an architect. Surprised that he knew so little of his father's life-partner, he turned away to find his father's eyes cast on him.

"What's the matter?"

"Nothing is."

"Relax then."

"I am relaxed."

"You're restless."

Sameer moved his palms in circles over the surface of the couch. "I'm not sure why I came—"

"Why shouldn't you? I'm glad you came down. When did we see each other last? Three years ago—when we came up to Seattle, no?"

"I should have come to San Francisco in February."

"What? Oh. Is that what this trip is about? Your absence there? That's all over now. It's history. We bear no grudge."

"I should have attended. It was an important day in your life, your new life."

"Forget that now."

"Dad?"

"Yes?"

"I came because I'm worried about Nila. Also to see you, of course—"

"What's happened to her?"

"Nothing has. She's—well, she's not doing well financially. She's depressed. She has put on a lot of weight lately—she said so herself. She has fought with Anika and also with another close friend, she also told me."

The father, still standing, leaned toward him. "You're hiding something. You can't fool me. What is it? Tell me."

"I'm not hiding anyth—"

"Yes, you are. You're tense. Like some lamb on its way to the slaughter-house."

"Please. Can we go somewhere so we can talk in private?"

"Jerry can't hear a thing. The door to his office is shut. Plus, he listens to music on headphones whenever he works."

Sameer sighed. "Please make sure that Nila is taken care of," he said. "She senses an abandonm—"

"Taken care of? Has something happened to her? Sameer, tell me."

Sameer shook his head. "I told you. She's unhappy. She feels alone. She's lonely and bitter. She—well, she has no money, which makes matters worse. She needs your, our—"

"Is that what this is about? Money for Nila? You came down here for *that*? You could have asked me on the phone. Or she could have."

"No, no. That's not why—"

"Don't get me wrong. I'm happy you've come. Look, you must be tired. Why don't we talk about this in the morning? Go, get your bags from the car. You've just arrived. We can discuss Nila tomorrow."

Sameer rose with difficulty. The room seemed to have expanded and he felt small before the father. Jerkily, he embraced him, memories of his Garden Grove days pressed between their chests. He said under his breath that he was sorry he did not go to San Francisco, that he had trivialized his father's relationship—and courage—by not going.

The father patted Sameer on the back and let go of him. "Go now. Bring your bag from the car." He watched Sameer walk head-bowed toward the door.

"Walk tall, Sameer. Always."

Sameer straightened up. "You're at peace," he said, his back to his father. "Finally. That's nice to see. I'm happy for you. When I come in again, let's start all over. We could pretend the talk we just had never took place." He heard the father laugh and say that that would be okay with him.

Sameer stepped outside and took in the sunshine. He closed the front door behind him. He switched his cell phone off. Climbing into the rental car, he turned the ignition and strapped on the seat belt.

He rolled the windows of the car down and let the wind whip through his hair and skin as he drove up the Pacific Coast Highway toward Newport Beach. He'd done the best he could. He felt glad he hadn't brought up inheritance with a man still alive. It had to be a sin of some kind—children requesting their share before the time was right. Hurrying the future thus was sacrilegious in his mind. Some holy book somewhere probably had a verse or two on it. The parable of the impatient son he had cast himself in. Ask for inheritance and you shan't receive. Wretchedly, he thought of what he'd nearly done, what he'd been cajoled to do by Nila and Rosa. As he escaped from Laguna Beach, he thought bitterly of them. He ought to jettison them from his life for some time. He ought to turn around, speed back to the hillside house and beg the father's forgiveness. Instead he tore away from the Pacific and accelerated the car.

He took Route 55 inland and soon saw signs for John Wayne Airport. He'd leave by the scheduled flight tomorrow. He'd keep the cell phone off until he landed in Seattle. When Nila didn't even speak to the father any more, what right had she to expect him to do the dirty work for her? Their father was happy for the first time in his life, had arrived at last where he needed to be. How did it matter to her whom he spent his life with to sustain that happiness? Their mother was dead. Their father was gay. She had to accept that, as he had, and move on.

He'd tell Rosa he felt ashamed to bring up inheritance with the father. He'd email his father tomorrow to apologize for having brought up money in their conversation, for fleeing the way he had. The next time Nila called him at work he'd invent this for her: The father would leave Jerry out of his will and would agree to help her out on two conditions. One, she made every effort to accept the father for who he was; and, two, she never brought up inheritance again.

He raced the car toward the airport. He drove past it. He caught sight of the Airport Hilton in the distance and decided he'd check into it later. For now, he needed to drive listlessly for a while, air his mind out, let the breeze wash over him. The father had married out of self-preservation, he realized. When neither of his children had extended an invitation to him to live in their homes, the father had gone ahead with seeking a caregiver willing to love him and be by his side. In the end, we do what makes us happy *and* ensures our loving care.

Sameer read his wristwatch. He considered driving all the way to Garden Grove to glimpse the house he'd grown up in. He shook his head. Too far and loaded with the history of a family shattered and scattered by a lie that had been perpetuated by denial. He would bring the family back together one day, he thought. He'd devote himself to healing the wound that was tearing Nila and the father apart.

He drove on. He thought, suddenly, of the realty near the South Coast Plaza. He'd told Tokoyoda-Pfotenhauer he'd return. Why not do just that? The evening stretched open ended before him. He drove on, determined to get to the realty. He'd get a pleasant dinner later in the evening. First, he'd stride into Tokoyoda-Pfotenhauer's office, his head held high. He'd announce that he wished to move down to southern California to be near his father. He'd make up a story centered around the father wanting him in Orange County, begging him to return home.

Sameer chuckled like a little boy. "I'm back," he would tell Tokoyoda-Pfotenhauer, curious to know what condos her search had found.

The Music She Will Never Hear

by Kristin FitzPatrick

WINNER OF THE 2011 GIVAL PRESS SHORT STORY AWARD

On the way to the mine, the historian lets Jace control the radio, if there are any stations out here at all. After listening to some fuzz, the historian says he wishes he had some tapes, some of his son's tapes, lying around. He laughs. "What is it that they say? 'Not your father's music'?"

Then he asks about Jace's music. Jace reaches down into his backpack, pulls out a pirated album. He tells the historian that the band isn't on the radio much, that they are called Phish, a concert group, a live phenomenon, how they played at Red Rocks and you just wouldn't believe the sound. How the beats and chords blasted out from the stage in the half shell, that orange-pink cave. Then he stops himself.

"Guitars and drums and keyboards, but it's not rock?" the historian says.

"More like fusion. Jazz, rock, bluegrass, maybe, a lot of improvising. I guess it sounds like rock to people who don't know it or it looks like it from the long hair and the clothes."

"Sounds a bit like that Garcia fellow and his tribe. Hell's Angels and all that business."

Jace chooses his words carefully. "It's not exactly like that, Dr. Sims."

"Go on, let's have a listen," the historian says. "I like it already."

Jace pops the tape in. While it plays, the historian glances at the tape deck. On this field trip, the historian wants to know about more than just heavy metals. He has called in Jace to tell him about the harder stuff. Carbons. Mites, tites, rites. Complex bonds. School me, kid. Give the teacher a lesson in rock.

After a few songs, he turns the volume down and smiles at Jace. "How about your outfit? What do you play?"

"My band's not playing now. I'm drums. Brad, my uncle, he's upfront, sings and plays lead. Keiko, his girlfriend, she got bored and picked up tambourines, then took over for the keyboard player when he split. We lost our bass player too, so maybe she'll learn that." He laughs.

"What's so funny?"

"Girls can't play bass."

"What about those all-girl groups?"

"That's different. She doesn't get along with girls. Besides, she likes to hide on the platform, only show the top of her. Thinks she's fat."

"Ah," the historian says. "Yes. You're behind your instrument, too. All of you are."

"Didn't think of it that way."

The historian's hands shake as he drives west. They enter a tunnel. Jace imagines that a stone door closes over the entrance behind them, and then an animated bird pumps TNT ahead, to force a rockslide over the only way out.

Now the historian's face scrunches up. "Keiko? One of those in my world survey course."

"One of what?"

"A Keiko. She came to my office last week. Falling behind, she said. Otherwise I wouldn't remember the name. It's hard to pick out a face in a class of hundreds."

"Sounds like her. But she'll get there. Holed herself up all weekend to cram for midterms."

"Right. So, Keiko and your uncle?"

"He's only a few years older than us. My grandma said they needed extra time to recover from raising my mom before they could have another kid." He laughs, and the burst of air from the back of his throat surprises him, and then he has no air left.

"Your mum. Where does she live?"

"She doesn't."

After they stop for breakfast, once the historian's stomach is full and the coffee kicks in, he taps his thumbs on the steering wheel. A pebble hits the windshield. Clink. Then the shush of light rain and the swish that wipes it away. Jace twirls a pencil, a stick of soft graphite he uses to sketch impenetrable carbon bonds of diamonds, those bastards that last through the worst heat and pressure. That was how it started, the twirling and spinning, the drum stick tricks, over his muffled snare and in front of heavy metal videos, to imitate the stunts those drummers could do, the way they nailed not just the skin, but the rim and hi hat. With the whole body, all the force they had. That'll kill your ears, Grandma always said. He didn't care about damaging his hearing, but he couldn't lose it completely. The silence that followed the final crash would hurt more than the loudest pound.

Jace tries to make getting to the mine fun. "You said you have children, right, Dr. Sims?" he says.

"Sure, though sometimes I forget. My son is good at making himself scarce."

Jace has no answer.

"You know," the historian says, "my mates at the School of Mines said you're quite a whip in the geology lab and I should request you as my guide. Lucky for me, isn't it?"

"I don't know. Guiding's a job. It's not bad."

"So, Jace is an unusual name. What does it mean in Japanese? You must be half or—?"

"My name means moon, and I'm not Japanese. I'm white, and Ute." He mumbles this last part, because it's none of the historian's business, and because Jace is not used to the topic. His association with Keiko confuses people, but at least the historian won't ask any more dumbass questions about names and groups and who came from where.

The historian nods. Origins are his business. "My wife and I, we look different, too. She's what you call black Irish. White skin, black hair, dark eyes. Her family wasn't too thrilled when I came along. You know, another English invasion."

"Yeah, I know what you mean." This is a bullshit comparison, but the old guy is backpedaling. He is really trying.

"But before long, the differences fade away. Life will get easier for the two of you."

"You mean for my uncle and Keiko."

"Right. For them." He checks the rear view mirror. "It will get easier for you, too."

The tape has reached its end. The historian punches the power button. Tell me some mine legends, he says. So Jace indulges him. This is the true work of the guide, and it's harder this time because this client is not the tax lawyer or the curious senior citizen tourists, trying to escape through a cave, to be kids again, in the dark. Jace asks if the historian knows the one about John Henry's hammer versus the steam engine, if he knows how the tunnels were made. Of course he knows that one. The historian says his head has been in the Old West for years now, and he's touched a lot of the remains, but this mine, the one they're about to reach and one of precious few that isn't closed off, is a first for him. How many times has Jace been through this one? Twenty-seven. Will it look like the historian imagines, like the books say? Darker. Sound like? Twenty-seven leaky faucets. No, as many second hands, Jace tells him. Tick. Tick.

The historian's specialty is the mining era—the magnetism of the gold and silver rushes—what brought whom to the Rockies and why. Hunger, greed. And what kept them panning. Starvation, pride. So Jace wants to tell him not about wet caves and what grows within, but about other phantoms in tales he has learned outside of the School of Mines, echoes in a darkness for which the historian's research money isn't meant. The historian will think this myth is passed down from Jace's elders, that Jace actually knows his elders, rather than from old smelly books he dug up in the library.

"You ever hear the one about the moon versus the coyote?" Jace says.

"Can't say I have."

"The moon wanted the living to bury their dead, but his enemy, the coyote, was for cremation. Since the coyote was right on the ground, it was hard to stop him from swaying the living. Eventually the moon gave in."

The historian responds, but Jace doesn't listen. Out the window, below the interstate, in a valley town where even the trees are trucked in, the taller pines lean down, shelter the new growth as best they can, and their highest eaves rest on the halt of power lines.

Sometimes you can learn everything you need to know just by checking a window, looking through it, past your reflection, into what you can't see from any other angle at any other time. If you leave the blinds open just a crack, a moving object, say it's a rock, or a snowflake, or a man, a stranger, might come at you from the south, from the bus station. Or maybe he hitched. Maybe he walked, just wandered off. Maybe he parked, sat, waited. Just around the corner.

On a day in eleventh grade, when Jace stayed home from school, the man had walked the way only a messenger can, or a guilty child awaiting punishment. His hands were full, which made his steps slower, made his concentration more a part of the movement. His face poked up to check address numbers, and as he came closer, he appeared taller, the curves of his hat more defined, the thing in his hands more baglike than box shaped. Jace knew where the man was headed. He grew larger on the sidewalk until he cut a right angle, proceeded up the cement path that split the front yard. If Jace opened the window he would hear the man's boots: Click, tap, click, tap, click. No scuffs or drags. The bag lay flat over the man's palms, and Jace imagined him presenting it to Grandma. *It's a beautiful covering for the box, she might say. A nice way to wrap up my daughter, but we prefer urns. Have you people kept her in a box all this time?*

After the man disappeared under the cover of the porch, Jace dressed without making a sound. He wanted to hear Grandma say it. But what do you wear to accept your mother's ashes from your distant cousin, or would-be neighbor, or uncle? How do you prepare for a moment you'll have to remember and retell for the rest of your life? It was a Thursday in 1993, he'd say, eleventh grade, when I was out sick from school, so sick I'd lost my voice, and I was wearing my Rockies jersey, or my red t-shirt, or Brad's flannel. Not boxers. That wouldn't do.

At first all he heard from downstairs was a Do you need a ride to the station? But then, through the storm door, came the man's voice, the upward pull on the middles and ends of words, so that each statement sounded a dozen questions. It was that intonation, that tongue which to Grandma sounded foreign enough to wince at, lean forward into, that put Jacy at ease. Perhaps the women on the reservation, women besides his mother, sang baby Jace to sleep with that very pattern of rise and fall. Perhaps Grandma had to change his tune when he found his voice.

Jace threw on the best shirt and pants he could find. As he zipped up, he raised his head. A figure moved in the corner of his eye, through a crack in the blinds, down on the street, away.

Even with his hands free of the bag or box, the man constricted his movement. He shoved his hands into his pockets, he still hunched over. His hat hung by its string around his neck and onto his back. Jace could see the hairline now, just a slight receding, nothing like Grandpa's low tide, and a black crew cut. And then he saw the ears: tiny coils of brown.

Jace opened the window and heard the man's steps. They were not clicks or taps at all but thuds. Hey, he wanted to say. I know you can hear me.

At the kitchen table, once Grandma couldn't stand it anymore, she made Jace open what the man delivered. He untied the bag, pulled out the box.

"What is it?" she said. "Feathers? Beads? Turquoise?"

He opened the latch and held up the treasure: a rose quartz. Its mount had severed from the chain. The crystal was chipped and soiled, but still shined pink.

Grandma brought a hand to her mouth, backed her chair away from the table.

Once she had made it to the driveway, Grandpa said, "It was the last thing they argued about. Grandma didn't want her wearing it. She didn't want your mother doing a lot of things."

Jace knew this, knew how it all must have sounded to the neighbors: a good girl, a nice Arrowhead Academy girl, trying to civilize those people. And if that isn't enough, she goes and lets one of them work his charms on her.

***

Brad is Keiko's official boyfriend, and he is, officially, Jace's uncle. It's October now, and neither of them have seen Brad since July, since Jerry Garcia reached his deathbed. Brad called Keiko last week to announce his visit. If she hasn't failed out yet, Keiko is still on the historian's official roster of students. The historian is Jace's client this weekend, who pays to have someone with a permit, someone who knows rocks inside and out, to take him underground. Jace is the guide. But these labels are all coincidence, and fail to explain the actual roles each of them plays.

When Jace and the historian check into the motel at the end of the first day, the historian stares at the key in his hand and looks toward the east wing, where a bed waits. "I'm knackered."

"Okay. I'll get settled in my room, see what's on TV."

"Sure. Do as you please. It's your holiday, too." The historian reaches for his wallet, pulls out three new bills, and rubs them together until they squirm apart. He stretches his arm out, toward Jace. "Get yourself something to eat. This should be enough for a haircut as well."

While the historian sleeps, Jace dreams. All of last summer was a dream. Every day he spent with Keiko glimmered, even in the pouring rain. Pitter patter, rat-a-tat. Besides counting beats, and pounding them out of course, this is what Jace can do: judge a stone by its color, cleavage, hardness, and by its specific gravity. Sometimes you can find two stones in one. That's what his rock guidebooks say. Hold a purple stone up to the light and you'll notice the golden glow of citrine inside. One day on the Phish tour, a day when clouds threatened, when Keiko was asleep, he opened her bottle of thyroid medication. No capsules inside. Not two, not one. Without them anything could happen, any expansion or contraction of cells, tissues. It would show in her middle, and in the glow of her skin. Her hormones need a special transmitter, a daily call, to send messages—stay where you are—to those eggs stalled out on the sides of their roads, their pathways into the dark tunnel, and then outside. By October the signals sit stagnant with three months' worth of blood. *Wash me.* She keeps saying it's just her thyroid messing with her cycle, but Jace wonders if a new life is starting to grow.

But that's now. This was then: the summer Phish tour, the stolen moments alone with her. Like the day when Brad was off trying to score concert tickets in the parking lot of Red Rocks theater, when Jace and Keiko snuck into the cave on the side of the pavilion. The going rate was getting higher, and in there they could climb and pull and crouch and enjoy the show for free. No one would know. It was harmless. They just sat there, enraptured by the music, and stared into the golden-coral-pink-blue-everything-is-possible sky when Brad was nothing and nowhere, like everyone else but they two.

That's what it was like last summer when Phish played at Red Rocks, or Mud Island, or Finger Lakes. Once the music starts and you grease up and all your cylinders kick in and the pistons are really pumping, and you sweat and pulsate and start dancing around, you're not just one pathetic little engine anymore, you're on the superhighway: thousands of individual bodies moving as one amoeba.

One night in Vermont, at the end of the tour, when it was late but no one was tired and gone was the novelty of card games or Hacky Sack, Brad grabbed his flannel. "Going beer hunting," he said. But Keiko knew better.

"Hope your weapon backfires," she said. She did not look up from her knitting.

Just before sun-up, in that slice of night too late for activity and too early to start the new day, Jace heard a hum from the edge of the parking lot. It was the engine of whoever dropped Brad off, some floozy he met last week maybe, when he ditched Jace and Keiko to go to some nearby Grateful Dead shows. Jace bolted upright, slithered out of Keiko's s sleeping bag and into his own on the bench seat. It was a cold night, so he was already back into his clothes. Keiko did not stir when he peeled away from her.

Brad rolled open the door and grabbed Jace's foot. "Dude, wake up. Jerry's tweakin'."

Jace lifted his head, rubbed his eyes longer than necessary. It was a good act.

"It doesn't look good," Brad said. "The rest of the Dead tour's canceled. They're talking Betty Ford Clinic." He squeezed Jace's toes on that last part, then he leaned onto the feet, rested his chin over the ankles. "I should have seen it coming. The way he kept the volume down at Giants Stadium, and how all those chicks cried and clapped when he was barely making any noise at all. Just leaned onto the guitar pedals, like they kept him upright." Brad straightened up, let go of the feet. "If things don't get better, they'll send him back to California. A bunch of us are gonna meet there no matter what. So we gotta get going. I gotta get you guys home and be on my way."

Jace climbed into the front passenger seat as Brad started the engine and pulled out.

"I might need to take the semester off," Brad said, and Jace could hear it in his voice then: ten years of an older sister's records fading out, another chorus lost, another groove scratched. "I can graduate next year. School seems like such a joke now, compared to this."

It's not like it was a member of Phish on that hospital bed. Their band will still go on. It was just the old guy from the Dead, and old guys croak all the time. But Brad couldn't go on without the music's front man, the voice inside all that vinyl.

On the tour, sometimes Jace drove. Sometimes he navigated. That morning, on the way home, a somber morning because they'd just gotten word of Jerry Garcia's hospitalization, Brad just needed Jace close by. Once Keiko was up and in position, Jace sat on the floor between the front bucket seats, listened for the tempo changes or never ending drum solos on the tapes. At this spot, Brad could elbow Jace's shoulder when they reached a bridge, as the strings rose in pitch and speed, and the vocals held onto a note. And Keiko could cup the back of his head as he nodded on the accentuated beats. Sometimes she thumbed the edge of his ear, circled around toward the center until it tickled and he jolted away. On the floor he felt the bumps in the road.

It was during the return trip, the don't-worry-everything-will-be-fine movement west, that the pounding slowed to a thud at the right front. Brad pulled over. No cussing. No words at all. No kicking, and very little sound as he walked to the back. Then the click of the tailgate.

Keiko whipped out of her seat, opened her door, and followed Brad.

Jace took his spot on his bench seat and faced the back. He set his chin on the headrest, curled his fingers over it. He watched Brad shove blankets and duffels aside, and pull up the trap door. No jack. No spare tire.

"Where is it?" Keiko said. One hand dug into her hip, the other flailed.

No answer from the driver. The spare tire pit held only a quilt, the old pink one Grandma had threatened to burn. It protected something square. Brad looked up at Jace as he lifted it. It was heavy enough to strain his face and neck muscles, but Brad made the bundle look weightless. All that time it had been there, in the van's belly, and through a steel sheet felt every splash, every bouncing rock, the wind below. Brad let Keiko unwrap it: a stack of early Dead records, imprints of half-planned riffs and spontaneous jams. *Anthem of the Sun, American Beauty, Skeletons From the Closet.* Tracks useless to moving forward in a cassette and CD era, but necessary to remind them of their precursor, their source, their uncle father sister mother of sound.

When Grandma had finally cleaned out her daughter's room, Jace was old enough to get out of the way. It was a curse, she said, for anyone to wear a dead girl's clothing or shoes or earrings. Grandpa boxed and carried and dumped all of Jace's mother's things, but when Grandma wasn't looking, he placed one stack of records under each boy's bed, with a set of headphones to the hi-fi in the basement. There they could sift through what she had left behind.

Keiko didn't touch the records. She didn't whine. She set the bundle down and held Brad.

Jace shoved his hands into his pockets and hit the road. Eventually there were signs. Not just the green of this route or that, the white of watch your speed, the blue of filling station or rest area ahead, or the red of you'd better stop, but brown signs indicating an interesting turn off.

It was a cold and quiet walk at that hour, as blue-black gave way to lavender. Glass shards twinkled on the shoulder. A stray dog zigged and zagged, then rushed toward and behind a rock wall with watermarks at its base. Water was here, then one day it fell away, down chutes of dirt and stone, into pools, through valleys, and eventually released into the sea. Gone. And it left dried remains, sediment lines to help us remember a time we never knew.

With thumb pointed up, he trotted backwards on the shoulder. He stopped, jumped, blew on his hands. A car pulled over. Behind the wheel was a fat man in a beige jacket. The passenger window was down. Jace leaned in. The man offered a price, and stroked Jace's hand.

He walked another mile, maybe two. Head down, the chill burning him now. Lights poured over him, passed him by. Just ahead a station wagon sputtered onto the shoulder, crunched rocks, flashed one taillight. An arm appeared out the driver's window, waved him forward. It was chubby, a white blob against black pavement and sky, with dark fingernails.

When he told the driver how many miles he and his uncle had covered and how far west they were headed, she let out a low whistle and picked up the CB receiver. "You're gonna need a good tire. Up here's an honest mechanic, sells quality parts. Normally on a reservation, they'd bleed you dry, but not these people. Got the fear of the Lord in 'em." She made the call, woke up the man in charge. He would leave the door open. "Ten miles ahead," she told Jace.

"Thanks." He scanned the interior. A bumper sticker on the glove box said *On the eighth day, He listened*. No radio. No tape deck. The back seats were folded down, with boxes on them.

"What's in the back?" he says.

"The Good Word. That's what I got to give, or sell, sometimes. On my way to Burning Man now. Those kids frying in the desert, they need some inspiration. They're a tough crowd." She raised a finger, wagged it twice, then held it still. "But at every concert I hit, I always catch a few before they enter, reel them back out. Return to sender."

When they reached the gas station/garage/general store, Jace carried in a soiled and tattered sheet of paper with the tire's diameter written on it. The door creaked open and then slammed shut behind him. The lights buzzed. Two employees, husband and wife probably, spoke in chains of inflections until it was settled. A price. Behind the counter, the wife rubbed her eyes and said, "It must be quite a trip, to drive through the night like this."

When he stepped outside and loaded the tire into the back of the car, the sky was more purple than blue. The driver was pleased. She honked and waved goodbye to her friends, peeled out of the lot. "It's going to be a fine day," she said. "Like the days when I sell my lucky Bible, you know, the last in a box."

Jace bought her last three Bibles for ten dollars. She dropped him off a few exits from the van, where Brad and Keiko waited.

"Good luck at the next show," he said. Now, as dawn broke, he noticed the amulet that clutched at her throat. It was round and white and it stole the light from her skin.

***

Jace can't sleep. If he's going to try to win Keiko back, he should use the historian's money to buy her a gift. Across the street from the motel is a shop in a long barn, shined up and ready for traveler's checks. On its roof a billboard sized sign shouts up to the interstate: PRECIOUS GEMS. He enters the store and unzips his jacket, a heavy jacket that makes him worth watching. His hands stay in his pockets as his eyes scan the merchandise. He does not enter the shopkeeper's blind spots.

He peeks out the window, through the blank space between signs. The last slice of sun sinks behind a peak to the west. On the other side of it is the resort town where Keiko studies now, in her parents' ski lodge, where she begs her cycle to end, or to begin again. She is waiting for something to crack, to break down and pour out.

He passes over the dross and toward the shiny rocks. And then he sees a stone that looks just like the one in the driver's amulet: pearly, opaque, but too clear to call white. The shopkeeper tells him it's a moonstone, a gem whose main element is wind, and whose known to transmit magnified emotions, lunar energy, psychic perception. "It's a third eye," she says.

Once the shopkeeper unlocks the case, Jace holds the moonstone up to the light and tests its weight with a dip of his arm. Solid and full of complex bonds. Impossible to break. He sets it on the counter, and it clanks against the glass, as if to tell the stones below, *Hey, up here, look at me. I'm free.* Jace removes his billfold and separates two notes from the third.

The shopkeeper wraps up the moonstone and hands it to him. "Lucky girl," she says.

As Jace and the historian return to the mine the second day, the historian hands Jace a stray branch. It is pointed on top. "Here. You're the guide."

They walk for a while, crunching dried leaves until their feet fall into step. It takes a while for the bird noises to find his ear. There is a quiet that follows the tour, even months later.

Above them, the moon hangs low with a blue blanket tucked over its middle. Pines keep their arms down, but near the bottom, some reach straight out and curl up. They stretch wider down low, away from the trunk and its waterways. They brown and crisp easily this close to the dirt, and the roots below.

The soil hardens as they climb. Slate chips away and slides around. Their toes break it off, and their heels skate back a little on tiny sleds of it.

A hawk blinks, casts one eye down on Jace. He wonders what it sees from its perch, if it can make out the whole mountain range, or see what's ahead.

"Jace, over here," the historian says. He waves a hand and points to something important on a rock wall, a scrub tree sprouting out of a crack where stone meets dirt. What Jace notices is a carving off to the left, above the sediment lines: "100 years come around, 100 years underground, 1988 and where's my mother lode?"

The historian says he wishes his wife were here to name this sprout. "She really knows plants. So the soil, that's not completely foreign to me."

Up top, there's never enough traction underfoot. But below, in the mine, that's the world Jace can sink into. He knows it by feel, and by ready-made notions of what the underground world should be. Caves, holes, mines. Stalagmites, biotites. Lights on helmets. Chisels and scythes. Tracks, trains, engines. John Henry tried to beat the machine with his hammer underground. That's what they tell you in school. What Jace knows are tough rocks, knows what makes them burst, give way, tumble, hide under their neighbors. The historian wants to find out what's inside, what's bubbling, spitting, what's pulling them down.

Before they go in, Jace scans their surroundings, imprints the image: white aspen branches cast out what gold leaves they have left. Below them lies a wash of dirt slopes punctured by slouching telephone poles: crosses falling over tracks. Jace knows the wires they carry, how they hug the old trunk lines that lead the interstate along and then swizzle away. But they always veer back, always return to parallel the streets. They are, as the historian told him over poached eggs yesterday, the same routes to the same destination, but they stop now for shopping centers and resorts instead of bridges and county seats. Still, they follow the same rivers. These lines guided Eisenhower's construction and now his roads have made them obsolete. But they stay as Western flavor: an attraction, a reminder of how far we've come.

The historian stops Jace. He is short of breath from the altitude and the excitement. He can't wait to start a day of time travel, to fill the gaps in history books. Maybe Jace will get a thank you in the fine print of the historian's next book.

He pats Jace on the back and motions toward the mine. "Artifact is history where there is no memory," he says. "All that ever happened or might have been lives inside of something we can touch. It must, or else it never was."

Maybe it's the coffee pulsing through him, but Jace wraps his head around this. Yeah, he thinks, we feel a surface, judge its heat, blame its simplicity, praise its usefulness, its place in the evolution toward what we want need gotta have can't live without today. Right on, old guy.

Jace pats the historian's back and leads him in. He is ready to move Dr. Sims beyond the basics of rock. Igneous, volcanic, metamorphic. Mites, tites, rites. Those are easy. Jace is here to tell him about what else is down there, what can distract or obstruct, what can console. And he does. He leads, listens, and nods at every question, even if it's too dark for the historian to see him. In here Jace does important work.

When the historian asks him to pound, Jace says, "We're not supposed to, Dr. Sims. Mine access permits are pretty strict."

"I'll take the heat. Just find a spot and nail it." He pauses as he hands over the instrument. He does not have to show Jace how to use it. It is the guide's tool. Jace has been here before.

Jace finds a target and taps. The historian steps away and finds his own spot. They pound in unison for a while, and then their paces stagger, like a gang of hammers forcing spikes through railroad ties and into dirt, or slate, or impossible rock below. Clink clink. Clink clink. For a long time nothing breaks, but they make a rhythm, tap out a pattern. Veins bulge above the historian's brow, sweat slides down his neck. His breathing offers a loud wind accompaniment, but it can't keep tempo with the percussion.

"I'll try over there," he says, and points around a bend. The words barely come out. He smiles and grips Jace's arm. "Feels good, doesn't it?"

Jace stares at the wall in front of him. They are supposed to be taking samples, photographing the site, getting a sense of the everyday reality of the prospectors' search, like they did yesterday. His boss told him that's what the historian is known for: sniffing out the real story behind the mining myths, getting into character. Jace is just paid to identify stones, explain formations, point out hiding places of gems that may have been passed over. He is here to demonstrate the safe spelunking practices he absorbed from expert geologists. Some guide.

When it happens, Jace is just around the corner, pounding the daylights out of a certain groove, as the historian instructed. Then he stops, doubles over, and hears only silence. The dripping has stopped, and the steady beat of the historian's hammer is gone. No echo. Done. Over. This is what Jace will tell the paramedics when they arrive.

In the darkness, he reaches for the historian. He kneels next to the old guy's body, and he takes the moonstone from his own pocket. He presses it to the historian's pulse points at the left wrist, then the right, moves it over his torso, over the cavity of organs to upper chest, holds it over the place where he thinks the pounding happens, where the blood landed once it reversed its flow, where the force begins and, if he doesn't do something quick, where the force might end. He knows he should press hard, should lean onto the historian and smother him with a chance at resurrection, bounce him back to life. And so he removes the stone, pushes and pumps, covers the Dr. Sims's lips with his. Puff times three. Jesus. They made it look so easy on St. Elsewhere.

He runs away. Through the tunnel, down the slope, wet and muddy sorry excuse for an exit, and then he's back on the trail, where he hurdles erupted roots and ducks under branches and shrubs sprouting from rock. He hears only feet and breath, feels the downward pull of the historian's wallet and keys in his pocket. Each step stays on the ground too long, each stride too short, wasting time, wasting air, losing another minute, second, instant. He is not supposed to hear the slap of feet and breath, not supposed to concentrate on his own sound at a time like this.

He stays upright, no tripping or wheezing, all the way to the parking spot, where he finds a cellular phone in the historian's glove box. He punches the buttons, gasps under the beeps. "Come on, motherfuckers," he says. "Answer."

The paramedics appear like a hologram. They work their magic—one two three one two three, listen, again—and they blow used air into the mouth from which the history flows, oxygenate the blood that stills in blue trails beneath graying skin. They beg life from this stranger, give him breath, help him draw in and expel the stuff on his own. But the heart takes its time in responding. It slows as it comes down from the fight, the return of blood to its sender.

They say Jace was right to let the historian lie, to resist the urge to drive him away, that a miracle kept him alive. That it's not every day you see a cardiac down in the hole. Not anymore.

The ambulance shrinks as it rushes toward the nearest hospital, a hospital that fixes a lot of heart problems, in the closest of Colorado's resort towns. Lots of old guys feel the pressure on the chair lift, or in the hot tub, or by the fire, where the blood starts to boil, hits obstacles, bottlenecks between build up on the walls of its paths, its closing tunnels, and rushes back home, overflows. So they keep specialists close by to clean up the mess.

Before the paramedics left, they told Jace to call the patient's family, to follow the ambulance in the historian's vehicle. He knows the way, right? But instead he stays, lets his feet sink into the mud as he watches the ambulance shrink away, and as the rain pastes his hair over his face. It feels slimy, and it narrows his view. In the distance a train gives warning. *Here I come. Fear me.* Jace is supposed to move faster, to hurry up and follow the historian to the place where he will heal, where he will come out a better man.

The moonstone. Before Jace gets in the car, he has to go back down into the mine, to find what he left. It is a slow walk—no hurry now that the life is saved—slow enough for him to notice that out here the aspens have dropped most of their yellow leaves and that the chill carries a warning of impending first snow.

In the mine, the darkness swallows him and the air thins exponentially. He wheezes and searches. Fingers travel walls, then ground. Beams of head-lamp and flashlight bounce and swing. They catch the usual debris: shreds of rope, pencils, loose pennies. Too dark in here to retrieve any object that might slip out of hands or pockets, especially if it's brown, yellow, or copper.

He stands where he stood just minutes ago as he pounded the wall. It was foolish and illegal to follow the historian's whimsical orders. He walks around the curve, into this alcove the historian found, where his heart stopped. Jace kneels down into the mold his knees made earlier, beside the indentation that the historian's back left in the dirt.

This is where he set the moonstone down. It was a silent release, softer than you'd expect at a time when your heart is an Allman Brothers drum solo at a million decibels, to compensate for the other guy, who's lost his volume, his treble, his bass. Jace holds it up now, and his headlamp draws out the gem's pearly coloring, that shade between clear and white that's so hard to name, even in full light.

Keiko will hold the moonstone under a lamp, too, once he gives it to her. She'll either say what the hell kind of gift is this or she will say Oh, Jacy, you know me so well. She will embrace him and stroke his ear with her right hand and rub the stone with her left. Together they will hold it, test the weight of all it offers: lunar energy, a third eye. But it will still feel light after all, because, as they will remember without saying, the moonstone's main element is wind.

Right now, he thinks, she must be sitting by the window, watching the last of the aspens' gold eddy down, away. Maybe the altitude will affect her cycle, apply some pressure to her stubborn female organs.

Outside again, Jace dials the people in the historian's address book. No answer from the wife. The son is at work, working on a Saturday at a place where they play classical music to pacify callers on hold. Jace waits. The music does not calm him. Frantic violins and cellos burst above the kettledrum's

THE BEST OF GIVAL PRESS SHORT STORIES   105

thunder. It is a tune to be performed live, so that the musicians in the pit can strum and strike with the appropriate violence in the neck and fingers, and on stage a ballerina can dart here and there in a fury. Keiko would know this tune. After all the running around, she would finish with a slow, soothing flourish. He is sure.

Over the phone, the historian's son stays composed. Just a low Jesus Christ and a Shoulda known this was coming, then a sigh. He gives thanks to Jace, the witness and rescuer, the messenger of this not shocking news. It's lucky, he says, because the hospital is close to his workplace, to the restaurant in a hotel Jace has seen in glossy advertisements. The son will be there in no time. "Drive yourself home in my dad's car. Call us at the hospital and tell us where to pick it up. Might not get there for a few days, but don't worry, we'll pay you for your trouble."

As he starts the engine, Jace pictures the historian's son behind the wheel instead, a miniature version of the father: short and wiry with curls more gold than silver. He is driving his father home. A small, dark-haired woman stares out the passenger side window, knitting and crying small diamonds. They fall into her lap, shine up to her face. She turns around to check on her sleeping husband until they approach their house at the end of a dirt road. Maybe it rests on a hill, sits apart from the others. Maybe it is humble, or dripping with ornate artifacts as proof of the historian's life spent sifting through forgotten days. It is a bi-level with an entrance down below, or a colonial, with two shuttered bedroom windows for eyes in its face, and blinds open just a crack.

When you're on the road, like Jace is now, alone in the historian's car, you think about other travelers. Those who've gone before you, those who've turned off here or at that exit back there, and you wonder whether they strayed from their routes, or continued over the pass, and where they ended up, if they made it, and who they thought about along the way, on this road or that. The last thing Brad said to Jace was a hook. He wanted to fight. "What can I learn at school that I can't pick up out here?" It's been a while since Brad has played. He must be ready to burst.

In order for Brad to visit Keiko, he has to skip the Phoenix show between the northwest and southern legs of Phish's fall tour, where things are really blowing up now, because since Jerry's death Baby Dead has really struck gold. Brad stays close to see what's inside, but he has a day or two to spare for Keiko.

He probably can't wait to tell her all about how the band has changed, bigger and more popular, but still better, to assure her the sound hasn't lost its magic, that it was okay for the band to sell themselves out to MTV just once, that it was worth it for a song like "Down with Disease."

Brad travels light. That much Jace knows. Some practical and some useless items sag in his pack, with the photo of Keiko, taken when they met, when she still danced, in her thinner days. In costume, in position, under lights that ignore the fleshier parts that shine up the muscles and bones. She looks away from the camera, to something higher, out of reach. Since the doctors committed Jerry and Deadheads called Brad in for support, the moon has cycled three times, but Keiko's cycle has stilled, frozen up. Without regular cues, you lose your rhythm. Jace thinks that tonight, on his way back from Oregon Washington British Columbia, Brad drives with the photo propped on the dash. He taps a beat on the wheel and serenades the photo as he drives, tells it that he's almost home, that he's okay, that everything will be different now. The photo stares back and says *I'm dead. It's a new me that awaits your return, that swells with new life. Maybe.*

The historian's glove box vibrates, and a high-pitched ring shakes Jace back to right here, to this road. He answers the call.

"Hey," the son says. "The old man's still ticking. My mom wants to repay you. If—"

"No, it's nothing, really."

"Oh, well, okay. Hey, which class are you in? Nineteenth Century American?"

"I go to a different school, in Golden, for geology and chemistry." But I take the bus to Boulder every weekend, he wants to say, and sometimes I help Keiko with history.

"Chemistry. That was my thing." He pauses. "Don't drop out like I did. I predict you should get hell from the old man if you do, and I sure don't want to hear about that."

The son grew up here, after his father left home, migrated west. Jace heard the difference when they spoke earlier, but something in the intonation, in the way a guy not much older than him could sound like an old English historian, put so many years between them. Something protective and concerned and underscoring the shoulds and sures sounded a rhythm learned early on, through regular listening. Repetition and imitation. It was a natural pattern, an imprint.

From the south, the mountain moves closer. So tall and official and useful now. It still blocks Jace's view, hides the town of heated sidewalks and patient lovers. *Respect me*, it says. Snow blankets not just the mountain top but its face, too: white and opaque and silent. The cover is highly anticipated, and around here it falls harder and faster and earlier than anyone can predict. It is the impromptu high, the call to action, the moneymaker. The sounding: come forth and conquer the Rockies. They're all yours, the ads say. Name a star for your sweetheart up there, or here, name a peak or a ski run, or just one little mogul, after yourself.

On the Verge

by Tim Mullaney

WINNER OF THE 2005 GIVAL PRESS SHORT STORY AWARD

"Do they really drink blood?"

Ethan's lip curls as he asks the question, as if to indicate he already knows—is already mocking–the answer. But his irony is mitigated by his directness, and Toady struggles, as he has all summer, to formulate a reply.

"Piet took a bite out of a raccoon that got run over in the parking lot. Supposedly."

Toady has settled on the safest way of answering Ethan: with specific information tempered with a tone of casual skepticism. It is a technique he has refined since the day he graduated from Jackson High, which was the same day Ethan got back to town and asked if Carousel Kitchen had changed its menu since his last time home, during winter break. Toady had said no, the menu was still the same; he had been a little puzzled by the question and a little hurt when, after he answered, Ethan had laughed and said, "Never mind." The memory of this laugh, a condescending note rising and falling in Ethan's throat, still hovers close to Toady's skin, threatening as a yellow jacket. To avoid being stung he assiduously avoids answering "yes" or "no" to Ethan's, or anyone's, questions.

"Bullshit."

Ethan spits this out straight, and Toady is reassured by such definitiveness. For an instant, he has the feeling that the ship he is on has crested a dangerous swell and is sliding easily back into the calm pocket of the trough. But then Ethan exhales cigarette smoke through his nose and squints in a peculiar way, as though he's found something covertly sought-after. Toady narrows his eyes in the same direction as Ethan's, but can't focus through his feeling that something is off kilter and won't right itself. There's a rustle where there used to be a sigh, and his ship is again climbing the wave.

The night is warm, with an inviting heaviness in the air, but Toady wishes it was cold. He wants to sit in Ethan's rusted hatchback, the way they used to on winter nights, wants to listen to the radio until the car's battery dies and the music cuts out and they are left to fill the silence with their talk. Then they would be alone, the windows steamed with their breath, the crowd in the parking lot rendered invisible. He doesn't like the way Ethan's attention wanders as he smokes, slouched against the hood of his car, scoping out their old schoolmates loitering in the parking lot and under the restaurant awning. These are the people he and Ethan discussed on those nights when the car's power failed, leaving them separate and superior in a cocoon of ripped leather upholstery. Ethan has been uninterested in private gossip sessions since the beginning of summer, when he perfunctorily asked Toady how everyone was doing, what they were up to. Toady, thrown off by Ethan's apparent disinterest, aimed for nonchalance but felt petulant and defensive when he said he wasn't really sure, didn't really care what was going on with people. Ethan shrugged off that response and stopped pumping Toady for information, but during the first few nights of June, the first few nights everyone gathered at Carousel Kitchen, Toady reluctantly trailed Ethan as he made his way from one table to the next, then through the throng in the parking lot, asking everyone how they spent their last year and how they planned to spend their summer and the next year. Now Ethan has stopped this kind of mingling, but the old order is still disturbed, and it is increasingly difficult for Toady to master his desire to take Ethan's face in his hands and sift his expression for clues as to what excites his curiosity and why. He wishes they had talked more often during the last year.

Tonight, as on many recent nights, Toady's palms sweat with the exertion of secretly reading Ethan's inscrutable expression, tracking his attention as it is directed here and there. He follows Ethan's gaze across the street. The parking lot at Lou's Diner is swarming with the usual crowd dressed in shades of black and purple, shot through with electric stripes of green or pink or blue.

Many faces are accented by heavy makeup that glows in the neon light of the *Lou's Home Cookin* sign. Lately a rumor has circulated through Carousel Kitchen that these freaks on the opposite side of the street have stopped ordering food at Lou's and instead drink coffee and smoke cigarettes and then peal out to go in search of their real meals: squirrels and raccoons and opossums. Rumor has it they thrive on fresh blood, that they are, or least have deluded themselves into thinking they are, vampires.

"I should go," Toady says, hoping Ethan will look at him when he replies.

". . . Okay." Ethan looks at the ground in front of Toady's feet and then away again, quickly, back across the street.

"I mean, I'm not really tired. But I've gotta be on the line at seven."

". . . 's a shitty job." Ethan closes his eyes as he says this, as though in pain, and then squints at Toady like someone who's stared at the sun too long.

". . . Yeah . . . well . . . waited too long to try to get a job, I guess this is what I get."

"Should quit."

"I need the money."

"Yeah. I guess."

Men work on the loading docks or the mechanized lines, the lines with big machines that dye pistachios red and wrap gift baskets in three layers of plastic. Women and students assemble the baskets on the stationary lines. Standing behind long tables, they pass the baskets down from one hand to the next, each person adding another item: a sausage, a block of cheese, a small bag of just-dyed pistachios, a tin of dog biscuits.

Dell is the only man over the age of eighteen who works on the stationary lines. His hands are just as callused as those of the men who spend their days unloading trucks and driving forklifts and oiling the gears of the primitive machines on the mechanized lines, and his skin has the same sheen of metallic sweat. From these similarities, Toady figures Dell must have once worked with the other men, but he can't tell whether Dell wants to rejoin them. Occasionally Dell mutters something—"clucking hens" or "fucking tired" or just "fucking"—but usually he is quiet. Toady senses menace in this quiet. During their fifteen-minute mid-morning and mid-afternoon breaks, Dell loiters alone under a stand of pine trees and smokes a cigarette. He eats his lunch there as well, alone. Toady sits on the hood of his car to eat lunch; he often watches Dell and imagines what must have happened to send him to the stationary lines. A fight. Sharp words spoken, fists clenched, an Exacto blade drawn. There are times, usually in the dead heat of mid-afternoon, when Toady catches himself examining the faces of the forklift operators and the bare forearms of the men on the loading docks, searching for a scar from the cut Dell made with his blade. Sometimes Toady sneaks sideways looks at Dell's exposed flesh, at his hands and arms and neck, and, when he bends over, the small of his back, try-ing to find the mark that has set him apart from the other men. But aside from the calluses on his hands and a few strands of violent, wiry hair poking from the places where his flesh folds when he bends, Dell's skin is smooth and dark beneath its oily film, and Toady is left wanting physical proof of Dell's differ-ence, of his past violence. Still, Toady has sometimes caught eyes with women working on the line and detected a warning in their glance, a warning he can't decipher but that he senses is meant to alert him to one fact: Dell is dangerous. This is why he is kept apart from the men, why the men keep their distance. This is why the women defer to him and stroke him with soothing words when he seems particularly tense. Because they know his secret. They know the ter-rible things of which he is capable.

"Theodore . . ."

There is a delay before Toady looks up, in which he is just able to regret that he was too embarrassed to introduce himself as Toady at the factory. He isn't sure which of the women cooed his name. They are all looking at him. His finger is wrapped in the ribbon decorating the handle of the basket in front of him, and there are two more baskets beside him. He has fallen behind.

"This one . . . head's always in the clouds."

Leona, the retired schoolteacher who is the unofficial manager of the sta-tionary lines, says this with the air of doting chastisement Toady assumes she perfected in the classroom.

"Leave him alone, he's a good worker."

There is silence after Dell says this, a pause, and then Toady grabs three blocks of cheddar from the box in the middle of the table and goes to work packing the baskets he let pile up. He blushes at the words spoken in his de-fense and can't look up to confirm his feeling that Dell is looking at him, and that all the women, though they have returned to their work, have their feath-ers raised in warning.

It is drizzling at lunchtime, so Toady abandons the hood and eats in the front seat. He plays the radio softly and hopes he doesn't kill the battery. Dell isn't eating under the pine trees, although it appears the branches would keep him sheltered from the light rain. Past the pine trees, on the other side of the train tracks running behind the factory, the tops of four brightly colored golf umbrellas are just visible over the high grass and reeds which border both sides of the railroad embankment and mark the edge of the eighteenth hole of the country club golf course. The umbrellas bob and sway in an indecipherable puppet show, then disappear. On sunny days, Toady eats his lunch accompanied by a chorus of shouts and splashes from the club's pool, punctuated now and then by the dull crack of a golf ball being teed-off or the hydraulic hiss of a forklift unloading trucks a few dozen feet in front of him. Toady imagines the scene in the clubhouse: a few kids who showed up hoping the rain would die down, his brother probably among them, eating potato chips and watching TV as golfers walk in and shake off rain-slicked windbreakers, tally up their strokes on soggy scorecards. Toady dwells on this conjured tableau with a fascinated intensity, as if it is a newly discovered photograph of some long-forgotten festivity, until the percussive spiel of a used-car salesman blares through the speakers. He snaps the radio off. He is about to take the key out of the ignition when he sees Dell, leaning against the factory between docks three and four, smoking. The glowing tip of his cigarette is dramatic in the day's gloom. Toady sends the windshield wiper in a single arc across the glass. In the sudden clarity, he is certain that Dell is looking straight at him, and for a moment, Toady doesn't look away.

Piet balances on the exposed root of an elm tree in the yard. As usual, he is dressed entirely in black, and the light of the street lamp filtering through the leaves hits him only in certain places, making him look, Toady thinks, like a spirit struggling to materialize. Toady stuffs his hands deeper in his pockets when Ethan tells him to relax. He resents Ethan for bringing him here and subjecting him to the moment that is now fast approaching, when he will be tested by Piet on Piet's own turf. Already, Toady senses Piet's eyes narrowing and back straightening at the approach of something vulnerable. Toady isn't sure how to guard against the coming attack.

When Ethan suggested going to the party, Toady regarded the proposal as just another of the ridiculous plans Ethan had been pulling out of his hat all summer. Most of these schemes—like replacing all the menus at Carousel with stolen menus from Lou's—were self-consciously elaborate and not pursued with any seriousness, so Toady felt it was safe to encourage Ethan's plotting tonight. But now, with Piet only a few yards away, Toady regrets supporting Ethan's determination to show up at this party. He sets his jaw against all of Ethan's directives to loosen up; his teeth grind as he considers the curious, prolonged looks Ethan has been giving the crowd at Lou's. Toady tries to count the times he has left Carousel early, before Ethan, and wonders what Ethan has been doing when they haven't been together. It seems that Ethan has already won approval from Piet, that Ethan's presence here won't be challenged. In fact, it seems Ethan expects a warm welcome. A vague fear keeps Toady from asking Ethan how this all came about, and Ethan's unwillingness to volunteer any information, coupled with the confidence in his step, has Toady suspicious and irritated.

When they are close enough to make out the glint of Piet's eyebrow ring, they stop. Piet and Ethan share a nod, and Piet casts his eye over Toady, who clenches his stomach as if he is about to be hit. Piet asks his question.

"Are you a faggot?"

"I'm here with Ethan, aren't I?"

Toady, surprised by his quickness and the real venom in his answer, is instantaneously giddy, close to sick, at hearing someone pin down and give voice to that question which has long darted about, playing in his mind and the air between Ethan and him, always disappearing before exposing its true contours. He looks at Ethan, apologetic and hopeful. Ethan smirks in a way that strikes Toady as approving, but this smirk quickly widens to a strange, complicit grin. It occurs to Toady that the half innocent, half bullying tone of Piet's question was in a register that Ethan himself has been using lately. Piet smiles, wide, and Toady, startled by the pale yellow glow of his teeth, is frustrated by the satisfaction he and Ethan seem to be milking from this complicated moment. Considering their pleasure, Toady is certain that he has somehow betrayed himself by implicating Ethan in his reply to Piet. Just as Toady is gripped by this apprehension, a sudden foreboding of imminent collapse, a dread that his entire universe is a house of cards held together by a thin glue of accumulated assumptions, Piet disappears, swallowed by the night, the relative brightness of his teeth leaving a sickly impression in the blackness that fades as Toady's disquietude plummets into fear. His fright is only partially relieved when he realizes Piet has not vanished, but has crouched on his root-perch like a tree-dwelling animal about to pounce. Sure enough, in one, smooth, feral gesture, Piet spits a stream of tobacco juice onto the tree, leaps down and licks Toady's face from his chin to a spot just behind his ear. The metal stud in his tongue is cold and sudden against Toady's skin. Toady instinctively puts a hand to his cheek, sticky with fast-drying saliva, while Piet, squatting on the ground, emits a low growl, like a dog warning off a challenger. Ethan grabs Toady's arm, roughly, just beneath the shoulder, and leads him toward the house. Piet barks at them. Ethan holds the door open, and Toady goes inside as Piet howls, long and mournful.

The house is more brightly lit than Toady expected. Curtains or blinds are drawn across all the windows, and from outside the house was distinguished from the darkness only by the porch light flickering over the three oversized wooden numbers of the address, 785, tacked to the brown-stained siding beside the door. But low-wattage, exposed bulbs on the ceiling of almost every room give a washed-out yet emphatic glow to the interior. The kitchen is particularly bright, the overhead light reinforced by a shadeless lamp sitting on a card table doubling as a bar. Scanning the collection of bottles on this table, Toady runs a hand along his face, retracing the path of Piet's tongue as he mentally retraces Piet's history. It is a history tangled with this address, dating back to the days when the house, just a block away from Thomas Jefferson Junior High, was notorious among the middle school students for its beer-can and cigarette-butt littered yard, the mean, scraggly cats that lived in the overgrown shrubs out front, and the snowman that appeared in the winter wearing panties instead of a stocking cap, with a carrot and two pieces of charcoal arranged to approximate the male anatomy.

"Hey, Toady."

Lisa Prue appears and plunges her plastic cup into the bag of ice. Toady knows he shouldn't be as surprised as he is to see so many familiar faces. In the Carousel Kitchen parking lot everyone might whisper disapprovingly about Piet and the crowd at Lou's, but among the Carousel regulars, rumors about the goings-on at 785 were long ago replaced by certainties. Toady knows he is in the minority of students to have gone all four years at Jackson without venturing even once to this address.

"Glad Ethan convinced you to come," Lisa smiles as she struggles to light a cigarette without dropping her drink.

". . . Yeah." Toady holds her drink and tries to pick out Ethan's voice through the static of the party, braving his fast-rising sense of abandonment by focusing on the task.

"Cool. Thanks." Lisa takes a satisfied drag and offers the cigarette to Toady. He refuses and she smiles, winks and walks away. Marilyn Manson starts playing somewhere upstairs and Toady feels a sickening slipping, the threat of a curtain falling, or rising, the fear that he is the victim of systematic lies. Ethan's strange interest in the nightly assemblage at Lou's, his elaborate schemes, his new kind of impatience and sarcasm, these fragments of thoughts, duplicating as though reflected off opposing panels of glass, persistently crowd Toady, as if trying to assemble themselves into a meaningful shape, an explanation for the misgivings lodged like buckshot in his chest. The house is a network of narrow hallways and sticky floors, and as Toady wanders he feels he is a mouse trying to make his way through a maze in which other mice have made their home. Returning to the kitchen, he tries a rickety screen door, all but invisible in a dark nook beside the refrigerator. It opens onto an unlit, screened porch. A large plastic trash can occupies one corner, surrounded by loosely tied black garbage bags that camouflage three or four bean-bag chairs in which people lounge, passing a joint. A sagging couch with ripped cushions exposing disintegrating foam occupies the other corner. Two people are lying on each other on the couch, grinding their hips. Toady releases the screen door and it whips back on its tight hinge and slams shut. The people on the couch glare at him with the quicksilver animosity of two animals interrupted in the midst of mortal combat. The girl on top has long, tangled black hair with bangs cut straight across her forehead; the black mascara and lipstick obscure her features and lend her a pale, androgynous aspect. Ethan lies below her. He grins at Toady, half-wicked, half-shy. The girl's dark make-up has rubbed off and smeared his upper lip and the skin under his nose, bruising him. Toady sees teeth, bared and dripping. He quickly backs into the kitchen and goes directly to the drink table.

Was he looking at her? Toady rubs the salt off his wrist and watches it fall into the crack between the armrest and the seat cushion.

"Toady, you okay?"

Up to this point, each successive drink had dampened more and more the thoughts jockeying for position in his head, making him feel increasingly aware of the things going on around him. But the world was flipped inside out by the last shot he took, and now the music and conversation are distant and indistinct, and his thoughts are loud, coming one word at a time. *He. Was. Looking. At. Her.*

"*Toady!*"

Lisa Prue is offering him a drink, but he ignores her. A uniformed police officer is standing in the doorway. Toady has drunk too much to be afraid, but his face drops in surprise.

"It's okay, he's my cousin," Lisa explains as she thrusts the cup into Toady's hands, and the cop raises his drink, takes a sip, and disappears down the hall. Lisa follows him, and Toady downs the water he has been given.

Ethan appears and disappears, and Toady loses track of time and falls into a rhythm. Like a child in a pool, content to simply move through the water and experiment with the ways a body can feel alternately heavy and light, Toady wanders through the party caught in a hypnotic cycle of expectation and disappointment. His imagination has been blunted by alcohol, so when Ethan is not by his side he can trust a certain blankness will descend. His mind will not re-create too vividly Ethan's odd grin, or his laugh. Still, every moment Ethan is not beside him, Toady waits. And each time Ethan comes back, it is without any significance in his step, and when he speaks his tone is flat—normal—and he doesn't make any reference to the girl with dark make-up. It is when Ethan is standing next to him that Toady is sure, finally, that he doesn't inspire in Ethan any feeling of muscle-tightening suspension, of possibility, and this certainty unspools his memory, which plays footage that is suddenly painful: a look Ethan once gave him while they were singing along to the radio, the time Ethan playfully ran an ice cube down his back, the "love you, man" Ethan awkwardly spat through his car window just before he drove off to college. Toady prefers, in a way, the forgetfulness he can enjoy when Ethan is absent. Finding that the stench of garbage has finally driven everyone out of the porch, he sits on the broken couch to be alone.

Closing his eyes, Toady is aloft and spinning, so he leaves them open just a crack. He hears voices in the kitchen. Piet and Lisa and someone he doesn't know. They go away. Somewhere else in the house, the music blares for a second and is gone. A tree branch brushes the porch-screen. There are more whispers in the kitchen. Or are there? Toady opens his eyes completely. Someone is close by, but Toady can't make sense of anything. He realizes he is about to throw up. A few seconds of intense concentration succeed in dispelling the acute nausea, and as he feels the perspiration gathered on the hair beside his ears, he realizes he is surrounded. People are crammed onto the porch. No one is talking. Someone hits his arm. He looks up, recognizes Ethan, makes room for him on the couch. The girl with dark make-up sits on the floor between Ethan's legs.

Piet enters stealthily, holding two bottles. One is half full of whiskey, one almost entirely full of a dark red liquid Toady doesn't recognize. Piet hands the whiskey to someone propped on one of the bean bags, then uncaps the bottle of red stuff and takes a long swig, which sets off a round of muted hisses. He smacks his lips and offers up the bottle. It is taken by a hand that seems unattached to any arm, and then a voice, rising like a plaintive wind, comments on the stench of garbage and is swiftly told to shut up. Piet says, startlingly loud, "It's cool."

There is a short, expectant silence, and then Piet continues, more quietly, "Ethan. Shoot, fuck, marry. Mandy Czaplinski, Jenny Sturwitz, Jenny Stern."

Ethan's immediate response, "Fuck Jenny Stern, marry Jenny Sturwitz, shoot Mandy," is met by muffled giggles and groans, and Toady is struck by the impression that everyone is acting out some sort of well-rehearsed routine. He panics, realizing he doesn't know how to play his part, or even if he has a part to play. He turns to Ethan, who mouths, "The cops." Toady looks for Lisa Prue, but can't find her among all the people pressed together in the dark. The whiskey reaches him and he passes it to Ethan without taking a sip. Ethan tosses back a quick swallow. The girl with the make-up drops her head so that it rests on Ethan's lap. She opens her mouth and Ethan pretends he is about to pour whiskey straight down her throat, then he bends over, wags a playful finger in her face and says, "No more for you." She grabs the bottle, which Ethan relinquishes as he leans close to Toady and explains, with a harsh edge, "Lisa's cousin's talking to them. Relax."

Toady looks over Ethan's shoulder, through the screen, and zeroes in on the top of the high flagpole of Thomas Jefferson Junior High School, visible above the roofs of the houses across the street, flashing silver between the streetlights and the moon.

Toady is halfway through the line at the country club brunch buffet when a new pan is brought out and placed in an empty chafing dish in front of him. The blast of steam that escapes when the cover is removed is pungent and milky. Before the steam clears to reveal a mound of scrambled eggs, the back of Toady's throat constricts; his eyes water as he stumbles in a sick panic to the sideboard, where he sets down his plate and tries to pour a glass of water. A piece of ice lodged in the spout of the pitcher diverts the flow of water into a trickle that dribbles onto his plate and runs down his arm, soaking the cuff of his shirt. Toady gasps at the cold and nearly drops the pitcher, but at the shock, the crisis is past. He succeeds in pouring himself a glass from a different pitcher and after a few sips is breathing with ease, but the sight of his plate—toast and hashbrowns, soggy in spots from the spillage—roils his stomach again. As he steps away from the sideboard, abandoning his plate, he spots his father at a table in the corner, reading the paper. Exhausted by the previous hour at church, spent clutching a missal and trying to swallow away his nausea, and disgusted by the thought of watching his family eat, Toady slips into the hall and out to the patio. The clubhouse chatter and the clatter of silverware diffuse into laughing overtones hung in the humid air. The patio is wet, the mist gathered at the edges of things. His heart beating fast, Toady trots across the damp stone, through a gap in the hedge, over the putting green, past the pool, into the men's locker room.

Sitting on a bench between two rows of small gray lockers, his eyes closed and his head between his knees, Toady breathes deeply, settling his jitters with the familiar scent of mildew and chlorine. A pleasant tingling in his neck is soon accompanied by a feeling of expansion and relaxation in his stomach. He opens his eyes and savors the sensation of relief. He presses first one foot and then the other into the carpet, perpetually squishy, and recalls past summers, relives tortured minutes in the pool spent dreading the inevitable moment of crisis, when he would no longer be able to hold it. Then he would come in here and walk across the slimy carpet with his bare feet, an unpleasant tingle scurrying up his spine with each footfall. Toady shivers at the thought of these excursions. He looks up at the saloon doors marking the entrance to the urinals and showers. A flutter in his stomach reminds him of the reason why he never put anything on his feet before entering the locker room. Why he never just went in the pool. There was a kind of possibility in the waterlogged carpet and the chill of the tiled bathroom floor, and while this possibility might make him grit his teeth, it also made him tremble with anticipation. It was a generally expectant feeling he still has sometimes, right before he does something that will make him feel guilty.

He treads to the saloon doors, remembering what it was like to stand in front of the urinal, bare-chested, drops of pool-water beading on the hem of his trunks and falling onto his feet. He thinks back to the occasions when, while he peed, he heard the showers running. He is alone in the locker room now, as he usually was on those bare-footed afternoons, but whereas on those afternoons he would feel disappointed in his solitude and sometimes even linger with a vague hope that someone else might come in, now the quiet invites him to contemplate what he might do in a stall or at a urinal. On the verge of stepping through the swinging doors, a memory of the previous night, a memory of Ethan on the couch, partially blocked by the body on top of him, paralyzes Toady; indistinct thoughts regarding Ethan have nagged at him all morning, spiking his hangover with confusion and disappointment, but now these thoughts are amplified. Impatient for an immediate replacement, for something else to excite him with the same kind of tension he enjoyed with Ethan, Toady leaves the locker room.

Without any sunlight glinting off the water or bobbing bodies disturbing the perfect flatness of its surface, Toady can see straight down to the bottom of the deep end of the pool. When he looks up, a gray-white shroud obscures everything more than a hundred yards in front of him. He squints through the haze, trying to see a place beyond the fence, beyond the caddy shack, beyond the red tee boxes of the eighteenth hole. He tries to locate the spot where the manicured grass of the golf course gives way to the wild weeds growing beside the train tracks, and then he narrows his eyes to see beyond the tracks, to the pine trees towering next to the factory parking lot. He is sure of what is in front of him, but can't see anything through the fog.

The sun beating down on his face lends an orange tint to the darkness behind Toady's closed eyes. The hood of his car is warm on his back, and he knows what is happening to the turkey sandwich in his hand. The mayonnaise is melting in the heat, and the bread is becoming soft and gooey where his fingers are pressing into it. But he remains still, allowing the sun to fire this moment, to make it hard and strong. He thinks back to the night before, to the way he and Ethan said good-bye in the Carousel Kitchen parking lot. It was casual, barely more prolonged than any other night's good-bye. It wouldn't be the last time they saw each other. Ethan even suggested Toady come visit him the next weekend, before the start of classes, but the idea of visiting Ethan had already become abstract and improbable. Toady decides he won't go. He will tell Ethan he is too busy preparing to leave for school himself. And this excuse won't be a lie, but Toady knows it will feel like one. Toady feels the weight of uncontrollable forces acting on him and all at once is grasping at straws, trying to come up with a course of action that will somehow put him in the driver's seat. He sits up and suffers a slight pain, the sensation of a marble rolling from the back of his head to the front, as he opens his eyes. His vision distills slowly, and as the flashes darken and drift away he tries to come up with a number, the number of times in his life he will know he is leaving something behind him for good, the number of times he will be able to mark a moment of definite departure. As he is seized with the desire to at least mark this moment, insignificant as it may be, he sees Dell, leaning between the loading docks, looking at him.

Dell's skin shines. His short sleeves are rolled to expose his shoulders, glistening like polished fruit. His face is nearly blank, an expression of challenge cancelled out by one of invitation, leaving a tension at the corners of his mouth. Toady reads a promise and a question in this tension, and when Dell turns and walks toward the pine trees, the tension doesn't break, but extends like a lengthening cord between them, and Toady doesn't so much follow Dell as get pulled behind him by this rope woven in their mutual stillness and silence.

Dell goes through the pine trees and disappears into the tall grass beside the train tracks. Toady trails him. He halts with one foot in the grass and one on the bed of pine needles, until his foot sinks slightly into the weeds and slides a little forward, and he wades in. The growth is thick. The marshy ground descends steeply into a gully running beside the embankment. The reeds, many of them taller than Toady, are snapped and matted where Dell stepped through them. Toady follows this path and finds Dell standing with his back to a cluster of towering cattails growing at the spot where the soil gives way to the rocky roadbed of the railroad.

Toady meets Dell's gaze and after a flickering moment takes a few last, slow steps, narrowing the distance until they are close enough to touch each other. The tension warps and quavers, their stillness no longer perfect at this range where every small shift is perceptible. They meet each other's adjustments, swallow for swallow, sigh for sigh, as if trying to synchronize themselves to find a moment to act by common consent. Toady sees something else now in Dell's face, in his posture and presence, something urgent, about to spill out of control, and again senses his potential for violence. A trembling in his chest makes it difficult for Toady to breathe, and he exhales, abrupt and loud; Dell meets this with a sharp intake of breath that almost whistles between his teeth, and then he seems to hum a word from his chest, something that sounds like "Yeah," and his right hand drifts from his side to his thigh, and up, and he extends his thumb and runs it along the ridge running

at an angle beneath his fly. Toady looks from fly to face and Dell mouths the words "You want it?" and Toady's answer, something between yes and no, gets stuck in his throat, and he gags, chokes, and forces his hesitation down into his lungs, to make himself heavy, so that breath after breath he sinks and sinks, but still he's frantic because the sensation is of rising, of being just on the verge of breaking the surface. He closes his eyes and Dell's thumbs press against his temples, his cheekbones, the skin between his nose and lip. Dell stretches this skin, peels Toady's mouth open and for a flashing purple and yellow second Toady smells wood chips, mud, oil and steam and then nothing; he can't breathe or open his eyes. He's suffocating, but is paralyzed, as though his mind has been knocked into a separate orbit from his body by a terrifying, slapping, sudden impact with steel or rock or water, so he drifts, riding secret vibrations in the ground until there is a rushing and crashing, like a cascade, like oblivion. The train hurtles past and is gone, and as the dying wind descends on Toady, on every freshly exposed part of him, he opens his eyes, takes a deep breath, and comes back to himself. He is squatting; he kneels, leans back, looks up, holds Dell's legs for support. The sun, radiating behind Dell's head, blinds Toady, but before he turns away he discerns a submissive glow in the murky silhouette of Dell's face, a grin of helpless gratitude. Toady runs his tongue along his teeth, then covers them with his lips and rocks forward, and Dell is in his mouth again. Toady's head thrums; he's not sure if he is hearing his own blood circulating or Dell's, and then the surging, lapping, waves-in-a-conch vibrations coalesce into a rhythmic pounding. As it beats against his tongue, Toady clocks the inevitable thump of Dell's pulse, and like a rope falling from his neck, the hard knot of Toady's hunger unravels and unravels and unravels.

Progressive Linkage

by Steven J. Cahill

WINNER OF THE 2014 GIVAL PRESS SHORT STORY AWARD

Harlan never knew what his brother had under the hood. Always something new. Hotter plugs. Bigger carburetor ports. An electric fuel pump. Anything for that extra kick. Harlan couldn't keep up, not on the highway, not in the garage, not anywhere. Garrett was older and stronger, had been winning at everything forever, and now his Chevy was a little quicker than Harlan's Ford. A little faster. But they'd been racing and chasing since Harlan could remember, so that was the way of it. Fact of life.

Like today at the stop sign with Garrett pulling up beside him, saying, "Let's release the beasts, little brother. Zero to sixty. Let the horses out of the barn." And like that, they were revved up and counted down and fishtailing down River Road. Side by side at the get-go, tires screaming and smoking, with Harlan close, almost staying with him till second gear. . . almost. . . then shifting hot and almost gaining ground, but almost was never quite enough. And never would be. Not when it came to Garrett. Not when they got down to going at it head to head.

Driving back to the garage, Harlan told himself it didn't matter, but still. One of these days he'd find a way to saddle up his own horses to catch Garrett on the highway. Give the big boy a little surprise. Better yet, get the jump at the giddy-up and leave him sucking wind. Let those Chevy stallions eat some Ford dust. Harlan imagined the surprised look on Garrett's face. Imagined pulling away and giving him the old Sanderson wave.

Harlan swung around the gas pumps and pulled in over the grease pit in bay one. Garrett drove in beside him, parked his Chevy in the second bay and opened his hood. He gave him a thumbs up and came over with his big-brother smile, saying it had been a good race. Close.

"My engine was screaming like a bobcat in heat," he said. "That Ford may get into my pants yet."

Harlan felt a little rush of pride. "Second gear felt good," he said. "But I think I shifted early."

"Watch the tach," Garrett said. "And listen to your engine. Wait until she's begging for it."

That was Garrett. Everything hot and sexual. Today he was putting on new valve covers. Edelbrocks. Chrome-plated like his carburetor—a four-barrel Holly—special ordered from J. C. Whitney. Garrett liked having the best.

Harlan took a wrench off the work bench and went down the pit steps to change his oil. Chrome valve covers were fancy, but speed and power mattered more. The real trick was balancing the horsepower cubic inch equation. Finding the magic one-to-one ratio.

He took out the oil plug and watched it drain. The old Dodge in bay three needed an inspection—farm trucks took a beating—but that was on Garrett's list. Harlan was still looking at a front-end alignment and a tune-up before he got to his homework. With Pop scheduling so much work lately, Harlan was lucky to find time to change own his oil.

A busy garage, *Sanderson and Sons*, a business destined to be theirs when Pop ran out of gas. Meanwhile, the old man ran the pumps and kept the books but turned all the mechanical work over to them. He liked claiming he was sending his sons to school to become doctors—engine surgeons. Recently he'd begun telling customers his boys were mechanical magicians.

"Healers," he'd say. "With mystical powers."

Pop's bragging embarrassed Harlan, but he could usually diagnose an engine problem by listening. Hear the rattling of tappets and say, "Sounds like a valve job." Garrett would slip into his mechanic's coat and add, "Push rods and rocker arms too." Harlan would reach for the hood latch and say, "What about those sticky lifters?"

Garrett and Harlan, fine-tuning their routine. But they did have the magic touch with internal combustion engines—intake to exhaust—everybody knew it. It was in the Sanderson blood.

Garrett was kicking ass down at the track too—driving test cars for Summit Teams—which was bringing in new business. Harlan was finishing up at Hastings High plus working extra hours to keep his '56 Ford running hot and looking good. The money part made Ma crazy.

"You boys," she said. "There's more to life than a fast car."

"Maybe so, Ma," Garrett said. "But it takes a fast car to find it."

"I know what you're finding at that track," she said. "Racer-chaser women looking for faster cars with leather upholstery."

"Not a faster car in the state." Garrett gave Harlan a wink. "And leather seats are too cold for making out in the winter."

"Don't get cute, Mister." Ma looked at Garrett over her glasses. "And don't think I don't know about you and that hairdresser."

Harlan laughed. Ma would have a conniption if she knew half what Garrett was doing.

"Pop had a flashy car," Garrett said. "Didn't that catch your eye?"

"Oh my, yes. The '34 Ford." She paused, laughing and thinking back, then gave Garrett a warning look. "But your father wasn't running the roads every night and tomcatting around. He was serious."

"Pop's '34 was a roadster, Harlan," Garrett said. "Tomcatting in a rumble seat is serious business."

"Garrett T. Sanderson! Mind your mouth." But she laughed. Garrett was her favorite and always made her laugh. "Time to stop chasing skirts and driving crazy." She pointed over at Pop dozing in his chair. "The old crankcase is waiting for you to settle down and start running the business."

And Ma had shifted into high gear about the business: The family business. And her boys being heirs to a dynasty. About her sons being more than good mechanics. More than simple gear heads exchanging ratchets and wrenches for Christmas. They were executives and businessmen, the bloodlines of the business, and somebody around here better get busy and jumpstart the next generation. Because if he didn't Harlan would get interested in girls and beat him to it.

Garrett had laughed and said Harlan would need lessons to operate that kind of internal combustion engine. Harlan blushed and said that wasn't the race he wanted to win.

Of course now, waiting in the pit while his oil drained, Harlan couldn't stop thinking about the race he did want to win but knew he couldn't. His '56 Crown Vic couldn't beat Garrett's '57 Bel Air. Clearly. Not running stock. It was that simple.

Meanwhile, Garrett was carrying on a running commentary and ratcheting down his new Edelbrocks. "Looking good under the hood," he said. "Silver catches a woman's eye."

"Pop saw the invoice," Harlan said. "Said it was too much cash for a little flash."

Garrett laughed and tightened a bolt. "Flash this chrome at a woman and she'll let you peek under her hood."

Harlan didn't think it was that easy, but Garrett was ahead of him in that department too. Way ahead. And running the roads with a married waitress from *Denison's Diner*.

"A corn-fed woman," Garrett said. "And she can serve a three-course meal."

Other nights Garrett went down to the *Hair Shed* for a little session with Jolene. "A beauty-shop chair is like the tilt-a-whirl at the county fair," he said. "And Jolene knows how to curl my short hairs."

Harlan loved hearing his brother talk about it. Telling him what to do and how to do it, filling in details about what women liked to hear, where to touch them and how, what to tickle and when, how to start their engines and get them into second gear. Garrett was his big brother with big-time good looks. And he was fast, fast, fast.

"Time you got saddled up and broke in," Garrett said. "Show some little pompom girl what your Ford has got and she'll strap you on. Give her a hundred-mile-an-hour ride and she'll cream her jeans."

Harlan knew he was blushing and hoped Garrett couldn't see his face.

"A hundred's easy," Harlan said. "When the Vic is running right I can bury the needle."

"Exactly." Garrett laughed. "I couldn't have said it better. She'll be hotter than a cowboy's pistol on the Fourth of July."

Harlan didn't know many pompom girls. They didn't have much to do with shop boys, but Faithlin Hardy was a cheerleader and she was in his English class. And she'd smiled at him when he read his poem. He wondered if she liked going fast. Some girls didn't.

"I don't know," he said. "What if she just gets scared?"

"All the better." Garrett came over and sat on the pit steps. "Her heart will be hammering like an engine throwing a rod. Like your first time on the cross."

The Sanderson Cross. Garrett's little trick of switching lanes when they met out on the highway. A heart-stopper that first time. The crazy bastard crossed the center line and came straight at him. A head-on about to happen. Harlan read his mind at the last second—swung left and changed lanes—a double cross—both cars on the wrong side of the road, meeting and passing in one split-second of life-changing terror. It had been a close one.

Harlan drove home pissed, his blood still up, and found Garrett washing the Chevy. Garrett grinned at him over the top of his car. "Did you come home to change your shorts?"

"Jesus Christ, Garrett. You could have killed us both."

"I knew you wouldn't wreck your car. You had to cross."

"What if Ma had been driving?"

"There'd have been some skid marks in her bloomers." Garrett laughed and wrung out a chamois. "If your Ford is coming that fast, I know you're driving."

"What if I seized up? Some drivers freeze."

"Just get over when I cross or you'll be sitting in the front seat of my Chevy."

Garrett was crazy as an outhouse rat. And always on the edge.

Now it only happened up on the Flats. And now Garrett accelerated when he swerved into his lane. It was cross or crash. Even with Harlan expecting it, the adrenaline always kicked in and started something in his belly -- something hot.

"Speed does that?" he asked. "Being scared gets a girl going?"

"Better than a horror movie at the drive-in," Garrett said. "You'll have that cheerleader doing cartwheels in the back seat."

That was his brother. Fast women, fast cars. And Garrett's Bel Air had the Power Pack with dual exhaust. Plus it was a rag top. A black convertible. No wonder women loved him.

"When I drop the top and drive through town," he said, "I feel like the pied piper."

Harlan adjusted the mixing valves in his carburetor and changed his air filter, but he was thinking about the three carburetor setup he'd seen on a T-Bird in *Hot Rod* magazine. A row of shiny Hollys sitting on top of a 312 engine. He imagined harnessing them to his accelerator and releasing those beasts. Be like wild stallions coming out of the barn when he floored it. And catching Garrett in the stampede. He was wondering about the complications of progressive linkage when Faithlin Hardy walked in.

***

Faithlin's mother had been getting on her case again. Little nagging questions about the future. About being a senior and her plans after graduation. What about one of the Cosmetology Colleges?—Jolene had an extra chair at the *Hair Shed*—Didn't the Medical Center have On The Job Training?—Practical nurses and LPNs always had jobs. And how come shorthand and typing weren't on her schedule this year? Secretarial skills always came in handy.

"To help out when you're married. Just hope you'll never need to."

"Nurses have to work nights." Faithlin checked her hair—time for a trim—and gave her mother a hug. "You said night shifts are hard on a marriage."

"Yes they are, Honey. But you wasted a year on a boy that left town."

Push was coming to shove and Faithlin knew it was time to make a decision. Get on with being a woman and find herself a man to go the distance. She'd gone steady with Dolby Rainer her junior year which was a total waste because he'd gone off to college after he graduated and she guessed he wasn't coming back. But she wasn't about to sit and wait, and she sure as hell wasn't going to go trotting after him and waste her life chasing his dreams. Besides, Hastings was her home town. She knew better than to run off to New York and get used up by the city. This was her place, thank you very much, and she'd stay right here. No varsity cheerleader was going to have a problem finding a replacement. She did a slow pirouette in front of the full length mirror.

Yes indeed. Faithlin Felice Hardy had the goods. Not to be conceited, but she had the moves and if she played her cards right it wasn't too late to get the pick of the litter.

Not all the big dogs were on a short leash and half the varsity athletes still dropped hints or gave her the look. Most boys checked out her chest or looked at her legs and were forever sneaking peeks at the satin panties cheerleaders wore. Not that she didn't admire their physical talents too—she loved behind-the-back passes and fade-away jump shots—but she hated the athletes' sense of entitlement. After the team won regionals and went to state, half the boys stopped doing homework and started treating cheerleaders like property, acting like hot hands on the court was a license for hot hands everywhere.

She wanted sensitive, maybe not a writer—Dolby had gone off to be a novelist—but someone with enough heart to get hers going. Romance and passion, that's what she wanted. Someone subtle but exciting with a little substance. But with the mother smother getting worse, she'd better get a hustle on.

Harlan Sanderson appeared like a bolt from the blue. Actually he'd been sitting behind her all year—the shop boys sat in the back—but today he was called up front to read his poem. Harlan, blushing and embarrassed, but reminding her of his older brother. Dark, sultry Garrett, the race-car driver hunk. Harlan had the same muscular build. She was admiring his football shoulders and wondering why he never played sports when he walked up to the podium and read the title:

"*Heart of ICE*," he said. "I-C-E is all capitals. It's an abbreviation for—"

"It's better not to tell us Harlan," Mr. Porter interrupted. "Let us figure it out as the metaphor is revealed."

Metaphor. Really. Faithlin was surprised Harlan had written a poem. Never mind one with a metaphor. She liked his shyness and the way that curl of hair fell across his forehead. And she liked how he looked standing behind the podium to read. Pleased that his poem had been chosen, but not carried away with it. He really was quite good looking. She was surprised she'd never noticed before.

Harlan nodded and cleared his throat. "*Heart of ICE*," he said, and began reading:

'Blood is the fuel flowing into the heart
Waiting to combust with a flickering spark.
Then the air is mixed by a butterfly's wing,
And the sound of thunder begins to sing.'

Harlan paused and looked up. He met her eyes—a soulful look—and blushed again, but his voice gained confidence as he read. Lines about passion in the blood becoming fire—erotic really—about turmoil in the chambers of the heart. Faithlin liked the kind of poetry Mr. Porter called accessible. Robert Frost and Emily Dickinson, poets she could understand. And now she could almost feel the heat of the engine as the vehicle in Harlan's poem chased the white lines on a dark highway.

'Building power and gaining speed.
A chariot racing beyond earthly need.'

Faithlin was fascinated when the lines built to a climax and the metaphor became clear. She loved that he called his car a chariot. A chariot with a carburetor heart that mixed air and gas to feed the fire. The passionate fire that drove his Internal Combustion Engine. ICE.

The shop boys whistled and clapped when he finished, but Mr. Porter held up his hand, explaining extended metaphor and how the chariot's human feelings and passion were an example of anthropomorphism.

Faithlin liked that it hadn't been one of the college-bound kids getting his poem analyzed, and some of the lines stuck with her all day. Carburetor or not, she knew Harlan had deep feelings. Hard to imagine him having a brother like Garrett with a slow-eyed Elvis look and reputation for being so wild. He drove like a bat out of hell, and there'd been rumors about a married woman. But today she knew Harlan was different—still waters run deep—and brought up the Sanderson name at dinner.

"Watch out for that older one," her mother said. "A car will always mean more to Garrett Sanderson than a woman's heart."

"Well, that convertible is a head turner," Faithlin said. Which was a fact. Every varsity cheerleader on the squad was dying for a ride in that Chevy. Most of them would give it up just to get close to Garrett. "And I heard he's winning at the track."

"Garrett Sanderson will be racing cars till they kill him," her mother said.

"But that younger one would clean up nice."

"I think he may have potential." And she did. Faithlin had spoken to Harlan after class. Stopped him in the hall and told him how much she loved his poem. Told him she admired the way he'd explored his deep feelings. 'You know, in a symbolic way.' He went shy, but she could tell from the look in his puppy-dog eyes that he had feelings for more than cars.

She liked his car too—a Crown something or other—plus Harlan was practically running his father's garage. He wasn't headed for the swing-shift waiting list down at the plant. Harlan Sanderson had a future.

"I imagine him ending up with the family business," her mother said. "And he's still young enough to be trainable if you start putting down papers."

Faithlin's father cleared his throat and rolled a toothpick around in his mouth. "Garrett met Richard Petty at Daytona last year," he said. "If he gets a ride with NASCAR, he'll have tickets and passes to pit road so the whole family could—"

"This family doesn't want tickets to that circus," her mother said. "Her ticket's right here, and Harlan Sanderson won't be out burning rubber while she's raising babies. He might have grease under his nails when he comes to the table, but he'll be home for supper."

That was the Good Housekeeping Seal of Approval for Faithlin, and she went down to the *Hair Shed* for a trim. Jolene added a few highlights and gave her a summer look. A little bounce. Faithlin was leaving the shop when Garrett Sanderson came down Main Street in his pride and joy. He slowed and stopped, his engine burbling like a log truck while she crossed the street in front of him. The top was down, his hair was combed back like the King himself, and he gave her such a long Elvis look that she felt the heat.

Faithlin hadn't worn a bra and knew he was watching her jiggle. Her sweater was so light and tight that her nipples showed. But she'd gotten used to lingering looks from cheering and expected them. Now she was even wishing she'd worn her shorts and that her legs were tan. Give him the big picture. A pair of short-shorts on North Main could tie up traffic.

Faithlin hadn't given it all away to Dolby Rainer, saving herself for the main event, but she'd come close—given him a lesson or two in the back seat—so she knew all the moves. Walking past Garrett's car, she went loose at the waist and put a touch of salsa on her hips. Take that, you old hound dog.

But when she looked back, he was waving at Jolene inside the shop. Didn't matter. Faithlin wouldn't be spinning her wheels chasing that good old boy around the circuit. Her sights were set on the brother.

Harlan didn't have a girlfriend, not that anybody knew, but Raelene Bailey had gone giddy about his poem and put a little extra on it when he was around. Like she was looking to get something started. Faithlin wasn't worried about competition—she could handle that—but she didn't want to back-stab Raelene.

Friday afternoon she checked with the girls after practice and found out the coast was clear. Raelene had been working some serious moves on Billy Stebbins and was ready to put him out of his misery. Lately she'd been thinking maybe she'd like to have a baby to get a little head start on her future and nail Billy down. And what did everybody think of that idea? Her father could get Billy on the day shift at the plant and who wouldn't jump at a chance like that?

Saturday morning Faithlin put on the sweater again. It was Orlon, powder blue, and buttoned down the front. Oh yeah. Then she shimmied into her short-shorts and went down to Sandersons' garage to get a driving lesson.

***

Harlan was thinking to ask Garrett about progressive linkage setups when Faithlin Hardy walked in. Taking her time and pausing to look at the Continental Kit on Harlan's Ford before coming up along the driver's side. Garrett was talking solid lifters and a new camshaft for his Chevy, but Faithlin's shorts shut him up for a minute.

She traced the chrome V on Harlan's door with a lazy finger, saying, 'So this is The Chariot,' and started talking about how it was too bad the Driver's Ed car at school was an automatic. "I got my license with my uncle's car," she said. "But I need to learn stick shift. My mom's car is standard."

Garrett nodded knowingly. "Manual transmissions are tricky, Faithlin, but I could give you lessons." He patted the hood of his Chevy and winked at Harlan. "And this chariot is a real fire-breather."

Harlan wished he could be more like Garrett. Casual and confident in a flirtatious way. When girls talked to Harlan at school, it always came around to his brother. Who was he going out with now?—Or—Is it true he's being recruited by NASCAR? When Garrett drove by the school with the top down and glasspack mufflers rumbling, the girls fluttered around like there was a rooster in the hen house.

Sometimes he cruised by just to get them started. Garrett was twenty now, too old for high school girls. He called the younger ones 'Jailbait' and 'San Quentin Quail'— but Faithlin was eighteen.

Harlan couldn't believe she was here. So beautiful, her face thoughtful and serious while she considered Garrett's offer. He wondered where Dolby Rainer had gone off to and when he'd be coming around again. Then he realized that Faithlin was looking at him.

"I was thinking Harlan would be the one," she said, and gave him a warm smile. "We're in English class together, and I really like his poetry."

"Poetry." Garrett rolled his eyes. "Hard to imagine."

Harlan's pulse jumped when she ran her hand up the strip of chrome on the roof of his Crown Vic. She had a profile that put her in a class by herself. "I don't know," he said, feeling himself blush. "I help out in the shop, but I've never taught driving."

"Harlan's right," Garrett said. "He's a rookie when it comes to teaching. You'll be wanting someone with experience to get you started."

"What about it, Harlan?" Faithlin leaned over and looked inside his car, shorts so tight the lines of her underwear showed through. "Don't you want to get experienced too?"

Harlan shrugged, but she was watching him, eyes bluer than her sweater, and waiting for an answer. He kept his voice even and said he'd been driving stick since he was nine and guessed he could probably hold up his end of it.

"That settles it for me." Faithlin gave him a high-beam smile. "Besides, with your brother so experienced and all, he'd probably be too fast for me."

Garrett laughed and studied her for a moment. "Maybe," he said. "But I don't think so." He shook his head after Faithlin left and clapped Harlan on the shoulder. "She's faster than both of us," he said. "You'll be the one that gets a lesson."

"What do you mean? Learning stick shift will take ten minutes."

"Be a hot ten minutes," Garrett said. "That girl wants to pop your cherry."

Harlan felt a surge of heat in the pit of his stomach. An electrical tingle in his groin. Like running the Sanderson Cross and being scared half to death.

Garrett was already giving instructions, telling him to take his time and listen for her breathing to change before he shifted. Telling him to get her engine into second gear before unhooking her bra and going for bare skin.

"And writing her a poem." Garrett shook his head in wonderment. "Smooth move, little brother. She's breathing hard already."

"The poem wasn't about her," Harlan said. "It was about cars."

"Hot cars always turn women on." Garrett rumpled Harlan's hair. "But if she's too hot to handle, I may need to take the wheel."

But Harlan was only half listening. He had an image of Faithlin stretching for the chrome crown on his car and wasn't worried about unhooking her bra. He didn't think she'd been wearing one.

***

Synchronizing the pedals wasn't half as tricky as going from a cartwheel to a split—varsity cheerleaders were athletic for God's sake—just another maneuver that required timing and coordination. And practice.

Harlan turned out to be a good teacher. He was patient when she raced the engine, knew enough to keep quiet when she grated the gears, and gave her gentle reminders about not developing bad habits like riding the clutch. She drove around town to practice shifting at traffic lights, and he took her on routes that had stop signs on hills.

Harlan's car was a '56 Ford, a blue and white Crown Victoria with a modified V-8 engine which needed, according to Harlan, a little more gallop. Cute. Calling 225 horsepower 'gallop.' The car was scary fast and sexy to drive. By the time Faithlin felt comfortable shifting and was working on smoothing out the ride, she discovered how much she loved to drive. Nothing felt quite like it. Standing on a pyramid of cheerleaders in the gym was the end of a performance, a pose. Cruising down North Main behind the wheel was a performance in motion, one with potential. The Crown Vic—Faithlin loved the name—was sleek and lethal as a jungle cat, but she was taming it and learning what it could do. What she could make it do.

Harlan began teaching her things that weren't in any Driver's Manual: Revving the engine and popping the clutch, burning rubber and blowing smoke, how to spread a patch and leave a loop. Redlining, speed shifting, and just plain driving fast. And faster. Faithlin was loving it.

And she loved the cheerleaders being jealous, checking Harlan out when he picked her up from practice, admiring his car and making little comments.

"Stick shift. Like you need lessons for that."

Laughing and talking about parallel parking. About Raelene Bailey taking Billy Stebbins to the gravel pit for some real back seat driving. Girl talk, curious and asking questions about Harlan, but Faithlin let them wonder.

She had decided to break him in slow. After all, he was a rookie and this was going to be her first rodeo too. Dolby Rainer hadn't amounted to much so he didn't count. She could take her time with Harlan, parcel it out and let it build so she could enjoy the ride.

She liked the way his breathing quickened when they kissed, the medicinal smell of Vitalis in his hair, and she loved to hear him moan when she arched up and let him press himself against her. A little more each time. She felt it building too.

But everything was building. The sound of a V-8 engine, the smell of hot tires and asphalt, the feeling of being transported when she got her hands on the wheel. Acceleration and speed were intoxicating, and Faithlin was in ecstasy when she caught rubber in second gear. There were feelings she'd never had, and she was discovering what Harlan meant when he said, 'Let the animal out of the cage.' Wild things were asleep inside her, and they were waking up.

Tonight she kept the accelerator on the floor in second gear until the tach ran into the red. Six thousand RPMs in second gear. Incredible. And then, out on the state highway, she had the speedometer pushing ninety, driving faster than she'd ever driven before. Faster than her mother's car would even go.

Laughing at her expression, Harlan took the wheel and drove out to Hastings Flats. "This is where Garrett and I open up and turn it loose." He began doing things behind the wheel that had her heart pounding in her chest. My God, doing doughnuts and skids and spins, doing emergency brake turns.

Going from zero to sixty was like being on a carnival ride. Faithlin timed it while Harlan trimmed it down, getting quicker and faster every time.

"Let me try, Harlan," she said. "I can do it."

"Not here," he said. "In case we meet Garrett."

Faithlin pulled away from him. "You don't want your brother to know I drive your car?" She felt her good mood slip away.

"It isn't that." Harlan laughed and pulled her back. "We've got a surprise."

Men's surprises were hard to imagine, but Harlan held the accelerator down and told her to watch the speedometer. She was holding her breath when the needle quivered up and passed a hundred. Definitely over. My God. And Harlan said it had flattened out. That the engine was starving.

"Incredible," she said. "I can't imagine going any faster."

"Garrett's Chevy will. He even polishes the ports in his four barrel carburetor."

"A four barrel." She remembered carburetors from the *Heart of ICE* poem. "Can't you do that too?"

"Better than that," he said. "And I've sent for the parts."

Harlan told her he was working on a setup to make Garrett Sanderson eat their dust. How he'd love to beat his brother at something, anything. He'd never been first at anything around Garrett. And after that, if Faithlin wanted, she could put the speedometer out of sight. The Crown Vic would be ready to do a buck twenty plus change and she could bury the needle. After they beat Garrett, he'd let her do some real hot driving.

Faithlin slid over and put her head on his shoulder. A hundred and twenty miles an hour, maybe more. With her at the wheel. Just thinking about it made her hot. Beating Garrett would be special too.

The Vic was running smooth and they cruised the back roads while the sun went down and filled the pewter sky with dusk. Faithlin loved that word, Dusk, and Elvis was singing 'It's Now or Never' on the radio. She pressed her breasts against Harlan's arm—no bra today—and rested the warmth of her hand on his thigh. Harlan was shy, letting her take the lead, and she suggested stopping in the gravel pit. For a little while, you know, if you want to.

When the car was full of heat and heavy breathing, Faithlin's nipples were tingling and she decided to undo the buttons. Go that far at least. Going a hundred miles an hour had started a fire inside. Stirred her in ways that were showing. She wanted him to see her breasts, her swollen nipples, and she wanted to watch his face.

She sat up, straddling his lap and watching his expression change while she undid the buttons on her sweater. Slowly. Unbuttoned every one and then held the sweater open and let him look. It was worth it. He was begging to touch them. Next time she'd let him.

They were quiet driving back to the garage, and Faithlin rolled down her window to cool things off. The throaty sound of the engine blended with Roy Orbison on the radio doing *Pretty Woman,* and she felt like her life was filling up and coming true.

Garrett was in the work bay of the garage when they came in. Faithlin knew her face was flushed and that Harlan was still hot and bothered and walking funny. Garrett looked at the buttons on her sweater and grinned. He knew what she'd been doing to his brother. Faithlin smiled right back. She wasn't about to be intimidated by Garrett being Hollywood handsome.

"I did over 80 tonight," she said. "Harlan says I'm good with speed."

"I guessed you'd be a natural." Garrett winked and looked at the blonde streaks Jolene had put in her hair. "The question is, what are you teaching him?"

Harlan jumped in and changed the subject. "The engine was getting mushy at the top end," he said. "It felt like I was getting valve float or running bad gas."

And easy as that, they were talking about high-octane fuel and compression rates. Usually she didn't listen, it was like a foreign language. But now it was interesting. Now it all sounded like sex. Solid lifters and big pistons. Short-stroke engines and faster windups. My goodness.

***

Harlan's parts came in the mail. The intake manifold he'd special-ordered from J. C. Whitney with three two-barrel carburetors—triple deuces—he'd gotten the Strombergs. Hooking them up would be tricky, synchronizing the system and adjusting the linkage without Garrett knowing would take time, but he'd gotten a calibration kit and an electric fuel pump. Besides, Faithlin was developing an ear for engines now and would help with the fine tuning.

Harlan loved the look on her face when he explained the linkage. How they would be cruising on one carburetor at quarter-throttle with the other two waiting to kick in. The engine purring like a kitten at a stop light until some gear-head in a jacked-up street rod pulls up and gives them 'the look.' The light changes and the Vic becomes a roaring lion and eats the kid alive.

"Flooring it opens the door," Harlan said. "The linkage lets the animal out of the cage."

Faithlin hugged him and slid her hands into the back pockets of his jeans. "I can't wait to drive it," she said. "I'm excited already."

Harlan moved his hands onto the flare of her hips, getting excited too, but she leaned back, eyes half-closed and dreamy and said, "And we'll beat Garrett?"

"That's the plan," he said. "A little surprise for big brother."

"I want to be with you," she said. "I can't wait to see his face."

Harlan couldn't either, and wanted her there. But lately Garrett had been weird about Faithlin.

"She's got you by the balls, Brother. Your pecker will shrivel up and fall off if you don't use it soon."

Harlan was sorry he'd told him about that night. About hitting a hundred with the Vic and Faithlin undoing her sweater.

"And you sat there like a deer caught in the headlights." Garrett laughed. "But then, that girl's headlights are always on high beam."

Harlan didn't like him talking that way about Faithlin's breasts. "We're taking it slow," he said, but thinking about her nipples made him hard. And he wouldn't be asking his brother for any more advice. This was private now, something special with Faithlin, and he hated it when Garrett called her a tease. Saying to bring her up to the Flats and show her the Cross. Nothing like a near-death experience to get a girl ready to rock and roll. Harlan said he'd give it some thought.

He didn't like the way his brother was today either. And he kept hanging around after they finished old lady Bartlett's transmission and put away the tools. Faithlin had been in and out all afternoon, talking recipes with Ma and pumping gas for Pop. Harlan had her put new Blue Jewel taillights on the Ford while they waited for Garrett to leave so they could get started.

But Garrett was still bragging about his Chevy taking them apart up on the Flats. Even beating some of the new '60s. How he'd nailed a Plymouth Fury and a Pontiac Star Chief, and just last night he'd kicked some Chrysler ass.

"But you do things to your car," Faithlin said. "Add extras."

"Racing is about winning." Garrett gave her a knowing look. "Everybody thinks they've got something special under the hood."

As much as the attitude and arrogance annoyed him, Harlan felt a surge of confidence. He and Garrett had been playing cat-and-mouse with cars and horsepower since they started driving. Extra carburetion was fair.

"Of course there's weight and the gear ratio of automatics," Garrett admitted, being modest now. "Torqueflite, Hydramatic, even the Chevy Powerglide is sluggish. Show me a heavy car with automatic, and I'll show them my exhaust."

"What about new Fords?" Harlan asked. "Have you run a Galaxie?"

"Bad news, Good news." Garrett laughed. "New Fords don't have the power to pull a sick whore off a piss pot. Even your '56 will blow the doors off a Galaxie."

Harlan winced. He didn't like that kind of talk around Faithlin, but she ignored it.

Garrett was putting the top down on his convertible for a night of cruising. "This is the car to beat, Little Brother." He winked at Faithlin. "I've got the fastest stick in the state."

When Garrett finally left, Harlan pulled the Vic into the garage and they went to work. Changing the manifold and mounting the Strombergs took longer than expected. Connecting the linkage was trial-and-error and making constant adjustments to smooth out the engine. But Faithlin was patient and helpful, learning the language of mechanics and handing him tools: wrenches and screwdrivers—flathead and Phillips—deep-well sockets and ratchet extensions. And she adjusted the idling screws while he lengthened the linkage.

The language Faithlin was teaching him required no words: reaching for tools and brushing hands, working side-by-side underneath the hood, and resting her hand on his leg during road tests. Language with a physical vocabulary, and Harlan was feeling it.

But he knew not to rush things:

Garrett ran high test in his Chevy—93 octane—saying, "Vitamins for my horses."

Harlan filled up with aircraft fuel—120 octane—thinking, 'Vitamins for race horses.'

Garrett had a Mallory dual-point distributor.

Harlan put in a three-quarter cam and solid lifters.

They were getting to it and Harlan planned to be looking at his brother in the rearview mirror. And then he'd wave.

The Sanderson Wave, Garrett's signature move. Lift a lazy hand and draw a big S in the air. An arrogant, slow-motion S. And put a period at the end. "Punctuate it," Garrett said. "Because it's over. A Sanderson Wave means goodbye; it ends when you point at the guy you beat."

The Sanderson Wave. Garrett even did it when they made the Cross, but that happened so fast Harlan always kept both hands on the wheel. But this time he'd give Garrett a dose of it. After they came off the line and his Ford jumped out front, Harlan would hit second gear and raise his hand to draw the big S—Goodbye Garrett—pointing while he pulled away.

Faithlin laughed when he practiced tracing a sensual S in the air in front of her, like he was drawing her profile. She smiled, stepping into the space, and arched her back. Her face was flushed and expectant, beautiful.

"You Sanderson boys have sexy moves," she said. "But when are we going to race?"

Harlan was ready to take on the Chevy. He had a mathematical advantage: Three twos vs a four-barrel. The Vic had the equivalent of a T-Bird engine and accelerated like a striking cobra when he jumped on it. He hoped his transmission could handle the torque. Three wide-open Strombergs blasting through BBK headers sounded like a top fuel dragster. A crazy one that burned nitrous oxide and went about a thousand miles an hour in two seconds. Then needed a parachute to stop.

"Tonight," he said. "If Garrett heard the rumors and takes the bait."

He had, and he did, and he was fuming. "Faithlin has been blowing smoke," he said. "Your little Twinkie told Jolene that your car is faster than mine. Half the girls at the *Hair Shed* are believing it."

Harlan felt a small moment of deceit, but Garrett was already talking about the run. Calling it a 'Moment of Truth' and saying he hoped it wouldn't break Harlan's heart when his girl wanted to ride home in the Chevy.

Honest to God. Sometimes Garrett was too much. This wasn't like a movie where the girl goes home with the winner, but the look on Garrett's face gave him a cold chill.

"Faithlin's not the prize," he said. "Just to be clear."

"Let's make the run," Garrett said. "See how it goes."

With the summer heat yet to come—and graduation two weeks away—it was a perfect night for racing. Harlan picked up Faithlin and drove up to the Flats, listening to the music of his engine and feeling the thunder of the Strombergs when they opened up. They were tuned and ready with the kinks smoothed out of the linkage. Tonight they were responding without a single cough or stutter, going from idle to wide open without an instant's hesitation. The Vic was ready; Harlan felt it.

Harlan loved *Rebel Without A Cause* where Natalie Wood stood between the cars and dropped her arms to start the race. But Faithlin would be riding with him—she was part of this now—and drag racing in Hastings was simpler. Two vehicles lined up at the south end—on a start line painted years ago—revving up while they counted down—then raced to the Route 5 sign halfway down the flats. More than a quarter mile and far enough to answer any questions. Harlan had done the ritual a hundred times before, beaten every kid and every car at school, but Garret always pulled away. Got him by a car length doing zero to sixty and still gaining in the quarter. Tonight would be different; Harlan knew it.

More than a dozen cars had parked in the roadside pullout where a crowd—mostly kids from school—had started a small fire in a barrel. Billy and Raelene were sitting on the hood of his car, and Billy gave him a thumbs-up when they went by.

"The word got around," Harlan said. "How did they know?"

"I told the cheerleaders." Faithlin opened her window and waved. "I wanted them to see."

Garrett was waiting at the start. His convertible top was up for better aerodynamics and he was looking down at the crowd. "I'm glad you brought witnesses." He grinned at Faithlin. "You should have sold tickets."

The arrogant tone settled Harlan's pre-race jitters. "We're ready to go," he said. "Do you want two out of three?"

"Let's wind them up," Garrett said. "One run for all the marbles."

It was a clean start: screaming tires, a cloud of blue smoke but coming off the line together with the Vic nosing ahead. It was finally happening. A quarter car length in low gear—incredible—redlining through the power curve and catching rubber in second. Zero to 60 faster than he'd ever done before—unbelievable—with the Vic out in front and still gaining.

Sound layered on sound for the sweetest moment of Harlan's life. His engine screaming in his head, Faithlin screaming in his ear 'Yes, Yes, Yes.' It was a decisive win. Over a car length at the sign and Harlan so excited he didn't even look at the speed. Both of them so excited they'd forgotten to wave.

It happened so quickly; it was over so soon.

Harlan's heart was racing when they turned around and stopped at the end of the flats. He wanted Garrett to ask for another run, but he didn't. Garrett did come over to the car and ask for a look under the hood.

Harlan showed him the Strombergs, filled with pride and wanting to talk linkage, but Garrett shook his head. "That's a great set up," he said. "But now it's not a stock engine."

"Neither is yours," Faithlin said. "Can't you just admit we won?"

Garrett studied her for a moment. "The Ford was hot tonight," he said. "But we'll run again."

"Anytime," she said, pulling on Harlan's arm. "We can't wait."

They parked in the old gravel pit beside the river. The sound of peepers filled the air with Elvis singing *Are You Lonesome Tonight* on the radio. Harlan slid across the seat and reached for Faithlin. He'd finally beaten his brother, and she'd been with him. No, he wasn't lonesome, but the sultry voice and the lyrics of the song made him ache inside.

They were kissing now, long slow kisses, with Faithlin melting against him and filling the car with heat. He kissed her again and slid his hand underneath her blouse, but she pushed him away.

"Wait, Harlan," she said. "So you can see."

His protest died in his throat when she slid back against her door and unbuttoned her blouse. Slowly, undoing it top to bottom, then taking it off completely. She reached back to undo the bra, slid it down her arms and let her breasts spring out. Ivory white with the nipples pink and erect. Harlan reached, his hands trembling.

"Not yet," she said. "Take off your shirt."

He did, holding his breath and watching her unzip her skirt and push it down over her hips. She kept her underpants on. A wisp of pale blue silk with lace trim and a monogram. FFH. Faithlin Felice Hardy, posing for him in her panties, sexier than *Playboy* magazine.

Then they were kissing, skin against skin, and she drew his hands up to her breasts. Telling him to hold them and kiss them. Jesus. She held his head against them and let him suck her nipples until he felt like he would explode. My God, he was so hard it hurt. Then her hands were on him, pulling at his belt and unzipping his Levis. He almost couldn't breathe. She reached in to hold him, her hands warm and moving until he made a strangled gasp and collapsed against the seat. And like that, it was over.

But Faithlin was smiling when they got dressed. "Next time we'll go slower," she said. "This part is not a race."

***

Faithlin was surprised at how much the race had turned her on. Like an aphrodisiac. But speed and power were seductive, and Harlan's car was fast and sexy. She wished she'd been driving. And she really wished she could have seen Garrett's expression when they won. Like watching Harlan's face while she was taking off her clothes. Maybe better.

Just thinking about it got her hot. That whole night had been wild—half the kids in school came to watch—like cheering at center court, but she'd been a player. A participant, and she'd been riding in the winning car. She almost couldn't breathe at the start, but she'd gone screaming crazy when Harlan pulled ahead. And every nerve ending in her body was on fire when they won.

Of course Garrett hated to admit losing. He'd practically ignored them after they won the race, then claimed that Harlan's engine wasn't fair. And acted like Johnny Thunder when he drove off in his convertible to fast-talk some woman into the back seat. Probably tell her how he won so she'd get all hot and bothered and go all the way.

Faithlin felt like it herself. Down in the gravel pit, still tingling inside, and getting Harlan so excited that he came right in her hand. She'd loved him being that needy and so helpless afterward. And grateful. It made her feel like a woman.

Harlan had been quiet driving home. She slid over and pressed against him until she realized what he was thinking. "Garrett didn't like it," he said. "I thought he'd be impressed."

"He was," she said, and straightened up. "He couldn't believe we won."

"He'll come up with something faster." Harlan shrugged. "He always does."

She put her foot on top of his and pushed it down on the gas. The Strombergs opened up and filled the night until she felt the sound down in her core. "You won, Harlan," she said. "We're faster."

There'd been lots of talk at school, but with Senior Projects coming due, the week had practically flown. Faithlin had yet to pick a topic, but Harlan's was about Henry Ford. Of course.

Saturday morning now with her mother drinking coffee and getting motherly. "You're spending lots of time with Harlan. Why not bring him here?"

"He has to work," she said. "And I thought you liked him."

"I do like him, but be careful. Especially if he's like his brother."

Careful. Her mother's code for sex.

"Don't worry Mom. I know the rules."

But the rules were changing. Half the senior girls were doing it, or practically. All the ones that were going steady. And last month Raelene Bailey missed her period. She planned on telling Billy right after graduation.

"Don't forget the car rules either. The Sanderson boys didn't get cars like that to drive to church."

Faithlin hoped her mother didn't know about the race. The brother competition. Or that Harlan was letting her drive a little faster every time. She couldn't wait to really open up those Strombergs out on the flats.

After she cleaned her room, she helped her mother with the laundry before going down to the garage. The *Sanderson and Sons* sign needed repainting which reminded her that Raelene would be having a baby. Someday, she thought. Someday she'd have a son with Harlan to carry on the tradition. But not until they finished having fun and were settled down.

The work bay doors were closed, but she heard the clink of metal and ratchet sounds and found Garrett working on his engine. He looked up when she came in.

"Harlan's making a hot run to Auto Supply. Poppadoodle needed parts in a hurry." He closed his hood, giving her his Elvis smile. "And now that his car is faster . . . well . . . you know."

Faithlin felt the usual quiver of attraction. He was something.

"It is faster," she said. "You could have said 'Congratulations.'"

"That would have been premature."

Something in Garrett's tone set off an alarm. He was putting away the tools, but she saw the J. C. Whitney boxes on the workbench.

"What have you been doing in there now?"

"Get in." He grinned and opened the passenger door. "I'll show you."

The top was down, and her hair blew everywhere. Her skirt was blowing halfway up her legs, and she pinched it between her knees to hold it down. Garrett headed up River Road to the flats. Once or twice, when the car began to skid, he smiled and turned into it, driving with one hand and accelerating. He was quite the driver, but she'd always known that.

The wind blew the engine sound away, but a muted roar followed them onto Hastings Flat. Garrett did a couple fast starts, letting her feel the acceleration and ran the tach into the red in second gear. Then he opened up, telling her she'd probably wet her pants if they met Harlan now Half his words were blown away and she ignored the rest. It was just Garrett talk.

"Let me drive," she said. "I want to try it."

"What if it's more than you can handle?"

There it was again, that infuriating tone, but he stopped to let her slide into the driver's seat. Faithlin knew he'd changed the engine; she'd known it from the sound, but she really felt it now. Felt the heavy throb of power when she revved up. The car was like a living thing when she let out the clutch and it almost got away—it was lighter than the Vic—but she corrected and kept the pedal down. My God. The car was very fast. She accelerated out of second and into high with the wheel so sensitive it felt like flying. Incredible. Faster than she'd ever driven.

Her hands were trembling when she stopped and shut the engine off. Garrett opened the hood and showed her what he'd done. There were two air cleaners in there now. Big ones. He'd added another carburetor.

"Dual quads," he said. "Two four barrels, in case you didn't know."

She did know. He started to explain but Faithlin shook her head. "Harlan told me this would happen," she said. "He knew you'd do something,"

"It will be more fun if Harlan doesn't know."

His voice was low and husky and he was smiling, more superior than ever. He stood so close she could smell his after shave. Her stomach fluttered and she didn't trust herself to speak. She walked around the passenger side and got back in the car, but Garrett followed her and stood so close she couldn't close the door.

"Harlan's just a kid," he said. "He'll always be sucking hind tit."

"You've got such a mouth," she said, but she was remembering Harlan's lips nuzzling at her breast.

And Garrett's hands were on her shoulders, pressing her down against the seat. "Garrett," she said, but he was leaning in and kissing her. And she let him, going with it. Not exactly kissing back, but curious. He tasted of coffee and kissed her hard, trying to overwhelm her with passion, like she'd be swept away She nearly was. Because Garrett Sanderson was faster than the car he drove. His hands were under her skirt and sliding up her legs. Fast. His fingers twisted in the waistband of her panties and pulled. She didn't mean to—no time to think—because she lifted her hips and let him take them down. They were off and gone before she could change her mind and stop the momentum.

She'd always known it would come to this. But now she knew how it had to end. She pushed him away, saying, "Garrett, No!" feeling dizzy, almost sick inside. She told him No! again, and then again, afraid he wouldn't stop, afraid she couldn't, but kept saying it until she felt the animal heat begin to fade.

Garrett swore, but moved to let her up. "What are you saving it for?"

"For Harlan," she said. "I want it to be Harlan."

The sun came through the trees and dappled light played on her legs. She pulled her skirt down, still naked underneath, and pulled herself together. Garrett watched her, but he didn't try again, and she tried to believe it was because he loved Harlan too.

***

Harlan drove the Vic into the second bay and opened the hood. It was running rough, skipping a beat and pausing when he floored it. He pulled down a drop light and got the tools to start adjusting. As much as he loved progressive linkage, the constant tuning was a nuisance. He turned up the idling screws and tinkered with the fuel mixture, but he'd been expecting Faithlin and finally gave her a call.

"Raelene is here and needs to talk," she said. "I'll be over later."

"Garrett's acting weird," he said. "Pop sent him out with the fuel truck, but he wants another run today. Probably cranked up something on the Chevy. Planed the heads or something."

Harlan thought she'd love to race again and was surprised at her reaction.

"But we beat him," she said. "You won, Harlan. Why race again?"

"He's my brother." Harlan laughed. "I have to give him another chance."

"Do you?" Faithlin hesitated again. "I'm not sure he'd give you one."

Garrett was right about women. Don't expect them to make sense.

It was still early afternoon when Billy Stebbins pulled in with his old Plymouth. It was a '49, ten years old, but the body still looked good.

"The clutch is going," Billy said. "Can you fix it so Raelene can use it while I'm gone?"

"Where you going? Didn't her Daddy line you up for the day shift at the plant?"

"I enlisted. Two days ago, when I turned eighteen."

Harlan whistled. Here was Billy Stebbins raising his hand and volunteering to leave town when everything he needed for a great life was right here.

"What about Raelene? She may not wait around for you to come home."

"I haven't told her yet," Billy said. "It's a graduation surprise. The car too."

Harlan had been thinking about getting Faithlin a ring. Not engagement or like that, just a nice one that fit. She'd been wearing his class ring around her neck on a chain. It looked good but sometimes it got in the way.

They talked school for a while: graduation and parties, beer blasts and skinny-dipping, and then Harlan looked at the Plymouth. He'd worked on it before and guessed he could make some adjustments. Girls always rode the clutch, but if Raelene drove it right she could make it last until Billy came back. If he did.

"She'll like the car, Billy. Park it behind Garrett's and I'll get to it next."

Harlan found Faithlin's panties when he was moving Garrett's car. They were under the seat. The wispy blue silk with lace trim and FFH. Under the passenger seat in Garrett's car. An icy fist gripped his heart.

He'd worried about Dolby Rainer. Faithlin promised him nothing had happened, but now this. He stared at the monogram, remembering Garrett's women and willing the letters to change. There'd been a Farrah and one called Foxy, but no FFH. Nothing even close. Harlan held them up and looked again. They were hers.

He went into the bathroom and pressed the silk against his face. His legs went weak and a wave of nausea twisted in his stomach. The shock of understanding took him to his knees and he began to cry. Dry, wracking sobs tearing him apart inside. He slumped over the toilet, crying and retching and tried to stop the rush of images flowing through his head.

He kept seeing them together, like they were in a movie, but Harlan was creating all the details and visualizing what they did. It was a strangely erotic torture, but he couldn't make it stop. Nor did he want it to. Being the director, giving them directions and moving them in his mind brought a strange measure of relief. It gave him the perverse satisfaction of somehow being in control. He replayed the scene again, horrified but fascinated when he ran it in slow motion. The scene that would repeat forever in a movie that would never end.

When he finally stopped crying and the nausea went away, a sense of resignation settled in. His head felt cold and numb, but he was filled with an icy calm. The world was coming back and he'd have to face it soon. Because somebody was out there now, rattling around in the office.

It was double-crossing Garrett—his son-of-a-bitch brother—knocking on the bathroom door and running his motor mouth. "Quit playing with your dipstick in there? You can't check Faithlin's oil if it's all worn out."

Harlan flushed the toilet and turned on the water in the sink. He didn't trust himself to speak, but didn't have to; Garrett's mouth was in overdrive.

"She's been holding out so long it'll be like putting a railroad spike into a BB Gun." Garrett rattled the door and laughed. "Fire up the Ford and follow me out to the Flats. I'm ready to get it on again."

Harlan put the panties in his pocket and opened the door to look his brother in the face. Expecting to see . . . what? Deceit in his eyes? Guilt and shame for the betrayal? But there was nothing. Harlan should have known. Garrett didn't even understand that it mattered. It was as though it never happened. Nothing bothered his brother. Garrett was the way he'd always been; Harlan saw that clearly now. And he understood that Garrett would never change; it was the way he would always be.

But Garrett was already outside calling back, 'Let's go,' and smiling when he started his car. He closed his eyes and listened to it rumble to life. Harlan followed him, fighting to control his emotions but hearing the throaty resonance of the Chevy's engine. He knew why his brother wanted the rematch.

Garrett grinned and gave it a little gas. "Did you look under the hood when you moved my car?"

Harlan forced himself to speak. "Not under the hood." His voice was detached and cold, like it was coming from an observer far away.

But Garrett was oblivious. He grinned again before he slipped the Chevy into gear. "Bring Faithlin when you come," he said. "We'll give her a little thrill before the race." He revved his engine and pulled away, heading for the Flats to beat his brother and take his girl. Same as always.

Harlan was working on Billy's car when Faithlin drove in. Knowing that she'd been looking under Garrett's hood added fuel to his smoldering rage. He watched her park her mother's car and check her hair in the rearview mirror. Once an endearing gesture, but he was seeing her clearly now and steeled himself to meet her eyes.

"Garrett's up on the Flats," he said. "Waiting for us to race."

"But what if he made changes to his engine?" Faithlin's blue eyes were filled with guile. "You always said he finds a way to beat you."

"He always has," he said. "So we'll surprise him."

Harlan slid his hand into his pocket and touched her panties. They were the confirmation of her betrayal, but the contact gave him courage. He went over to the Vic and opened the driver's door. "Warm it up for us," he said. "Give it a road test while I finish Billy's car."

"Do you want me to—"

"Run it out to the Flats. I'll be ready when you come back."

Faithlin was a beautiful girl, and Harlan felt his heart twist when she started the car. He traced the chrome V along the door. The Vic was a beautiful car too and it was not too late.

But the movie was running in his head and the moment ended; it was too late for regret.

Harlan gave her the Sanderson Wave when she drove away. The animal was out of the cage. He went back inside to work on Billy's car. Raelene would need a lot of clutch with Billy gone, and the pressure plate was worn. Harlan was making the adjustments when he heard the sound of sirens heading for the Flats.

Fat Tails

by Daniel Degnan

WINNER OF THE 2010 GIVAL PRESS SHORT STORY AWARD

One by one I grab the salmon as they wriggle, spit, hiss — some with fins ripped off from their struggle in the net, some disemboweled by crabs. I stick the knife behind their gills, pull it forward through their throats, toss them to the other side of the hull. I'm calf-deep in salmon when I start, but have only bled forty fish when I slip and fall against the edge of the skiff, still clutching a creature in its death throes. Its blood pours over my gloved hands. Its mouth opens and closes mechanically. Its cold eye stares out to sea.

"It's much easier with three people," Meg says. She releases the last length of net and it splashes overboard. "We tried putting a lawn chair in the boat so Dad could help, but it slowed us down even more."

With its hull covered in salmon, the vessel barely has room for the oar, machete, and two gas tanks.

"When will your brother get back from hunting?"

"Soon, I hope," Meg says, taking the knife from me. She slices and tosses the fish as methodically as she dealt poker hands the day we met at Stanford. I played perfectly — crunched probabilities, measured bets, redirected risk. "Better lucky than smart," I grumbled when she flipped her winning pocket pair. She bet me dinner on one more hand.

The skiff bobs in the blue sea while Meg bleeds the fish. I sit back on the bow platform to catch my breath. The sheer granite cliffs and lush green hills slide past the distant gray-and-white peaks of the mainland. Meg starts the engine with a pull of the cord. We push our way towards the refrigeration boat across the bay, weighed down by our catch. Fish flop across each other at our shins.

"Not a bad first pick," she yells over the engine's groan. "What do you think of Kodiak?"

Meg's rolled the sleeves and pants of her orange rain gear, but the fabric still drapes over her slender body. She pulls back her hood and unbuttons her jacket, which blows behind her like a cape. The sun glistens off her yellow hair, pink cheeks, moist skin. She's vibrant against the backdrop of sapphire sea and emerald hills.

"Gorgeous," I say with a wink. "Though more effort than I imagined."

She plows into a wave, splashing me. Saltwater drips down my face.

"We're just getting started," she says with a wink.

I smile, remembering she used that same phrase at the outset of several of the adventures she convinced me to join: biking Death Valley, kayaking Half Moon Bay, snow-shoeing Alta Peak.

The skiff rises and falls as we approach a cove surrounded by soaring rock cliffs stained white and yellow with seagull excrement. Hundreds of the screeching birds perch in every available nook, scores more circle or hang in the wind drifts. Meg cuts the engine and we float towards the refrigeration barge. She rushes to the bow and ties us to it. Then she hops into the vessel, checks the console, and removes the plywood coverings of three large bins still half-full from a recent pick.

"Doctor," she jokes, "use that big brain of yours to keep the reds in the left bin, silvers in the center, pinks in the right." The fish are all silver with dark gray backs. Other than their various sizes, they might as well be identical.

"How did your father react when you told him about your job in San Francisco," I say, keeping my stance wide to compensate for the rocking of the boat. "About moving in together."

Meg hops back into the stern of our skiff. She squats down, grabs a salmon in each hand, and lifts with her legs to launch them, two at a time, occasionally crossing them in midair. Each precise toss, timed to the rocking of both boats, just clears the rim of the appropriate bin.

"You haven't told him," I say.

She tosses a salmon at my chest. I catch it, dropping the one I'm holding.

"It's not that easy," she says. "My father depends on me out here. He and Matt can't afford to winter in Homer without a strong season."

"I thought we agreed Matt would get a winter job so they could hire one or two hands next summer. Hell, once I graduate we could even help them out with a little money."

"That's a silver," she says, nodding to the fish in my arms. I toss it into the bin and grab another.

"You think your Dad will have a problem with us moving in together, don't you?" My forearm and back muscles already ache. "Or maybe you have a problem with it."

"You've never depended on anyone, anything," she says. "And you've never had anyone depend on you."

She hurls the fish double-time now, briefly clearing a bloody circle around her feet before more fish slide into it. The wind blows her hood back onto her head, masking her eyes, but it hardly matters - she barely looks where she's throwing. Mechanical movements, concealed features, curves lost in the blanket of wet-weather gear — I could forget that this is the same woman who ran naked into the Santa Cruz Bay to get me to brave its icy waters. She removes her hood, wipes the sweat from her forehead, matted with blond hair, and I'm reminded.

"I'm depending on you," I say. "Besides, you know me. When I want something, I solve for it. And what I want is for you, this one time, to get what you want."

What I really want is Meg's spontaneity in my life: the off-trail hikes, midnight excursions, impromptu costume parties.

"Hold that," Meg says stepping towards me. She points to the giant striped salmon at my chest — it's easily twice the size of even the larger salmon, maybe fifteen pounds. Its silver scales shine iridescent. She's careful to place her feet firmly on the hull as she paces through the fish. "It's a king salmon, and a nice looking one at that." She pulls the knife from her belt. "I must have missed it."

I hold the fish as she slices its throat and spreads the wound apart. She wipes the initial gush of blood aside and peers at the meat within. "It's a white meat king," she says. "A delicacy!"

A large wave strikes the boat from the side, causing it to rock violently.

I drop the fish into the pile and in an effort to steady myself grab the nearest object – her knife.

"Shit!" I say. A pulse of adrenaline surges through me. With two sets of gloves between the blade and my hand, I suspect it wouldn't have broken the skin. But the pain lingers.

"Did it get you bad?" Meg says, putting the knife back into her belt.

She helps me remove my jacket then the armband. I yank off the wool and rubber gloves. My palm fills with blood. Meg rips off her own gloves and throws them to the hull.

"Let me see," she says, grabbing my hand.

The cut is about two inches long but doesn't appear very deep. She wipes the blood away, careful not to touch the wound.

"Is it a white meat?" I ask.

She lifts my hand to her face for a kiss.

"A delicacy," she says.

I grab her hood with my other hand and pull her to me. I taste my blood on her lips. We kick the fish from between us and press our bodies together. She pulls open my jacket, the buttons snapping in quick succession. We undo the clasps of each other's orange overalls and they drop into the salmon. We unbutton each other's shirts. Cool air blows across my chest, sensitizing my skin to the warmth of her hands. With one hand bloodied and another covered in fish and jellyfish goo, I'm forced to trace her body, salty from sweat and sea, only with my mouth. Her hand slips to my pants and I shift to make it easier, but it's clumsy with a hull slippery in fish-guts, our overalls at our knees, the rocking of the boat. She falls backward into the salmon, with me on top of her.

"Gross!" she yells, and we laugh.

***

We walk up the grey crescent beach littered with tangled piles of nets, oil drums, small creatures' bleached skeletons. We pass a ramshackle greenhouse and a tottering swing set manufactured from tall logs. Beyond the beach, stairs made of split tree trunks lead up to the deck of a simple plywood cabin with only two sides covered in shingles. Beyond that there is nothing but green and yellow hills rolling up to a white-capped mountain.

The crack of a gunshot from deep in those hills echoes off the mountains across the bay. A bald eagle launches from its perch atop an evergreen.

"Matt," Meg says, more to herself. She scans the hills, as if out of concern. "Is he OK?"

Meg shakes her head. "He's fine."

We climb the stairs onto the deck. The floorboards, where they are still in-tact, warp under our weight. Meg steps indirectly towards a screen door at the side of the house. I wait, then tread quickly in her footsteps. In the center of the main room, two beat-up couches are positioned around an oil-drum stove that sits in a bed of beach rocks. Above it hang sweatshirts stained with salt and blood. A propane-powered kitchen lines one wall, with mismatched dishware and cooking supplies. Above a door in the back of the room, a long loft holds a pile of blankets and two sets of couch cushions duct-taped together.

Meg's father, Jack, ducks under the doorway. Beneath a thick orange and white beard, his skin is red and wrinkled, especially near his eyes, which seem locked in a permanent squint. He limps to the couch, falling forward into each step as if hoping the next footfall will catch him. The whole cabin creaks and shifts under his heavy gait.

"We had a pretty good pick," I say, guessing Meg won't mention the knife incident. Jack thought we weren't arriving until next week, so when the sea-plane reached the beach this morning, he wasn't sure who it could be. He saw me step off the pontoon in my synthetic sleeveless fleece, the price tag still on my boots, and assumed I was with the Fish and Game Commission. Meg told me that when I was out of earshot, he joked, "Let's hope you don't need him to lift an anchor."

"Four-hundred fifty pinks, forty silvers, twenty reds, and one white-meat king," Meg says, holding up the prize. "Billy wasn't half bad." She nods at me and even though I know she's lying, a feel a tinge of self-satisfaction when Jack nods his approval.

Meg kicks off her boots and slides on her makeshift slippers — older boots cut down to fronts and soles. She grabs a frying pan and spices from the shelves.

"Ugly weather's coming. Fog. Maybe rain." Jack drops onto the couch and massages his knees.

"Summers in San Francisco the fog rolls in thick as smoke," I say, nodding to the thin aluminum chimney rising from the oil-drum stove. "It's one of the reasons I was happy to get away." I collapse on the couch opposite Jack. The cushions sink beneath me and a puff of dust rises into the sunlight. I smell fish and sweat and men. A spider so big I can see fangs scampers from the armrest. I shift away, pull my back off the cushions.

Around the room, boards hammered unevenly into the exposed wall beams support whalebones, eagle feathers, a rack of rifles and shotguns. Above the entranceway, a page from a magazine hangs loosely from a nail: "If you shoot the wolves to save the moose, and then you shoot the moose, you're either out of your mind or in Alaska."

"Your legs bothering you?" Meg says. She mixes brown sugar into honey.

"They're fine," Jacks says, but he grimaces with each rub.

"Can I ask what happened?" I say. Meg pauses her mixing. Jack stops rubbing his knees. "I mean with your legs."

"They're fine," he repeats. He stands up, towering over me in my sunken seat. Hidden beneath his scraggly beard, a scar extends from his left ear to chin. I don't ask about that.

***

The screen door slams like a gunshot, jolting me from my sleep. A man about my age storms into the room. He has a rifle on one shoulder and a knapsack on the other. He wears a skullcap and fingerless gloves, and his clothes are caked in mud. Each step leaves a wet imprint on the floor. With a shift of his shoulder he swings the gun into his hands in front of me.

"Who's this?" he asks.

"Dammit, Matt," Meg says. "Take off your boots."

"This is Billy," Jack says. "Remember? Your sister's boyfriend is spending the summer."

Matt places his rifle in the rack. He puts his hand in mine. There is no eye contact, no grip, no shake: a dead fish. His fingers are brownish-yellow – filth, cigarette stains, or both. He's missing at least three teeth and the others barely hang on. He bears no resemblance to the great hunter Meg often described, the boy who protected her by wrestling away a sled dog when he was eight, who cleared twice as many salmon as any other set-netter in '99, who shot a grizzly twice in the skull as it stormed this cabin.

"So you're the boss," I say. I slap him on the shoulder and he flinches.

"What's for dinner?" he says, retreating to the other couch.

"Rosemary-rubbed venison with green apple mustard," Meg says. "Assuming you shot something."

"No deer," he says, then chuckles.

"King salmon sounds great," Jack says.

Meg prepares it in the honey glaze, but it doesn't need it. The creamy white flesh is soft as butter. I even gobble down the skin when she tells me it's healthy. I eat white rice with soy sauce and banana bread still hot and corn that, even though it's from a can, tastes like it was harvested out back.

Matt doesn't touch the fish. He walks to a table in the far corner of the room with a plateful of rice and corn and a giant mug of black coffee.

"For dessert, I'll have the tiramisu," I joke. I resist the urge to stretch.

"Once you clean up these dishes, the three of us will head out for the late pick," Meg says. "Then we'll set up our beds."

"Billy stays in the guesthouse," Jack says.

"Not my room," Matt says.

"I'm happy to sleep on the couch," I say. I don't plan to sleep with the spiders. A celibate summer was not what I had in mind, and with boat sex seemingly out of the question, the offer affords me my only chance of sneaking up to bunk with Meg.

"You'll be more comfortable in the guesthouse," Jack says.

Meg mouths, "Sorry." She warned me sleeping apart was a possibility, not because her father was traditional, just that he had hang-ups. She takes my plate and clears the other dishes as compensation.

"Matt, you share the loft with your sister."

"God dammit," Matt yells, ripping the skullcap off his head and crushing it in his fist. "You always take his side."

His outburst doesn't faze Meg, who concentrates on the plates in the soapy sink.

"Whose side?" Jack says, straining against the arms of the chair to rise to his feet. "The guesthouse is for guests. Maybe if you spent a bit more time in the cabin I'd know what you were up to for a change."

Matt tosses his skullcap towards the gun rack. "You two will have to do the pick yourselves. I need to clear my room."

***

Meg and I push out to sea for the second time that night, a wet wind in our faces. Fog has rolled in, turning the bright greens and blues to subdued grays. The sun is merely a milky-white swathe in the western sky. Behind us, the cabin disappears into the fading hillside.

Meg drops the engine into neutral and we glide towards the basketball-sized red buoy. The strain of lifting it and the attached lines into the boat spreads pain like tiny needles across my lower back. I can't see it beneath the glove, but I'm sure my scab has cracked open. I imagine gangrene, my evacuation by helicopter. The afternoon was grueling enough without fatigue, heavy air, thoughts of amputation.

"Matt's not what I pictured," I say. I drag the lines between two vertical aluminum posts fastened a foot apart at the front of the bow. Meg puts the motor back into gear and the boat crawls forward until she stops it to feed the lines through identical vertical posts at the stern. Then she pulls forward again until gold-colored monofilament netting five fathoms deep bunches between these posts and runs the full boat-length. The first fish plops onto the small raised bow platform. It arches its body to one side, then the other. A steady stream of salmon caught within the netting pulls through the front posts. They pound the aluminum platform with metallic thuds.

"He's my brother." Meg rifles through the mess of monofilament, arriving where a fish seems hopelessly stuck in a Gordian knot of golden netting. The thin line is wrapped beneath the fish's gills, around its small beak of a nose; it cuts into the flesh behind its fins. She twists twine and fish, unraveling the mess in seconds, dropping the fish to the hull. Then moves to the next. The easy ones she simply shakes loose. The slightly tangled ones she attacks two at a time. The tough ones she rips free by brute force, often severing a fin or part of a tail.

"You never mentioned shirking work, rudeness. You never mentioned dental hygiene."

"What am I supposed to say? My brother is dirty? That he can be a dick?"

"If you had, I might have recommended a Caribbean cruise."

"He's a great hunter and a better fisherman. He doesn't like change."

"This summer was supposed to be a glorified campout, a break before my dissertation. I'm doing the work of two men."

"I'm doing the work of two men." She looks at my first salmon, still hopelessly lost in the net. If anything, I've entangled it more. "Make that three. What's the financial term for a drain on productivity? A liability?"

Meg snaps more salmon to the hull, working her way to where six fish convulse in the net beside me. I could correct her definition, tell her the real liabilities are napping in the cabin, but for two months I've got only her.

"So productive optimization is why you tried to stab me to death?" I say, holding up my wounded hand in a peace offering.

She untangles the fish I've been struggling with. She pulls a hand out of the net and clasps mine. "You grabbed the knife on purpose to get into my Grundens." She tugs the straps of her overalls.

"You make it sound so sexy." I kiss her cheek.

She steps back to the engine and drives the boat up another length. "I'll talk to my dad tomorrow. He'll make sure Matt doesn't dodge anymore picks."

By the third boat-length of net, salmon cover the hull. Permeating the boat, along with the thickening mist, is the ominous stench of dying fish, and worse, jellyfish. They come through the posts thick and slimy as bloody snot and slowly get ripped apart as they fall through the bunched net, dripping their mucous-y poison everywhere.

I shiver, wet with sweat, drizzle, and ocean-spray. I struggle to keep my balance as the boat rocks and the slick sludge of jelly-goo and salmon guts sloshes back and forth across the hull. I break after every two to three fish to breathe in the stagnant air. I search out the horizon, but the dense fog conceals it.

Meg remains fixated on the nets, continuing her methodic search and release. I press on. Releasing a terribly entangled salmon, I splash a small chunk of jellyfish just below my eye. It lodges itself there, stinging me as if a lit match had been pressed to my cheek. My gear is soaked in the same goop that burns my face. My hands especially, have been sloshing through the sickly jelly and the cheap white wool gloves are now pink with the thick slime. Helplessness exacerbates the irritation, intensifies the burn.

We bury ourselves deeper in dead and dying salmon. A difficult case frustrates me and I wrench the poor creature out of the net, ripping one side of his face off. I stare at the skinless head as it gasps for air through exposed gills. A fish out of water, I think, throwing it gasping and bleeding into the pile. I need oxygen. I need orientation. But fresh air and the horizon are nonexistent. I vomit over the boat's edge.

"I'm OK," I say before I finish. I want to wipe my mouth, but my gloves are covered in guts, blood, poison. Even the sleeves of my wet-weather jacket are splattered with jellyfish.

Meg makes her way over to me. She pulls a threadbare, discolored rag from inside her jacket and dabs my lips.

"No, you're not," she says, seating me against the railing.

I hate being a burden, but I hate being on this boat even more. I don't stop her when she lifts a post at the bow, then the stern, and the net, still full of fish, drops back into the sea. She puts the engine in gear and turns the boat around.

The swathe of light that was the sun has faded into the drab gray sky by the time we reach shore. My nausea dissipates as soon as my feet touch ground. I reach the guesthouse and collapse onto Matt's bed without removing my sweatshirt, soaked in spite of the raingear. I pass out to the steady rhythm of someone splitting wood and the distant drone of the skiff's engine, returning to sea.

***

The sun pierces my Plexi-glass window after only a few hours. I roll around to escape the glare, but light soon fills the guesthouse. I rise out of bed in spite of the cold tightness of my muscles and joints. I probe the room for something to cover the window and stumble into a five-gallon paint bucket filled with cigarette butts. Maps, some hand drawn, are nailed to the walls of the cabin. A detailed topographical one depicting the Kupreanof peninsula with an "X" at our cabin's location has notes scrawled across it. They categorize the soil in each square mile region by color and the vegetation it supports, but the colors are not earth tones and the plants are not indigenous — pink earth promotes squash and watermelon; yellow, celery and apple.

I find a hammer and nail one of Matt's dirty sheets across the window, but it does little to block the light. I'm barely asleep again when the door opens.

"Coffee's ready," Meg says. She stands in the doorway wearing the same plaid shirt and grey cargo pants as yesterday. "I'm making pancakes."

"Are we out of salmon?"

We duck under branches and step over mud puddles on our way back to the cabin. Inside the kitchen, Meg's as at home flipping flapjacks as she is bleeding salmon. When she won that poker bet, I complained about my limited stipend and tried to weasel her into a meal at the cafeteria. She showed up at the grad dorm with two paper bags full of groceries. Even with the limited ingredients and shoddy equipment of the communal kitchen, she prepared the most delicious Cornish hens with thick garlic mashed potatoes, followed by blueberry pie topped with fresh whipped cream. I assumed she learned from a great mentor, but watching her work her way around the broken cabinets, flickering flames, fractured measuring cups, I know it was necessity.

Matt shuffles a deck of cards in the loft. Jack sleeps on the couch, his chest moving heavily. Meg drops a pan in the sink and his head snaps to. He sits up and scans the room, alert.

"Meg tells me you're a college man, Billy."

"He's a doctoral candidate," Meg says. She hands us each a plate stacked high with pancakes drenched in maple syrup and butter.

"Once I defend my thesis" I say, "I'll finally get a job."

"And what's that," Jack says.

"One of my teachers runs an investment fund." I don't want to brag about the six-figure quant job Professor Rota promised me. It's not like Jack would understand anyway.

"No, no," he says. "What's the thesis?"

I consider giving him my dissertation title: Quantifying Pragmatic Options: A Generalized Approach From a Decision Analytic Perspective. "I use math to help people make choices."

"Math?" he says, chomping on a heaping bite of pancakes. "Everything you need to decide is right here." He pats his gut. "Did Meg ever tell you how I ended up here?"

"That's not a nice story, Dad."

"This lady told me she was on the pill. Then she tells me she's not ready for a baby anyway, least of all the bastard child of a mechanic. Next thing I know, the Honorable Judge Red Pumps tells me that even though I had no say in her having the kid, I had every obligation to pay for it. I said, 'If it's a portion of my salary you want, take it. A portion of zero is zero. And if it's fathering you want, good luck trying to find me.' Don't put me in a situation where I have no choice. I'll make one."

"You did have a choice," Meg says. "You didn't need to sleep with her. Besides, that's not the end of the story."

Matt rushes down the ladder, jumping halfway. He's got the deck of cards and a notebook in his hand.

"You're good with math?" he says. "I look for patterns in the cards." He opens the notebook. The results of hundreds of card flips are meticulously detailed on each line of graph paper, with symbols and notes besides each toss. "After the three of spades, I always get a queen or a red card."

Assuming no knowledge of the cards already thrown, I calculate the odds of it happening once at fifty-five percent, twice, thirty percent, three times, less than seventeen. More than three times, the likelihood falls off a cliff. "Let me see your notes."

The first column begins with numbers and crude symbols that correspond to actual cards. But halfway down the numbers are replaced by random misspelled words: presidents' names, animals, ingredients. Further down the words and numbers transform to intricate sketches of animals and vegetables. I look for some type of code but guess it's gibberish.

I point to a string of symbols — spiked images connected around a broken circle. "What's that mean?"

"Fire," he says. "You know, when you get cards of the same suit."

"Flush," I say. "But what's the significance of the symbol?"

Matt stammers and Meg puts a hand on his shoulder. She takes the pad from me. "We should do the early pick. Are you up for it?"

THE BEST OF GIVAL PRESS SHORT STORIES   165

I'm not sure which one of us she's asking but I say, "I think so."

***

"You know how to bleed?" Matt asks. He giggles as he jokingly thrusts the blade in my direction.

"Sure," I say with an uncomfortable chuckle. I carefully grasp the knife with my injured hand.

The weather is clear and crisp this morning and I breathe the fresh air deeply. With fewer jellies and three people we make much better time running down the net. Halfway through, Matt tosses a fish overboard. A flash of light glints off its side as it swims away. Meg doesn't say anything. I wonder if he saw something I didn't see: a parasite, some other problem. I keep picking and bleeding.

The next time he brings the fish right up to his face, mouths something to it, then throws it overboard.

"What the fuck, Matt," Meg says.

"It wasn't right," he says.

"Don't start that shit. I'm not busting my ass earning money for you so you can just toss it overboard."

"Sorry, Meg." He grabs the rail and faces the open ocean. "That one wasn't ready."

Meg's pained headshake, her exaggerated sigh, are borrowed from me. I've given her that reaction a dozen times since we met: that first dinner, when we discussed her plan to get a Master's in Social Work, and most recently when I argued against her decision to forego the telecommunications marketing job I found her for a low paying psych ward internship. She once told me all the men she met had problems. She liked me because I had solutions. So I was surprised whenever she ignored my advice. But watching Matt look out to sea, helpless and certain, I know now she withheld key information.

Meg won't look at me. She guides the skiff up another boat-length and idles the motor.

"You run the engine," she says to Matt, relieving him of his position in the thick of the net.

***

"Matt's hearing voices again, Dad."

"I accidentally dropped a fish overboard," Matt says.

"Dammit, Matt," Jack says. He sits in front of the barrel drum stove. He places a log inside and stokes the fire. "I thought we were done with that. If you can't keep your shit together, you can't run the site."

"Who says I want to? Let her run it. Let him."

"If you don't run the site, what the hell are you going to do?" Jack says. He points a log at Matt's face. "You barely have teeth in that head of yours."

Matt grabs a rifle from the rack.

"Put that back," Jack says.

"What do you think you're doing?" Meg says.

"I'm going hunting," Matt says. He holds the weapon by its stock, gesturing at Meg with it as if it's an extension of his arm.

"Watch where you point that thing," Jack says. He uses the log to lift himself up.

"Are you kidding me," Meg says, throwing her hands up.

She's more concerned about Matt's leaving than the rifle's implied threat - accidental or otherwise. I'm not sure what I plan to do with it, but I grab the meat cleaver off the kitchen counter.

"You talk to me as if I've never handled a gun," Matt yells back at Jack. He puts the barrel under his chin and pushes the trigger with his thumb.

"Stop!" Meg screams.

I cover my eyes with the cleaver's blade.

"Safety," Matt says, thumbing the trigger again. He storms out the door, slamming it behind him.

Jack launches the log at the door.

Meg grips her face in pain. "I can't do it, Dad." But already she pulls pots and pans out of the kitchen cabinets to prepare lunch.

"I'm sorry, honey," Jack says, calming himself. "Give him an hour to cool off. Then I'll go talk to him. He'll be all right."

"Not without serious help," I say. "Did you not see that?" I point the cleaver at the gun rack, then at Matt's notebook and cards. "He writes in code, sees patterns that don't exist. He talks to fish. He won't be all right. Not without professional help."

"No shit, Doctor," Meg says, taking a break from rinsing a pot to seethe at me. "You don't think we've seen psychiatrists? Tried medications? Dad's got Homer Medical on speed dial. We sprinkled Zyprexa on his goddamned pancakes for a year when he refused to take it. This isn't a puzzle you can solve with decision trees, so keep your diagnoses to yourself."

"Calm down, Meg" Jack says.

"Funny," I say pointing the cleaver back at the gun rack, "This is the first I'm hearing any of this. I'm thrilled to be stranded in the middle of nowhere with a rifle-wielding madman." I regret the last word before I finish uttering it.

"Settle down," Jack yells. He takes a heavy step towards me.

The cleaver feels heavy, clumsy in my grasp, and Jack's glare makes me realize that all of a sudden, I'm the madman. I step back and bump into the kitchen counter. Jack reaches out his sinewy arm, takes the cleaver from me gently, but firmly, and places it on the top shelf, out of my reach.

"I'll deal with Matt," he says.

"He thinks I stole his room," I say, trying to defend myself.

"He's not dangerous," Meg says, drying the pot. Her mouth contorts as she takes heaving breaths. She bats her eyes and her face turns red.

I'd never seen her cry before. Never saw her vulnerable. I used to assume she played strong to impress me. But she is that strong. Forget the rugged winters, the grueling summers. She's held this family together despite an absent mother, a disabled father, a crazy brother. She's performed the roles of fisherman, hunter, chef, and medic, captain and crew. It's her strength, but even more this inevitable chink in the armor that emboldens me to ensure she sees it can all be better, easier.

"Meg's not coming back next summer," I say to Jack. "She got a job in San Francisco. We're moving in together."

"I can't believe you!" Meg cries. The tears stop, anguish morphs to rage. She lifts the pot as if to throw it at me, but holds back. "You prick!"

Jack steps between us, holds out his hands as if refereeing a boxing match.

"Billy, go to your room," he says, shoving me towards the door. "Meg, go to mine. Don't come out until I tell you."

I slip out to the guesthouse guilty and frightened as a child. The brother who thinks I stole his place has a gun, the girlfriend who thinks I betrayed her has a knife, and the father - who knows what he thinks - has his callused hands. But I'm still exhausted. I look for something to secure the door shut, slide the bucket of cigarette butts beside it, then remember it opens out. I collapse onto Matt's bed.

***

I return to the cabin. Jack's passed out with a year-old magazine on his chest. I touch his shoulder and whisper, "Can we talk?"

He stirs, gets up. He grabs a bottle of whiskey and two glasses from a kitchen cabinet and motions me towards the door. The sky is cloudless and the sun has had time to warm the air, though the breeze is still crisp and carries the faint scent of pine. I follow Jack towards the edge of the deck but stay back a step - the boards are rotting and there's no railing. He holds both glasses in the palm of his hand and fills them to the rim.

"Sometimes fin whales breach just two hundred yards from here." He hands me a glass and with his own, motions past the skiff, the white mooring buoy, the outcropping of rock. "When they raise their heads near the skiff, you realize how small you are. But you chase them anyway. Cheers!" He clinks my glass and gulps his whiskey.

"She did find me," he says. "Matt's mother. She moved here from Seattle. We made it work together in Homer. We had Meg. We got this site license. We had some great years I'll never regret. But she was already tired of Alaska, and me, the day the bear attacked the cabin. She hid, hysterical, up in the loft. Matt grabbed the rifle and ran out to meet it. Sad thing is, that time of year, with all the food in the hills and streams, that bear had no business bothering us. It was sick." He taps his temple and takes another sip.

"Matt shot it twice as it charged him. It took off up the rocks there." He points toward the outcropping jutting into the sea. "Matt tracked it to make sure it wouldn't come back and found it dead on that cliff. Ma radioed for a seaplane that day." He downs the rest of his glass.

"Some people need the supermarket, electricity, 9-1-1." He refills his glass and tops mine off, emptying the bottle, which he tosses over the edge. "Me? I don't understand…I don't want to understand tax deductions, resumes, insurance premiums. Give me a fishing rod and a gun and get out of my way. Matt doesn't fit in either place. Meg's at home in both."

"I was out of line," I say.

"That's between you and Meg. I want her to not worry about Matt and me. If San Francisco is where she wants be, I'm happy for her. For both of you."

"But she does worry about you. And she won't be happy unless she knows you and Matt are OK. Can't you force Matt into a hospital?"

"Not against his will, not unless he's an imminent threat."

"He just pointed a gun…" I can't seem to say it out loud.

"He knows the rules by now, knows what to say."

"There must be some other way."

"I'd beg her to go with you if I thought it would help. Matt's problem is his head. Meg's is her heart. I can't change his mind. I wouldn't change her one bit."

"Talking about me?" Meg says. The screen door slams behind her.

Jack hands his glass to Meg. "I'll get a refill," he says, leaving us on the deck.

"Sorry I went all crazy back there," I say.

"Me too," Meg says. "I had an inkling to throw the fishing knife at you." She pats the holster at her hip.

"It wouldn't be the first time," I say, holding up my palm. "I shouldn't have broken the news to your Dad like that. I thought San Francisco was a done deal."

"I hoped everything here would have sorted itself out, or at least gotten better. He's worse than I've ever seen."

"Stick to the plan," I say. "All the other sites hire fishermen."

"Matt scares them away before they've learned the ropes. It's more hassle than help."

"Bring them to San Francisco."

"It's sad, really," she says, sniffing the whiskey and taking a sip. "Cabin fever keeps people from coming here. Matt's sickness keeps us coming back. My brother will never move. My father will never leave him. They can't live without me."

"And you can't *live* with them. If your brother doesn't get help, he's going to get himself into trouble. Or all of you. You're just postponing it."

"Then postponing is what I have to do." She says it staring off at the water, so matter of fact.

"And what do I do?" I say.

"You're the expert decision-maker."

"Exactly. So trust me." I turn her towards me and hold her tight by the shoulders. "You can't help here. Even your Dad will tell you that. There's often not a perfect solution, but there's always a best decision."

"Well, whatever that is, it doesn't need to be made this minute." She turns from me and I can see she's holding back tears again. "I brought you here to see a different world."

"You've certainly delivered," I say.

Meg pulls me to her and hugs me. "Let's try to enjoy the rest of the summer."

Jack returns with another bottle and glass and three foldout chairs.

"The fish can wait until tomorrow," he says. He unscrews the cap and pours.

We sit and drink and watch the skiff rock in the gentle waves as they roll towards shore. The sunlight flickers off each crest like a million brilliant sparks.

***

I wake to Meg lying in bed next to me. I'd been sleeping so soundly, I have no idea how long she's been here. She stares at me with a sinister smile. I put my arm around her, nuzzle closer, but she has a different idea. She grabs my arm and slides off the bed. She's fully dressed in a thick sweatshirt, jeans, and boots. She pulls me after her.

"What?" I say, resisting her efforts. "I'm exhausted."

"Let's go," she says. She yanks my arm hard, dragging me off the mattress. She tosses me a sweatshirt. "There's a hat and gloves in the pocket."

The night is clear and the sea, flat. I push the skiff back from the rocks and hop in while Meg starts the engine. We glide out into the deep blue darkness, past the cliffs, and on to the sea. The fresh chill air, the drone of the engine, the rhythmic splash of the water soothe me. I close my eyes and forget myself, half-sleeping – we may have cruised for minutes or hours.

Finally the boat turns and Meg cuts the engine. She hops on the bow platform and sits cross-legged, facing forward. I follow her lead. The sea opens up in this direction and its nothing but water for miles. The deep violet overhead gradually brightens to the dipping red sun in the northwest sky. But already that same sun casts its first rays across the northeast.

Meg puts her hands in mine and we snuggle close for warmth. The slow rotation of the skiff reveals sunset, twilight, a purple sky interrupted by the faintest stars, then sunset again. We float until the sun rises and everything shines bright blue-green.

***

The Fish and Game Commission radios in a three-day fishing hiatus while it assesses quotas. Once the nets are up and we've caught a nap, twenty hours of daylight seems like eight too many. We straighten up the grounds. It takes all four of us to roll a tree trunk, worn white and smooth as bone by the sun and surf, to the back edge of the beach. We do some old-fashioned rod-and-reel fishing without success. We read decade old news magazines. I even have time to review my dissertation. I'm editing a section on perceived value when Jack returns from the freshwater spring with a six-pack of cold beer. He hands me one. "What are you working on?"

"My professor surveyed a group of people to determine the dollar value they put on their own life," I explain. "He asked questions like, 'Assume that you were about to take a car ride that had a one in ten thousand chance of ending in your death if you didn't wear your seatbelt, and I offered you one hundred dollars not to wear it, would you take the money?'"

"I'd take that bet," Matt says from the loft.

"Well in that particular case, the person who takes the money values their life at one million dollars." I don't finish with the necessary caveat, "At most."

"That's a lot of money," Matt says.

"I once got a ticket for not wearing my seatbelt," Jack says. "I took the skiff to Kodiak City — two hours through cold rough seas. Driving my truck from the dock, I got pulled over for swerving. I must have been hypothermic. I'm shivering like crazy and the cop assumes its DTs. He asks me to walk the line — you can imagine how that went." He smacks his leg and we all laugh. "Anyway, he thought he let me off easy."

"Do you like to gamble?" Matt asks. He hops down the ladder. He's got a competitive spark in his eyes. "Let's play Texas hold em."

It's suddenly clear how Meg got so good at cards — during weather delays and Commission enforced downtime, there's not a whole lot else to do. I put down the thesis and brace myself for some tough competition.

"Winner skips the next three picks," Matt says, pulling a bucket of beach pebbles from a crossbeam in the wall.

"Have fun fishing without me," Meg says, dropping a pan into the sink. "But while we're betting, first one out does the dishes."

Jack hands out more beers. Meg offers fresh-baked banana bread. Matt distributes the beach rocks. I sit next to him at the corner of the table, keeping Meg across from me. Matt deals. Jack picks up the first hand, but I ascertain little about his and Matt's playing style. On the next hand I draw pocket kings. Meg and Jack fold after the flop, but I'm able to draw Matt in. The river card gives no possible help, which means he needs pocket aces to beat me — less than half a percent probability. I go all in, pushing my pile of pebbles to the center of the table, feeling a slight surge of adrenaline. I snicker when Matt pushes his pile forward, and cackle when he flips an Ace and a Joker.

"For real?" I say.

"Pair of Aces," Matt says, scooping up the rocks.

I look around to see if I'm crazy. "You play with Jokers?"

"Why not?" Meg says. "It's more fun, more unpredictable."

"Especially when you don't know they're in the deck," I say. "That's a regular Black Swan, right there." I point to Matt's hand. "I'm adding that to my thesis."

"Black Swan?" Jack says.

"Can I borrow this?" I say to Matt, grabbing his notebook. I flip to a clean page of graph paper. "Most events in life fall into what's called a normal distribution." I draw a tall bell curve.

"It looks like a fish in a net," Matt says.

He seemed so normal a minute ago, I'm surprised at how quickly this new delusion manifests. Matt picks up on my concern. He looks me in the eyes for the first time. He takes the pen from me, turns the page so I see it from his angle, and draws a small circle within the peak of the curve, off-center - the fish's eye. The gridlines are the net.

I hold the pad up so I can see it better. "Look at that," I say. "I always thought they called them fat tails because it's where the curve trailed off. But it's also the tail of the fish." I show the diagram to Jack. "Ninety-nine point nine percent of living is experienced here." I point the pen at the gut of the fish. Then I circle the tips of its tail. "But *life* happens here: bank runs, sovereign debt crises."

"Jokers wild," Meg adds.

"Those don't sound like life," Jack says.

"They are if you have a sound investment strategy," I say, tapping on the fish.

"Too bad you're out of rocks," Matt says, laughing.

"Yeah," Meg says, ganging up on me. "Go scrub the dishes. We have a game to finish."

I slink off to the sink.

***

The long days flow together in a rush of activity, broken only by brief nights of sound, but never fully satisfying sleep. We wake, we eat, we pick, we eat, we pick, we eat, we pick, we sleep. By the time the cut on my hand is lost among scrapes, rope burns, and calluses, I'm able to keep up with Meg in the nets. I captain the skiff and pitch salmon into the bins with ninety-five percent accuracy. I'm even put in charge of the weekly rendezvous with the cannery's barge – Matt's old job – to unload the refrigeration boat and pick up supplies. They toss me a fifth of tequila the day our haul sets a record.

Matt still dodges the picks and I'm happy for it. Meg and Jack treat him as if nothing is wrong, which is to say they ignore his outbursts, his delusions, his insistence on sleeping with his pistol. But I can't. I study him as if he's one of Professor Rota's term projects. I note his frustration as he clears the beach of clutter: rusted barrels, frayed lines, tattered nets. I time the frequency and duration of his disappearances into the hillside. I analyze his moods when he returns for his vegetarian dinners, muddied and giddy. And while Meg insists he's safe, I sense desperation, recklessness, violence.

"Have you thought about the patterns in the cards?" he asks one evening.

I'm mixing a cocktail I concocted to celebrate our award-winning haul – salmonberry margaritas.

"Not particularly," I say. "I've been busy fishing."

Matt laughs uncomfortably.

"You should get back out there and protect your record," Jack says, clinking my margarita with his. He ruffles my hair, and I'm strangely proud. Meg smiles at the gesture. Matt bristles. He returns to flipping cards for a moment, then tosses them to the floor.

"I'm going hunting," he says. He grabs the shotgun off the rack.

"In the dark?" Meg says.

"With a shotgun?" Jack says.

"You don't need me here," Matt says.

Meg places a hand on his shoulder, calming him.

"We do need you here. We just can't wait forever."

"It's not working anymore." He glances at me as if to signal I'm the reason, but then looks ashamed for suggesting it.

"What's not working?" Meg asks. But Matt's already halfway to the door.

"I'll show you," he says, "I'll bring back a deer."

***

The sun is warm and the breeze cool. We race through the morning pick in record time and Jack has lunch waiting when we arrive back at the cabin. We eat on the deck as the bald eagle hovers on the wind currents and a fox scampers across the beach. It's been three days without a sign of Matt, save the occasional echo of a shotgun blast.

Jack takes our dishes and returns carrying two rifles. He places one against the cabin and slides his lawn chair to the edge of the deck. He gestures for me to take a seat.

"Here's the scope. Here's the safety. Here's the cartridge," he says. He places the butt in the crook of his shoulder. There are two cracks as the shot's echo reflects crisp and clear across the water. The mooring buoy a hundred yards out dips briefly underwater and pops back up.

I have to brace my left arm on my knee to steady the rifle's muzzle. I center the crosshairs on the buoy. Another two thunderous cracks and the scope kicks back, catching me above my eye.

"Did I hit it?"

"Were you aiming at the water?" he says with a chuckle.

Meg loads another cartridge and places the rifle back into my hands. She stands behind me, places her hands on my shoulders and whispers in my ear.

"We're on the beach in Santa Cruz. Remember?"

I remember her naked in the waves, calling me to her. My heart picks up its pace.

"Not that part," she says, guessing my thoughts. She smacks my head playfully. "The warm sun, the light breeze, the soft sand. We weren't sure if we were awake or asleep."

Her soothing words relax me. Her fragrant hair refreshes me. Her gentle touch reassures me. The buoy looks fat in my sight. I pull back on the trigger and watch it sink beneath the water.

***

Across the green and yellow hills, purple lilacs sway like waves in the breeze, always out of reach. The terrain is tight with brush and thorny thickets. We try to stay on the ridgelines and under the evergreens where the ground is soft and mossy. But it's slow going, especially with Jack.

"If we see a bear, don't startle it," he says. "And don't run."

"We're going to see a bear?" I say.

"Probably not," Meg says.

"'Probably' doesn't put limbs back on."

"Bears have poor depth perception," Jack says, stopping to rub his thighs. "They only see through one eye at a time." He turns his head from side to side, demonstrating the motion. "The trick is to back away slowly."

"The real trick," Meg says, "is to file down the front sight on your rifle. That, and bring along someone slower than you."

Jack catches me sneaking a glance at his leg. "Why do you file down the sight?" I ask.

"So it won't hurt as much when the bear shoves it up your ass," Meg says. "Dad, why don't you wait for us at the cabin? We'll be OK."

***

We smell the carcasses long before we see them. Two full sized deer, three foxes, a few smaller rodents piled together. Maggots, worms, and all sorts of other critters writhe in the rancid flesh. The fresh body of a fox has the skin torn free from its face where the shotgun blast struck. The larger deer has a strategically shot rifle hole through its neck. Its purple tongue hangs in the dirt.

Meg rushes ahead, pushing her way through the brush. I find her squatting in front of a camouflaged tent.

"He's not in there," she says. She pulls out a filthy sleeping bag, a machete, and the cores of some green peppers. I wait until she moves ahead before switching off my rifle's safety.

The brush opens to reveal a large flat field. The earth has been turned and roughly ploughed. Stretches of fishing net section off and protect neat rows of various types of vegetation. A deer lifts its head above some tomato plants, red juices hanging from its chin as it chews. Meg's rifle instinctively rises to her shoulder. I place the beast in my sights too.

The deer's magnified skull collapses in an explosion of tomato, blood, and brain matter. It vanishes from my sight before I register the sound of the blast, which comes from in front of me, not beside me. Matt lifts himself from a prone position within the field. He stands directly in my line of fire, his chest in my crosshairs. He holds his shotgun above his head in a victory stance, his tongue flicking through the hole in his smile. His head is monstrous compared to the buoy I shot earlier. The trigger is cold on my finger.

"It's time to go home, Matt," Meg says. She slowly lowers my rifle's barrel with her hand.

We take turns dragging the buck back to the cabin. Matt grabs his deck of cards and climbs the ladder to his bunk. I join Meg on the deck to help her prepare the deer. She sticks her knife between the bones of the forelegs and twists it, creating two holes. She rams the end of a broomstick through them, lassos a rope around it, and throws the line over an overhanging beam. I help her lift the deer into the air, tying the rope off against the cabin. She places a large blue bucket under it.

"You're going to stay with them," I say.

Meg plunges the knife into the deer's chest, just under the neck, and pulls it down with both hands. The bones of the ribcage snap in succession. She presses the knife down all the way to the deer's crotch. As the chest cavity opens, blood pours into the bucket. The deer's entrails push through and hang below its torso, and again the smell of death hits me like a stiff wind.

"I can't leave them. I'll go back with them to Homer after the summer."

"I worry *after the summer* will be too late. And Homer will be inadequate. It's a bad decision."

She clears the insides with the knife. She places the deer's heart and liver into a frying pan. She cuts the skin around its neck, and uses the knife to pull at its hide.

"Are you breaking up with me?" she says.

"If you really plan to move to Homer I think you're breaking up with me." I pull at the deer's skin while she cuts it from the flesh with her blade, until the prey hangs without an outside or an inside, its decimated head rolled to one side, its guts stinking in a bucket beneath it.

"You could wait for me. You could come with us."

"Meg," I say, grabbing her arm to make sure I have her full attention, "why did you bring me here this summer? What did you expect to happen?"

"I wanted you to meet my family, to see my life. I told you. I thought he would be better." She puts the organs and a large chunk of flesh in a pan.

"Going to Homer doesn't solve the problem. It enables it. And in the process it will ruin your life. My life. Our life. I won't let him drag me down, too."

"That's up to you," she says. She turns towards the kitchen.

I turn her back to me. "Did you bring me here to chase me off?"

"This isn't about you!" She shakes free and storms into the cabin.

Jack joins me on the deck. We each grab a side of the bucket of guts. Jack stumbles across the beach rocks. We step out into the water and the waves lap against our boots. We put the bucket down next to a large boulder. Jack tosses the entrails and skin fragments on top of it. "For our eagle friend," he says, nodding toward the evergreen. "Or a nimble fox." He rinses his hands in the water. Rivulets of blood twist among the stones.

I squat down and dip my own hands, feeling the water's icy chill. I raise the salty liquid to my lips and feel the scruff on my face. I look down at my reflection, my full beard, and hardly recognize myself. I look worn but strong. I look like a man I would be frightened of.

"The herring run off Anchorage in the winter," Jack says. "An icy, snowy night a few years back, with visibility less than a few yards, I fell off the boat retrieving the net. I managed to climb back in before anyone noticed, then finished the job. I refused seeing a doctor until it was too late. I lost three toes and suffered nerve damage in my legs. The kids get their stubbornness from me."

"I can be stubborn too," I say, stroking the ragged hair on my face.

***

The cabin fills with the smoke and smells of broiling meat and steaming vegetables. Matt shuffles his cards in the loft. Meg puts the finishing touches on the meal.

I lean on the kitchen counter and speak softly to her. "I need to know something."

She spoons glaze onto the ribs.

"If things were better here, like you hoped, would you still be moving in with me?"

Matt stops shuffling. Meg nods.

"Do you love me?" I say.

She nods.

We eat tender chunks of venison steaks marinated in a garlic sauce, broiled ribs in a brown sugar glaze, rice pilaf, corn, peas, salad. Matt takes a healthy heaping of vegetables, a mug of coffee, and isolates himself in the corner. In between bites, he flips his cards and takes notes.

I slice off half of the fried fist-sized heart and sit beside him. He shifts away from me, further into the corner. I shift closer, blocking his escape.

"Some heart?" I say, offering him a bite-sized chunk.

"I don't eat meat," he says, focusing on his dealing.

"Why is that?" I say, popping it in my mouth. "It's not like you love animals."

"Billy," Meg says, "leave him alone."

"We're just talking," I say. "How's your three of spades theory working?"

"It never fails," he says. "A queen or red card always follows."

"I'll bet you it does fail," I say. "In three tries it will fail. If you win, you get your cabin back for the rest of the summer."

Jack gets up to get another serving, though his plate is nearly full.

"Sure," Matt says, shuffling the cards.

"But if I win, you have to agree to fly out of here tomorrow to see a doctor in Homer."

Meg glares at me. "What do you think you're doing?"

"It's a fair bet," I say. "He says he has a hundred percent chance of winning. I say it's one in six. Russian Roulette. For all of us. Because if Matt wins, each of us - especially Matt - loses."

Matt puts down the cards and gets up to leave. I don't budge.

Jack sits at our table, meat stacked so high on his plate it nearly topples. I make eye contact only briefly and it's enough to cause a shiver. But he doesn't stop me.

"You don't have to take that bet if you don't want to," Meg says to Matt. She stands over the table.

"Even if your theory is wrong," I say to Matt, "which I'm sure it isn't, you only have to talk to the doctor." I hold his deck of cards up to him.

Matt grabs the deck from me and sits down.

"What makes you think you'll have better luck now?" Meg says to me, her tone easing. She pulls a chair up next to Jack.

Matt throws out cards until the three of spades appears on the fifth toss. Matt takes a deep breath and tosses out the queen of clubs. He licks his lips and reshuffles. The second attempt, he flips a joker.

"That counts," he says. "Jokers are wild."

"They sure are," I say, dropping my head in my hands, furious with myself for not remembering. With two jokers in the deck and only one round to go, my odds drop to forty three percent. Better than a fifty-fifty chance of sleeping with the spiders for the next three weeks.

When the three of spades arrives in the last hand, Matt stands to deal the final card. A three of clubs. He collapses into his seat. I pop a chunk of venison into my mouth, vindicated. Jack studies Matt's reaction.

I pat his shoulder. "You only have to talk to the doctor."

"It will be OK," Meg says, reaching across the table to hold his hand. "I'll go with you."

"Are you OK?" Jack asks Matt. When Matt nods, Jack walks to the radio. He sets the dial and speaks into the microphone, "Outlet Cape requesting two passenger pick-up at oh-seven-hundred hours."

"Sleep in your room tonight," I say. "I'll take the couch."

***

Late that night, with the blood of the deer pulsing in my veins, I climb the ladder into Meg's loft. The smell of the night's feast hangs in the air. It mingles with the odor of a generation of summer meals, of fish and game. It mingles with the scent of Meg. Her body is taut from the summer's efforts. I'm surprised by my own body's strength, of muscles tightening in unexpected places. I take her in spite of, because of, the grit and grime that cover us.

***

We wake to the sound of the seaplane's engine. Meg holds me tight, then climbs down the ladder. Before I make it down, she has stoked the fire and placed a kettle on the stove. I hug her again. She hands me a cup of tea and I feel its warmth pulse through my hands. While Meg prepares breakfast I pull out my dissertation and review it. I'm jotting down some notes when Jack arrives and pours himself some coffee.

"What's that?" he says, pointing to the corner table.

A tower of cards rests on top of a page from Matt's notes. In front of the tower five cards are facedown. I flip them: the three of clubs and each of the four queens. I slide the paper out and the tower crumbles. On it, Matt has written, "I meant the three of clubs. Gone hunting. Love, Matt."

"Good for him," I say, crumpling the paper and tossing it into the stove's fire. "Me? I'm done hunting. He can garden all week for all I care."

"I don't know what you expected," Meg says. She puts the fourth dish back on the shelf.

"I expected him to keep his end of the bargain," I say, pointing out the door with my rolled up dissertation. "He lost fair and square."

"There's nothing fair about it," Jack says.

The double-crack of a rifle shot startles us. Meg drops a plate to the floor.

"He's too close," she says.

"On the water," Jack says, stepping towards the door. I follow Meg as she rushes past him.

***

I chase Meg down the beach, across a mountain stream, and up the rocky outcropping towards the cliff where Matt had tracked the grizzly. Jack lags behind us, maneuvering up the incline with the strength of his arms when he can't trust his foothold. Above us the bald eagle circles, screeching. Further out, the seaplane approaches, the sound of its engine amplified as it descends towards the water.

Meg's scream is bestial, primal, full of raw panic and pain. She yells, "Why?" and the response that echoes back across the water is her own twisted shriek. She squats on a grassy mound in a clearing, beside Matt's body. She places his bloody, broken head in her lap, bends her face to his.

Faceless fish, piles of prey, disemboweled deer. So much wasted flesh. I want Meg to stop screaming but I'm paralyzed in place, my eyes shifting from her rocking body to the approaching plane. I drop my dissertation copy, caked in mud from the climb, into the dirt.

Jack stumbles past me, rushing to Matt's side. He falls heavily to his knees and administers CPR, but it's useless. There are no paramedics, no emergency rooms. Meg lifts her head to face me. Her blond hair is matted with blood. Her eyes are blank.

She doesn't say, "You couldn't leave him alone?" But it's in there. I squat down next to her and pull her to me. She pushes away from me, pulls her father up, and they hold each other.

I step to the edge of the cliff. The air is clear and the water is flat and deep crystal blue. The seaplane lands with a splash. My bowels tremble and I remember Jack's words: it's not math, it's gut. I don't have the stomach for this. The plane glides towards the beach. The pilot steps onto the pontoon and waves to me. The world I came from is a half-hour flight over the ice-capped hills.

Jack grabs the spent cartridge from the grass beside Matt and turns it over in his fingers before slipping it into his pocket. He runs his hands over Matt, tenderly frisking him. He finds a stale biscuit, a knife with a broken tip, and a box of bullets. He tosses the biscuit towards the eagle's nest, attaches the knife to his belt, and loads a new cartridge into Matt's rifle. He stands and looks at me but I can't meet his gaze. I look over the cliff edge to the crashing waves below and am overcome by vertigo. I crouch to the ground, clutch the earth until a fingernail cracks.

"There's a shovel in the greenhouse," Jack says to me. "Tell the pilot there's been a change of plans."

***

We take turns digging in silence. I shovel furiously, distracting myself from thoughts that Jack, holding the gun, waits for me to finish digging my own grave. Distracting myself from the sight of Meg, pacing between the cliff, where she walks too close to the edge, and Matt's corpse, where she scatters flies. Distracting myself from the dreadful fears of isolation, responsibility.

Just as there is no doctor, pronouncement, or certificate, there is no priest, eulogy, or ceremony. Jack lifts Matt's body as if carrying him to bed and places it into the hole. We refill it. When we're done, Jack gives us our orders. I collect and chop wood and prepare a bonfire at the far end of shore beside the giant white tree trunk. Meg cooks a feast: salmon and venison with tomatoes and peppers picked from Matt's garden. There's even melon for dessert. Jack returns in the skiff with a bucket-full of snowcrabs, the span of their claws longer than my arm. We stab sticks through their shells and hold them in the bonfire like marshmallows. Their legs and claws stretch out, grasping at the turbulent air above the fire. We drink whiskey and when that runs out, beer.

Jack turns Matt's hunting knife over in his hands.

"You were barely walking when I gave this to Matt," he says. He speaks to Meg as if I'm not there. "Your mother worried the point was too sharp for her little boy. So he could keep it, he wedged it between the floorboards and snapped off the tip."

Meg laughs and I follow her lead.

"I remember one of my first fishing excursions with just him, after you bought him his first gun," Meg says. "He caught a halibut bigger than me. We couldn't lift it into the boat, so he shot it dead with his pistol and dragged it behind the boat all the way back to the beach."

"It was delicious."

They continue telling stories while I continue drinking beer, feeling out of place and unwelcome, as if I've invaded some personal religious ritual. They talk about Matt before he got sick — about his fearlessness, his selflessness.

Jack kisses and hugs Meg goodnight. He stumbles off to bed without a word to me. I inch closer to Meg, press my leg against hers softly. She loops her arm through mine and snuggles close. I feel slight, but enormous relief.

"I'm sorry," I say.

"It's not your fault," she says.

I meant it as a condolence, not apology, but I crave the warmth of her body next to mine. I want to pull it into me, but I'm afraid if I squeeze too tight I'll lose it forever.

"It's my fault for bringing you here," she says. "I should have known he'd be too fragile."

"You were only trying to live your life."

"I didn't need to throw it in his face."

"You did everything you could to protect him. You're the one who's self-less and fearless."

The sun dips below the hills across the bay and the landscape begins to lose its color.

"What now?" I say.

"It's up to Dad," she responds too quickly. "But I think we'll return to Homer to clean up Matt's things. Then go from there."

I guess I'm not part of the "we."

"What about your internship?"

"It can wait."

"What about us?" Her grasp loosens the slightest bit.

The northwest sky turns gray. The fire crackles as the logs settle into hot embers. They cast shadows across the rocky beach that give the illusion of motion.

"Do you want to come to Homer?" She knows I have to complete my dissertation. But I'm desperate. I call her bluff.

"If it will make you happy."

I think I see a fox sneaking towards the boulder offshore, but I can't be certain.

She let's go of my arm, shakes her head.

"I'm sorry," she says. She kisses me deeply and I try to hold it, save it, remember it like it's our first. "Dad radioed for the seaplane to return first thing tomorrow morning." She pulls away and walks to the cabin.

***

One by one the stars appear in the south, filling the indigo sky with faint white constellations. The bonfire's embers are searing hot and glow red and yellow in the gentle breeze. Past their light, little is visible. There's a splash in the water. Leaves rustle in the breeze. Preceding each lapping wave is the rhythmic metallic clang of the skiff, always out of place.

Returning to Matt's bed would be sacrilege and Meg's loft, off limits. There's the couch, but the spent shells of the snowcrabs, bleached white in the fire, haunt me, making the spiders seem even more vicious, threatening.

The night air is comfortable and already the hidden sun faintly cuts the darkness in the northeast sky. I slide off the tree trunk and lay in the warm rocks beside the fire.

I wake to a sharp biting pinch on my neck. I smack it and feel the hard writhing flesh of an insect between my fingers. A bug the size of my thumbnail — a sand flea or some sort of beetle — squirms in my hand. I toss it into the fire. Three more cling to my shirt. I jump up, swat them to the rocks. I ruffle my hair, yank off my shirt, wipe down my pants. Hundreds more emerge from the rocks. Like tiny jumping crabs, they crawl and leap past my boots. I swat one that wriggles on my thigh and scrape my boots together to clear some others. I circle the fire and watch as they close the perimeter around the embers. And always more and more emerge within the bonfire's radiant reach, continuing their mad march toward the light, where they bake themselves upon the scorching rocks.

Better Terms

by Mark Wisniewski

WINNER OF THE 2007 GIVAL PRESS SHORT STORY AWARD

There were at least thirty hornets in my medicine chest, which my land-lord insisted I keep closed until the exterminator opened it, so I hadn't brushed my teeth in two days. The exterminator, who my landlord said was a woman, didn't show the day she was supposed to, and then she was supposed to show the following morning—before I left for work—and now, on that following morning, I was at work, which meant I'd needed to leave my apartment un-locked for her, which I didn't like. Everyone knows an unlocked door means you could get robbed, but what got me most was I'd probably never see the exterminator—and there'd go a chance for me to talk to a woman other than the one who always came to the cemetery.

That's where I worked, the cemetery. How the exterminator could have shown at my apartment before my shift still bothers me. My landlord knew I left home at four-thirty a.m. to get to the cemetery by five, when any excava-tion needed to start. My boss Rich believed no one wants to see digging in a cemetery, so we had to finish all excavation before six, sixty-thirty tops. Any-way as I'd showered before work that morning, I knew the exterminator would never appear before I left, but still I sort of hoped she would, which then left me grumpy, maybe even downright pissed at my landlord for messing with me like that. You know: How can you lie to a tenant as ideal as me when you know I'll know you'll be lying?

And then there I was, at work, still grumpy, though there was no excavation scheduled, just leaf and littered item removal until lunch and then, after lunch, probably weed-wacking, but John Monilon wouldn't know until Rich rolled in and told us for sure.

John Monilon was one of those co-workers who's almost a complete friend. I'd sometimes think, while we'd be for instance watering sod, that one day we'd do something together after punch-out, like bowling or watching a game at the minor league baseball stadium you could see on the cemetery's highest hill, but somehow this never happened. You think you'll do something with a person like that, since there, at work, you and this person discuss yourselves so much this person knows all about you, like how one of your big toenails fell off for no reason, and you can laugh with this person, hard sometimes, but when it comes down to the last minute of a shift, while you're each holding a time card and waiting for the clock's final tick, you realize you and this person will part ways again, John Monilon off to a bar to eat a burger and drink beer and try for sex even though he has herpes and went to jail for dealing drugs, you back home to eat tuna and rice before you might browse through your stamps. Yes, I keep stamps, and, yes, I know stamp collecting isn't the best hobby for a guy who wants to talk to a woman other than one who always comes to a cemetery, but it's a truth about me.

At least it didn't help when I tried those over-the-phone dating lines. I should say right now that, through those lines, I actually have talked to women other than the one who always comes to the cemetery, but those conversations, when I'm honest with myself, don't count. For one thing, none ever lasted for more than fifteen seconds, usually because I'd lose nerve and hang up, once because I said "I save stamps" after the woman, whose name was Cheryl, asked me to tell her about myself. I still think it was rude for her to answer my response with silence followed by the tiniest laugh, but my experience with her did teach me that, if I ever do get into a conversation, a real conversation, with a woman other than the one who always comes to the cemetery, stamps are a topic I should avoid.

Unless maybe the woman raises it. And, yes, I'll admit I have wished for a woman out there, in the non-cemetery world, who loves stamps and wouldn't mind talking to me, but this wish, I know, could prove undesirable.

Have you tried the internet? you might be thinking, and in fact that's what

John Monilon once asked, and my answer was (and will always be) that if I'd meet a woman through the internet, she wouldn't count either, because what I want isn't intercourse but instead the satisfaction of having physically approached a non-cemetery woman, talked with her, and parted with her knowing we were both on better terms than we were before my approach. Maybe I'm old-fashioned, but that's all I want. John Monilon says I'm what shrinks call asexual, which, if you ask him, means I'll never have intercourse because my testicles won't cooperate. Between you and me, John Monilon might be right about this, but I'd never tell him so, because saying "Yeah, I'm asexual" to someone could, as I see it, end any chance that I am sexual—and, as I understand things, if I really am asexual, I'll probably never belong to any true family—not the one that got rid of me, not the foster ones I've lived with, not the theoretical one I'd create if I could father children with a woman who'd keep me.

Anyway what John Monilon and I did the morning the exterminator was supposed to show was leaf and littered item removal, which meant we needed to walk to the toolshed on the edge of the woods, unlock it with the key on John Monilon's chain, each take a drab canvas bag with a shoulder strap, each take a bladeless hockey stick handle with a beheaded common nail hammered halfway into one of its ends, then both wander the grounds in search of every leaf and littered item that kept the cemetery from being perfectly green.

Rich, our boss, believed in perfectly green. Perfectly green, Rich said, was essential in cemetery maintenance. If you asked him, people with dead folks need to see as much green as possible when they visit—or even drive past—a cemetery, because green means life in general, and life in general, to such people, can mean a hereafter. These people need belief in a hereafter so they can hope to see their dead folks again, so the greener we could make our cemetery, the more people would pay to keep their folks in it, which meant more money for Rich, which was supposed to mean a raise for me.

But the thing was, on that day (the day the female exterminator was supposed to show at my place), all I'd gotten so far was a fifteen-cent raise—even though I always attacked any leaf or littered item in sight, stabbing it as close to its center as I could, making sure it ended up well inside my bag, jammed toward a corner so it wouldn't escape into a breeze—and even though John Monilon and I, in the past few months, had been digging and sodding more plots than ever. If we'd earn more money, John Monilon once said, we'd meet more women—even if I was asexual, even, he also said, if we didn't use our raises to buy sharp clothes. Women, according to John Monilon, can smell money behind a guy no matter what he wears, and money, he said, is the main thing women want. Once I told him he blew more hot air than our newest leaf blower—since no way did he know what every woman wanted—and he told me to try to prove him wrong, then added that, so far, he and I both were living proof he was right. "Maybe they just don't want a guy with herpes," was what I said then, and he said, "No one but you knows I have herpes," which caused me to believe he and I could still be complete friends. But after punch-out that day, he hightailed it from the cemetery faster than ever, which made me wonder if, for me, complete friendship was a piece of pie in the sky.

Anyway John Monilon and I began leaf and littered item removal the morning the exterminator was supposed to finally show, and as usual, we started out side-by-side, with John Monilon telling me about what happened to him the night before, which this time was that he met a woman with large breasts. We walked all the way up and down one hill stabbing leaves as he focused my thoughts on her breasts, telling me how full they were, how she kept pressing the side of one against him because she supposedly couldn't always hear what he said, how he kept talking more and more softly and shoving quarters in the jukebox to play louder and louder heavy metal songs. He also explained how she must have wanted the breast to keep touching him, because no woman, he said, accidentally lets a breast that size touch a drunk guy that long—and how she must have known the breast was giving him a hard-on, and how, after the hard-on remained hard for at least a continuous hour, she excused herself to go to the bathroom, which he took as an excellent sign, but then, when she left the bathroom, she walked right out of the bar. What got him most, he told me, was that she walked out alone: it was one thing, he said, for a woman in a bar to make you hard and then leave with her friends, but to make you hard and bolt on her own was just plain vicious. Then, like John Monilon often did, he said, "You know what that's like, right?"—as if I always talked to friendless women who pressed large breasts against me, which he darned well knew I never did. And I said, "No, John, I don't know what it's like." And he said, "Ah, come on, man," and I said, "I'm telling you, John, I really don't know," and then he went off on a long speech, giving me the business about how certain it was that I was asexual. As usual when he did this, I didn't say anything, just looked ahead for leaves and littered items. Sometimes when he'd do this, I'd want to tell him to shut up, but then I'd tell myself to keep my own mouth shut—because if I asked him to shut his, we'd never be complete friends. It's better, I'd usually tell myself, to have anyone, even an incomplete friend, walk beside you giving you the business than it is to try to make a cemetery perfectly green by yourself.

And now, also as usual when John Monilon would tell me I was asexual, he tried a bunch of times to get me to admit that I was, but I didn't give in, and then, after I walked quickly toward a leaf well to our right, I stabbed it and angled off even more toward another leaf without hearing John Monilon or looking back to wait for him. And then there we were, on obviously separate paths, which meant we'd stab everything faster and end up finding each other back at the toolshed sooner, but in the meantime we'd be alone.

And when I'd be alone during leaf and littered item removal, I'd just zig-zag without plans from one non-green oasis to the next, and sometimes while I did this I'd think about some of my foster families, often about the last one I stayed with, the one that had me share a bedroom with my foster parents' natural child, a twelve-year-old boy (about three weeks younger than me) named Thomas. One night Thomas told me that, because his parents were poor, we'd never get an allowance like some of his friends did, and he decided we'd need to make our own money if we wanted to buy things, so we tried all sorts of businesses for kids, including selling tomato seeds door-to-door for this mail-order company in Illinois, selling Christmas cards door-to-door for this mail-order company in Georgia, until we decided that we weren't getting our fair share of the profits—and that we should start our own mail order company, which I suggested be a stamp company.

At first Thomas didn't believe a stamp company could make money, but then I told him what I'd learned from a family services lady years earlier—that people collected used stamps and even paid money for them—and soon we were tearing every stamp off his parents' mail, plus off envelopes we'd see in trash bins at our middle school, and then one night, while we lay awake in our trundle beds, we made lists in our minds of people who got lots of mail and might let us take torn-open envelopes from their wastebaskets. Nuns and priests at churches seemed like a good idea, as did dentists and doctors and insurance men, and the next day, after school, we asked quite a few of these kinds of people if we could look through their trash once a week, and most of them, after they asked why and we explained we were starting our own stamp company, said yes. Two of their secretaries even offered to put aside used envelopes for us so we wouldn't need to get dirty digging through their garbage cans, and one thing I noticed was that the nicest secretaries always faced Thomas while they were being nice, which, I decided, was because he had shiny yellow-white hair. Of course, in order to sell the stamps, we needed to remove them from their envelopes, which we did by tearing off the upper-right-hand corners of the envelopes, soaking these corners in lukewarm water in soup bowls (cold water took forever to unglue the stamps; hot water caused any colored envelope paper to bleed and stain the stamps permanently), then letting the stamps dry on our linoleum bedroom floor. The library at school had a magazine for stamp collectors, Lynn's Stamp News, and we put in a classified ad for $2.90 we made shoveling snow, and the ad said, "100 U.S. stamps in very good condition for one dollar postpaid—T & S Stamp," with our address. T stood for Thomas and S stood for me, and I'd been fine with the T before the S because I made Thomas president of the company one night after he said he was bored with peeling stamps off wet scraps of paper. Maybe six weeks passed with us checking the mailbox for not only cancelled stamps but also letters addressed to our new company, and the day after Thomas asked why we didn't just mow lawns for cash, the mail came with three one-dollar orders. And soon dollar bills were arriving almost every day, as well as a few checks for a dollar apiece made out to T & S Stamp, which meant we couldn't cash them until we went to a savings and loan and explained we had a stamp company, walking out that door with an official savings account plus a new source of cancelled stamps. Yeah, we had to keep sending in $2.90 for ads, but we were making an actual profit.

Anyhow Thomas and his parents were the foster family I'd think of most when I'd zigzag away from John Monilon, maybe because T & S Stamp was the closest thing to a group of people I'd really belonged to. Other families I'd stayed with had never kept me feeling as alive. I'm not saying Thomas and his parents made me happy, but their house was at least cleaner than the other places that took me in, which sometimes, when I stabbed littered items in Rich's cemetery, returned to my mind as a blur of cold fish sticks and the stink

of reheated macaroni and cheese. In some of those houses I wasn't the only foster child, and in those houses, you could actually feel the business of fostering
going on, as if you yourself were a cancelled stamp to be soaked and removed
and dried in a room and sent away for the profit of the parents, who'd argue
about which of them was president. In none of those houses did the parents
discuss my future beyond the next week, and in one I slept in the basement,
where the pilot light in the boiler sometimes went out, and once in the middle
of a night, when that landlord came down to fix the boiler, he asked me to take
off my pajama pants, which I was old enough to know not to do. But then he
told those foster parents I'd broken the boiler, and a few months later, I was
off to a house where my bedroom was half of the attached garage—where
a homemade curtain was supposed to keep me from knowing I was sleeping
beside a car.

My mind still can't get rid of the sight of that Fairlane's muddy passenger-
side tires, which I'd seen every night because the curtain wasn't quite long
enough. In fact it very well was a flash of those tires that stopped my thoughts
as I bagged a gum wrapper and glanced up to see the woman who always came
to the cemetery. She was singing this time, which she'd do now and again, only
today she was also visoring her eyes with her hand, looking ahead of her, at
the grass. The sun made the grays in her dark blond hair sparkle, and she was
wearing baggy blue jeans, and she saw me and smiled and said, "Greetings."

"Greetings," I said, and I thought, here we go again, because as much as
I wanted to talk to a woman, conversations with this one bothered me, sometimes even scared me.

"Seen any coins?" she said.

"No," I said. "No coins."

"I found two today," she said.

Here it occurred to me to mention my stamps, but then I thought: What's
the point?

So what I said was: "Do you find many here?"

"Coins are everywhere," she said. "You just have to be looking for them.
And where you find one, you tend to find more."

"But in a cemetery?" I said. "Maybe you should try—"

"You'd be surprised," she said.

Even right then, without considering that she might have collected coins,

I knew she'd be better off in a parking lot. Still, I said, "I guess they could be anywhere."

"People drop coins," she said. "It's just a matter of whether they hear them fall. And then whether they feel like picking them up."

"And you can't hear a coin hitting grass," I said, to make her sound more sane.

"And if you could," she said, "who cares about coins in a cemetery?"

"Uh-huh," I said.

"In a cemetery," she said, "people have their minds on other things."

"Probably so," I said.

Her eyes floated toward the hill that hid the minor league baseball stadium. "Do you know any?"

"Any what," I said.

"Dead people."

"No."

"So you still see your grandparents—that must be nice."

"Actually," I said, "I never knew my grandparents."

"You were adopted?"

"Sort of."

"Either you were or you weren't."

"I was in foster families."

"I was adopted," she said. Her eyes, my glance told me, were on my drab bag. "You didn't miss much," she said.

I wanted to tell her what I had missed: how, when you grow up in foster families, you're basically guaranteed to end up poor, because your foster parents themselves are basically poor, because they tend to be down-on-their-luck couples who take money from the state while trying (unsuccessfully) to raise you on less than the state gives them—not to mention that, after you've been fostered and you reach eighteen, you're all on your own, with no savings for college, no more laws that say you need care, so you end up with the kind of job no one else wants.

But this was the woman who always came to the cemetery, so why tell her this? Plus John Monilon had just crested the hill in front of the minor league baseball stadium on his way toward her and me, and that was one thing I liked about John Monilon: around him, I hardly thought about my childhood. As he walked toward us, we watched him the way two people watch someone else approach to silently admit they no longer want to talk to each other, as if, all of a sudden, they've decided to give up on each other, as if, all of a sudden John Monilon, as our current example, was about to say something that could put everyone present on better terms. Of course, three people on better terms after one conversation is less likely than two, which to me then meant it was impossible. But I still couldn't wait for John Monilon to talk.

Now his eyes were moving back and forth between me and her, and he was shaking his head.

"What is it?" I asked.

"It's about Rich," he said.

"What," I said.

"He was in a car wreck."

"When."

"A really bad wreck."

"How bad?" I asked, even though I knew what he meant.

"He rolled his pick-up," John Monilon said. "On the way home last night. His wife was just here."

"What are you saying?" I asked.

"Dude," he said as if now, finally, we were complete friends. "The guy's dead."

And here's where all three of us—me, the woman, and John Monilon—stood looking at one another like blood siblings might. How long we stood like this is something I couldn't tell you, but for however long it lasted, I believed each of us could have said anything about ourselves and the other two would have empathized. John Monilon could have said he had herpes; I could have said I saved stamps; the woman could have made her most peculiar statement about coins—and none of us, I was sure, would have minded. It was almost as if Rich had been our father, and then it was kind of as if every blade of grass around us had suddenly turned brown.

Then John Monilon said, "Do you realize what this means?"

The woman eyed him as if he always told the truth—which reminded me of how he always said I was asexual.

"What," I asked.

"We'll lose our jobs," he said.

"Why would that happen?" I asked.

"Because Rich's wife will inherit the cemetery. And she'll sell it. And who-ever buys it will probably decide to clean house."

"Why would she sell it?" the woman asked.

"She hates this place," John Monilon said, mostly to me. "Rich told me that once. She hated how much time he needed to spend here. And now she'll also hate it because he was driving home from here when he left her for good."

I saw an elm leaf behind John Monilon, and I walked over and stabbed it.

"What are you doing?" he asked.

"Leaf and littered item removal."

"Fuck leaf and littered item removal, Steve. Your boss is fucking dead. We might as well burn these bags and go to McDonald's."

"For breakfast?" the woman asked.

"For jobs," Rich said. "I mean," he told her, "for me and him."

"I find coins in McDonald's," the woman said. "A lot of pennies."

Rich gave her the kind of look strangers must have given her all the time, but she kept watching him like she and I had earlier.

"Why are you here, anyway?" he asked her.

"Because no one heard these coins fall," she said, and she reached into one of her pockets and took out a dime. "Wait a minute," she said. "Where's my nickel?"

She pulled out all four of her pockets, which were empty. Then she studied the grass around her, made fists with her hands, shook both at the same time, then walked off, up the hill in front of the minor league baseball stadium.

"We won't lose our jobs," I told John Monilon, who stood perfectly still.

"Sure," he said. "And you aren't asexual."

"John-Mon? Quit saying that to me."

"I'll say whatever I want," he said. "And you can believe whatever you want. That's your problem, you know. You never really face things."

"That's not true," I said, and I wanted to tell him that all I'd done in my life was face things: one foster family after another, then one day after another of stabbing sod that covered thousands if not millions of bones of dead people. Just because I didn't complain about what I faced, I wanted to say, didn't mean I never faced it. And it didn't help, I wanted to tell him, that all these days we'd worked together, he'd never been a complete friend.

"Like me," he said. "I face the fact that I have herpes. I face the fact that I have a criminal record. I face the fact that I can't get laid, and that now I'm going to need a new job—the lack of which won't help at all when it comes to getting laid." He cleared his throat, hitched his drab bag higher onto his shoulder. "But at least I try to get laid," he said. "And...at least I'm a square-shooter with myself."

"Go to hell, John-Mon," I said, and right after those words left me, I knew I'd destroyed any last bit of friendship we'd shared. And sure enough, he walked off, away from the hill that hid the minor league baseball stadium, and as he walked he yanked his drab strap off his shoulder, shook out his leaves and littered items, tossed his bag behind him—then, after a short but very fast running start, threw his bladeless hockey stick nail-first at the sun, letting only me watch it complete half a circle and stab itself into a grave. He then walked slowly but straight off the grounds and into the parking lot and got into his Toyota and drove off, and as much as I'd known him, I now had to admit I'd never been attracted to him, or, as far as I could tell, to anyone. Sure, I'd hugged various people in my life, given hello and goodbye kisses to several, and even considered what it would be like to have sex with one or two, but I'd never felt urged toward those actions, certainly not in the way you hear about in song lyrics, or from normal people, like John Monilon, who consider intercourse on par with food as far as human needs go. Over my years I'd liked a few people, but never for longer than maybe thirty seconds at a time, and never so much that penetrating our bodies, or even just exchanging caresses over our skin, seemed like a pleasant idea.

Maybe, I told myself, you are asexual. Maybe it'll always be like this.

But if it would be, I believed, I could still keep my job. After all, I didn't have a criminal record. That was the problem with John Monilon: he always thought that whatever he experienced would happen to me, too. It's different for me, I thought, and I kept on with leaf and littered item removal, figuring I owed it to Rich even though Rich was dead. And who knew: maybe Rich, wherever he was right then, needed to see perfect green in order to believe in a hereafter himself.

So I removed every leaf and littered item remaining on the grounds. Who cared about John Monilon anyway. Who cared about anyone. Then I re-policed the grounds all geared up for any new leaf or littered item, but there weren't any. The wind had died, like everyone beneath me. In many respects it was a beautiful day. If any excavation would need to be done, I wondered who'd tell me to do it. I returned to the toolshed for a weed-wacker, but the toolshed was locked, and I realized the key for it was probably still on John Monilon's chain.

Then, to avoid being seen by the day's visitors—as Rich had always required—I walked up and over the hill in front of the minor league baseball stadium and stood slightly more than my height beyond the top of it. The woman was nowhere. Inside the stadium, an old man was pushing a small aluminum box on wheels that drizzled white chalk to make the third base line. He walked slowly, placing the heel of one foot directly in front of the toes on the other, and I wasn't attracted to him, but all that really mattered was whether the line would be straight, which, as it turned out, it wasn't. If I can't work here, I thought, I can work there. Baseball needs perfectly green grass, I thought, and I felt better.

So I sat right where I'd been standing, just past the top of that hill, waiting for the end of my shift. Rich's wife, I was sure, would never come back that day, which made me my own boss. I avoided picturing the Fairlane's muddy tires by remembering T & S Stamp. Thomas and I had invested our profits in cancelled stamps you couldn't find on envelopes in the mail—far older stamps from a wholesaler who was about to go out of business—and we'd resold them, through the mail, at even greater profits. We'd searched garage sales for all but abandoned stamp collections and bought them at below-catalogue prices and sold individual stamps in them to strangers all over the country, and one in Guam. From the beginning we'd always saved half the profits and reinvested half, so roughly four years into our partnership, we were receiving at least ten dollars a day in the mail. School began to look pointless. Thomas' parents were proud of us, but they kept T & S Stamp secret from everyone he knew. I wasn't at all attracted to him or his parents, and I could barely stand the girlfriends he met in our high school—or any girl in any high school—and never, not for one moment, had I felt anything for that landlord who'd asked me to take down my pajama pants. I couldn't say, as I progressed through high school, that I was attracted to stamps, but I liked them. By my junior year, I'd sit looking at them longer than Thomas would.

The old man was now putting down the first base line. Then he made the two batter's boxes, which took longer than you'd think. But they were perfect.

Still, I wasn't attracted to him. I didn't miss the woman who came to the cemetery. I didn't miss anyone.

Then I walked home. I was surprised to find my door unlocked until I remembered the female exterminator was supposed to have killed the hornets in my medicine chest. Maybe she's here? I thought as I walked in, even though my apartment is only two rooms and a bathroom and she wasn't in the main room. She wasn't in the bathroom, either. The medicine chest was open, and the hornets were nowhere. How she'd killed them was a small mystery to me, as well as what she'd done with them.

I didn't bother to look for her in the bedroom. If she'd been in there, she would have left my apartment immediately, because she would have seen, on most of the floor and much of my bed, open albums full of inventory that had once belonged to T & S Stamp—that is, before I'd given Thomas our savings account balance of $1,462, which I'd done the week before Christmas our senior year, five days after he said he didn't want to sell stamps any more, even if he were president. At the time we'd made that deal, I thought we were both being fair, and in a way I sometimes still think we were. He had the money, I'd told myself back then, and I had an odd but growing business that would always stay with me. There would always be plenty of people who cared enough about cancelled stamps to pay ever-increasing prices for them—or so I'd thought back then. And the exterminator's perfume, I realized now, was everywhere.

For All the Obvious Reasons

by Lynn Stegner

WINNER OF THE 2013 GIVAL PRESS SHORT STORY AWARD

What you heard were the hooves of the three horses with the mule at the end clattering through the rounded stone along the river, the first and the third horse steady, carefully picking their ways, but the one in the middle, a small dark Arabian, skittering and taking too many steps to cover the same distance, some of the steps sideways and even back, *one jump ahead of a fit,* as the man downriver who had saddled her remarked.

"You can handle her." He nodded toward Harry. "Your man says you can handle a horse."

"Sure I can," Charlotte had said.

Harry believed everything she told him. He could afford to believe things and he was generous with that endowment, extending it to everyone. He had had the kind of upbringing that fostered commendable attributes like trust and courage and Honor, capital H. It was what she liked best about him, how clean-swept his life had been. Harry Fairbanks. How could she lose?

Of course it was easier to be honorable with nothing much to challenge those limits.

"I've ridden my share of horses," she added.

But the other one, the Indian, probably knew better. The Indian didn't look at her as she mounted, as she snugged up the reins, slipping her ring finger between the two strands of leather, her right hand clenched and holding the slack off to the right, her posture perfectly trained and the mare already jittering beneath her. The Indian, a thoroughly plausible individual who did not watch but who could assuredly hear the animal snorting and huffing—she knew that he knew the horse was too much for her. Already dark bands of sweat were spreading like ink along the Arabian's shoulders and inside her flanks, her skin twitching, and not from the flies. Abra was her name.

It was just another one of the things Charlotte had probably lied about. All those years of riding lessons, keeping her heels down and her eyes up, and she had never sat a horse well. Mr. Purdy had said that she wouldn't let herself become *one* with the animal—it was the sixties, and people had begun to say things like that, even riding instructors at fancy clubs—but now, seven years later, she knew it to be true. She had kept herself above and separate from the horses she had ridden, which had not been that many, all-told. Horses had been one of her youthful infatuations, and to her thinking infatuations demanded mastery, not union. Mastery, she thought, was a trick of the mind. Something you might try to sell yourself at the end of a long day when it was harder to believe that you knew what you were doing and were in charge.

They made a strange procession, the Indian, the girl, and then the tall man leading the mule, as they set off up the Fraser River, keeping close to the water where there were fewer mosquitoes and deer flies. For a while there had been sandy bars and shores and plenty of open sunlight, with the wet belt of alder, birch, black cottonwood and willow standing back and letting them proceed without trouble or interference. It was early June, the peak of spring runoff, so the broad banks were often wet from a recent surge, and the wildrye or mugwort or reeds flattened and muddy from the flood water's scouring rush. In the wide swaths of river rock, silt girded the larger stones, and there might be pockets of water warming in the sun from which the bugs lofted as they passed. On the drive up from Vancouver the smells had been of pulp mills and new asphalt where the Ministry of Transportation had been paving over one of the roads the map still indicated was dirt, and of course the smell of the peanuts Harry ate with compulsive intent—"Protein?" he asked, offering her some. Foodstuffs had been stripped of their individuality and trained into conforming ranks of dietary requirements. It was all very scientific. Protein was the thing in 1970, the superstar. VIP-for-protein, Harry once told her. Protein and the wonders of frozen vegetables, though they had conceded to cans for part of the trip.

Now in the midday heat along the river the smell was of rotting vegetation, and at random intervals, when the new obscure tension in her chest became too much, she clicked the mare into the shallows where Charlotte felt she could breathe again. Somehow it reminded her of what had happened, that smell. She could not yet bring herself to say "happened *to* her." She was not ready for that claim that would invite something for which she was not ready, some form of psychic catastrophe, a free-falling departure from the high mastery. She was not ready for much of anything yet, in fact, maybe only this trip, one week long, with Harry and the Indian guiding them up through the system of waterways and lakes that veined interior British Columbia.

It did not take more than an hour or so for Charlotte to give up trying to post, which anyway had been mostly to demonstrate that she knew how. The Arabian's trot was so fast, so frenetic, everything about her distracted and ready to bolt, that Charlotte could not settle into anything rhythmic. It would not have done to let Abra take the bit, but neither did Abra give Charlotte any indication of reliable consent. They were in some kind of standoff without having the least provocation. She was a beautiful little horse, spirited and athletic, big anxious eyes; and Charlotte, at 110 pounds, could not have been more than the lightest of burdens, insubstantial as a toy up there, or dismissible erratum. The standoff felt uncalled-for. They ought to have liked each other, made a pair—that seemed to be the idea back at the outfitter's. So Charlotte simply endured it, her bum, her spine jarred and twisted, Abra's hindquarters suddenly bounding out from under her, her head thrown down, her graceful neck swinging sideways. What a week it would be, battling this four-legged tempest. And yet Charlotte could not help admiring her defiance, her anger, so free and absent of cause. Abra was all heart.

On the first night they camped along the Mighty Fraser; Harry liked to call it that, liked to indulge in small flourishes of speech. The rest of the week would be spent east of the Fraser, in the area between Kamloops and north to 100 Mile House. The Indian was one of the Shuswap, an interior Salish tribe, and he knew the area well enough that even the man with the horses had called him by his Salish name, One-See, because he was the only one left who had seen each of the rivers and creeks, the lakes without names, the trails that vanished into the high timber. Harry's father had used him when Harry was a boy, and later, the boy grown, had tracked him down and hired him for fishing trips with his buddies. This trip was different, because of the girl and what had happened.

At twenty, Charlotte was not technically a girl any longer. But she was so petite and so well proportioned, so big-eyed and doll-like, that everyone treated her like a naïf. Or like something not quite real yet. On campus some of the guys referred to her as Harry's trinket, and there had been two occasions on which strangers had mistaken her for his child. He was ten years older, about to finish his degree in medicine at UBC. His mother had taken ill and he had had to leave school for three years to help care for her. It had devolved into one of those eerily satisfying romantic stories—she had died of cancer, and thirty-two hours later, Harry's father had up and died of a disease no one even knew he had, but which everyone decided was grief, pure and simple. They were a poor couple from the mountain town of Revelstoke, and Harry was the family star.

Charlotte was convinced that it would be the same for her and Harry— they would go more or less together. She did not think that she could bear it otherwise. People left: they broke down and were carted off, or they moved away, or they up and died. But not Harry, not this time.

The Indian unsaddled and staked the horses, then he offloaded the grub boxes and staked the mule too, graining them with hands cupped while Harry and Charlotte leveled out a tent site and gathered armfuls of wood for a fire. There was plenty lying about from the runoff and it did not take long.

"Reuben," Harry said to the Indian, for he would never know him well enough to call him by his Salish name, "shall we try our luck?"

Reuben was studying the surface of the river. He turned and nodded toward the rods, jointed and ready, propped in the crook of a cedar. After he had watched the water and the bugs skimming or dancing off the sheen, he came back and fingered up some flies from the box, then the two of them worked their way downstream while Charlotte put up the tent she and Harry would share. They were four months married but it still felt funny to her, spending all of the night hours with him. Even now, it was exciting to wake up and find him beside her, like a holiday morning surprise with its sudden extravagance of joy that sent a hum through her breast, anticipatory and guilty, as if she were getting away with something. *Still here*, she thought, *still right here*. She had developed a secret habit of happiness, trilling the sheets with her toes, before conceding that the day must end or begin. As a child there had been too many mornings when, awakening, there was no one there.

Charlotte's father was a G.P. in Ottawa. After her mother had been institutionalized, and then the years of him trying to conceal the women he saw, (because he was still a handsome man, after all, a vital man with needs, was how the maturing Charlotte came to understand the situation, his beard nicely trimmed, his shirts professionally pressed, no one could blame him, really), he moved to Ottawa so that he could see the women openly. In the tidy little city of Penticton where they had lived, people would have talked. Divorce was out of the question; one did not divorce someone who had had a mental breakdown. One did not abandon the elaborate beauty and comforts of social form for content, no matter how authentic. This was not America, after all, where messy realities throve.

That same fall when her father joined a practice in Ottawa and Charlotte began her freshman year at UBC, her mother was relocated to a Home in Vancouver. In the two years since, nothing had changed for Mary, and Charlotte's visits had dwindled to once a month. But a week ago just after what happened Charlotte had gone off-schedule to see her. Ignoring the rest of it, Mary was her mother, and this was the sort of thing you brought to a mother, something only a mother might be able to fix, or at least soften.

"Where are the bruises?" her mother asked her.

It was a reasonable question. Where were they? Why hadn't she fought?

Mary was having a bad day, they told her, and so the visit had taken place in the special room that was divided by a half wall, with heavy wire mesh rising from the low counter, their two chairs positioned on opposite sides. Her mother pressed her face against the wire, squinting at Charlotte's visible body parts, her face and neck, her forearms, searching for the bruises Charlotte had not thought to earn.

She had been hitchhiking. She hadn't ought to have been hitchhiking.

In a little while Harry and the Indian returned. She watched them coming toward her, their heads bowed in conversation, their boots sinking slightly in the wet sand and gravel. How she liked seeing him come toward her, like a marvelous and improbable piece of news. He brought the whole billowing world with him. And he walked like a man who knew he owned a place in that world. Harry, tall and lithe as poplar, was wearing the bright eager expression of a boy convinced he's about to figure out something grand, or very likely already has. His thinning hair was something she liked, confirming his seriousness of purpose. He took her seriously, too, her compact body, her moods, the things she said that often surprised him. Harry did not think that he was easy to surprise, but as it turned out, he was.

Beside him, shoulder-height and still black-haired despite his age, the Indian paced along with a great and serious fortitude, every step somehow both difficult and destined. The sun was down behind the broad canyon walls and with it, the wind had dropped too, so that all she could hear was the water coursing over the river stone, and the hollow knocking of an oil drum that had washed downriver and eddied between a gravel bar and the place where they had made camp; and then once Harry's laugh, cool, clipped and easy, as if he were trying to draw out a reluctant child. Harry was going to be a pediatrician and it seemed to her that he had chosen the perfect field, one that suited his encouraging nature.

"You didn't catch anything," she remarked.

He shrugged. "Wasn't the point."

Without quite looking at her, the Indian gave a languid side-wary acknowledgment and paced over to where the grub boxes sat beneath a stand of cottonwood and began rummaging through one of them. He was inscrutable, moving with a slight stoop that did not appear to come from any weariness but from contemplation to which, so far, he had given neither of them access.

She turned to Harry. "Aren't we here to fish?"

He squatted beside her, offering her a swig from his flask. "This is a salmon river. Sockeye, coho, chinook...mostly Sockeye. Steelhead if you're lucky. But Steelhead run at night. Reuben noticed a pool downriver, a pool with watercress where Steelhead like to hide."

It irritated her, his mini lecture. Sometimes Harry knew too much. "So what was the point?" Lately it was important to her that things have a point, a specific and well-defined objective, and it helped, too, to know just how long things would take, each task, each job, so that every bit of every day would be used up doing something good and productive, something worthy that an imaginary presence who was always watching you might tick off a list. She had become a furious housekeeper; she balanced the checkbooks to the penny;

she completed and then went back over her homework. Charlotte did this, she did that…. Industry stitched the day together, and so far nothing vital had bled through the open wound that morning seemed to bring.

He placed the back of his fingers against her cheek and gave it a feathery possessive stroke. "Oh, just to try it out, set the mood. We're after trout. That's inland, where we go tomorrow."

"I like it here," she said, tossing a pebble into the river, not wanting to belong to anyone at that moment, not even Harry.

In the flat light of dusk the river stretched away from her to the slanting and distant canyon wall, gray-brown, the water too, gray-brown like tea with milk, but cold, the surface a moving slick of indifference as it slid downward to the sea. The way the water moved, not flowing but huge and muscled from underneath as if it were pushing something impossible out of its way, and that one couldn't see but knew was there just around the next bend—that was what she liked, that pushing, that deep, heavy determination to shove the unseen thing down the canyon and out of the way. Lakes were motionless; lakes did nothing but lie there looking pretty and inviting and stupidly susceptible.

"You'll like it at the lakes too," Harry was saying just then. "You can swim."

"I might not want to swim."

"You love to swim."

"I don't want to swim. Not anymore."

"Sure you'll swim, Char. You'll do everything you were going to do. Nothing's changed."

She tossed another pebble in the water. "Everything's changed."

"No."

"I'm not going to swim."

"Don't be this way, Charlotte. Give it some time. Your feelings will change."

"I'm never ever swimming again."

He sighed, considered the flask in his hand, and then took another swallow. "The lakes are beautiful. You'll see."

"I don't care about lakes or how beautiful they are or how much you think I'll like it or won't like it, or hate it. I'm tired of swimming."

He seemed about to take her hand but thought better of it. "You're in a mood."

"That's right, Harry. It's just a mood. Nothing you have to think too long or too hard about. Call the next patient, order up another tray of animals to dissect, make notes in your notebooks, schedule a follow-up." A mosquito bite on her forearm had made itself known and she was scratching it down to a dot of pulp to put a quick end to the itching. "Consult with Alex," she thought to add.

Behind them the woods crowded down a narrow wet draw ending in a hedge of young cedar so dense that she could only worry about what was behind it. She took another sip of Harry's whisky and glanced over at the Indian to see if he'd been listening. Harry unfolded his long self to help with dinner, leaving her alone. She had wanted to drive him away but was equally disappointed in having succeeded.

She had missed the bus. And she'd seen others, friends of hers with their thumbs out, catching rides with other students into the city, or across the Lions Gate Bridge to North Van where it was cheaper to live. Where she and Harry lived now. Plenty of them did it.

They heated two cans of beef stew over the fire and sopped it up with bread. Afterward, the Indian rinsed the cans in the river, burying them and marking the place so that they would not have to carry them but could pick them up on the way back a week later. He did not drink and he did not eat the candy bars that were Harry's weakness, his only one, so far as she could tell. Reuben and Harry were familiar with the routine and with each other. They did not need to tell stories, the way men did, establishing who they are and what measure of deference or disregard each warranted. Even among men like her father, men who cared for a living, Charlotte had heard late-night versions of Great White Hunter tales, about patients with problems the books never told them about and that were usually the result of some strange thing they had managed to do to themselves, and these were the stories that had bothered her the most—the unavoidable exposure, the hoped-for and foolish trust, then the hunting tales that betrayed them. Once, even, she had overheard her father talking about her mother—'*will you just stop doing this, Mary,*' Bellows said *to her.* Bellows was another colleague of theirs in the practice. Charlotte had seen the cuts, too, but until that night, she had not known how they got there.

Around the fire the three of them sat. Reuben had found the desiccated root of a cottonwood five to six centimeters in diameter, and had begun carving it. His nose was striking, the kind suburban women with stereotypical views about Indians might want to paint, with a strong straight center bone, the flesh planning down evenly like the sides of a tent, one in shadow and the other a coppery gleam against the firelight. Harry was reading aloud from the fisherman's guidebook about Dolly Varden, the trout they were after, "*maximum weight, six to seven pounds, 18" long, hearty and colorful, stunningly spotted in scarlet with halos of pale silvery blue.*" A log had settled out of the fire and he poked it back in among the embers, releasing a miniature outburst of sparks. "*Dollies are anadromous—seagoing.*"

Over in the river shallows they could hear the hollow *booming* of the oil drum against stone. It was so deep and muffled by the current that the sound seemed to come to them subliminally, like some kind of animal, a moaning beast out there calling to them, *needing, needing, needing* and not about to give up.

"*Expect strikes to be savage,*" Harry read.

Charlotte had recently begun biting her nails again, a habit leftover from childhood and the time after her mother's breakdown, a habit now revived with a vengeance. The sound of the drum banging restlessly in the eddy was getting to her. Abruptly, she tore her hand from her mouth and leapt up, plunging into the water. The drum sent up a great rumbling commotion when she reached it; under the trees the Arabian began to dance nervously.

The Indian didn't rise to help. Harry scrambled his boots off, but Reuben extended one hand, palm down, and Harry stopped, and then the two of them stared into the fire, listening to her struggle to shove the oil drum out of the shallow eddy and into the main current.

Harry put away the guidebook. Reuben's knife hesitated, then a thin curl of cottonwood grew from it, and then another and another.

"The doctor said to talk about it," Harry whispered to her later in the tent.

It was pitchy inside the tent walls, but somehow she could see the negative white of his eyes. "I don't really want to talk about it."

"He said it would help."

"I told them everything."

"Char."

"The hard parts too. I told everyone everything." She was thinking at that moment of the younger of the two RCMP officers doing his level best not to expose a twitch of emotion about what she was being asked to tell them, what she heard herself having to say to strangers, to herself who had now become a stranger. "I'm through with my talking."

The officer had not been much older than she. It was worth hating him for, that and his fumbling inexperience, his dropped clipboard, his fat tender face and the tiniest glint of excitement she was sure she had detected in his eyes. It was like having to talk to a brother, if she had had one to talk to.

Harry propped himself up on one elbow, trying to see her through the darkness. She hadn't cried yet and they all seemed to be waiting for that— signs of release and metamorphosis. A proper lamentation. But what was it that she had lost? What had slipped from her hands? What had died and what could she grow into, now that she had been ruined?

"Charlotte," he whispered, "I'm *almost* a doctor." She could hear in his tone an attempt at some misguided order of distracting levity, a detour onto the sunny well-tended boulevard that was Harry's life and career where it was always safe to talk or cry, or to be yourself, because everybody would still love you. Harry was not afraid to be at anyone's mercy. "Why won't you talk about it, even with me?"

She rolled over. "For all the obvious reasons."

Adoration was a dangerous proposition, potholed with hazards, obstructed by roadblocks, strangers asking intrusive questions that challenged your assumed identity. One day, one look across a room at *him*, and there were things you knew you didn't dare reveal about yourself. Parts of you were quarantined as abruptly and dismissively as if officials had nailed a sign to your forehead—*until further notice*—or until you had somehow determined his receptivity—or his immunity—to the bad habits, the nasty thoughts, the lies that lacked any real point, the silly female rituals of love, the regrettable but not forgettable deeds of youth that you were convinced said more about who you were than all the make-up days that followed or coincided with that downfallen, down-at-the-heels version of you yourself.

She hadn't told them everything. She hadn't told them, for example, that she had been hitchhiking. They might have thought that she had been asking for it, or at the very least, that she had been reckless. Or that she was some sort of girl that she was not, a girl who hitchhiked.

On the second day they rode east along a creek that cut through the mountains, traveling in and out of shadow and then, leaving the creek, they found themselves beneath the tall fir and cedar and hemlock, resolutely in shadow. A disturbing quietude enveloped the Arabian. Charlotte began to worry that something important had gone out of her; began to wish for the fire and fight of the day before. From the trail a damp fecundity issued, and clouds of mosquitoes materialized, with single or double deer flies orbiting her dark curls and buzzing protest whenever one or the other became entangled. The thumping echo of slow hooves marched them along steadily, the Indian, the girl, and the tall young man leading the pack mule, and for a while no one broke whatever spell had been cast once they had left the sound of moving water and entered the silent forest.

Not long after, the Indian turned his horse, a stocky old stallion unexceptional but for a striking compliancy, and came back alongside Abra. "They like hair," he said to Charlotte. "Hair like ours." It was true: the deer flies did not bother Harry with his thin colorless wisps. Abra lifted her nose against the old bay and snuffed as Reuben handed Charlotte a tin of some kind of homemade salve, sharp and bitter smelling, that she was to rub around her neck and tousle into her thick curls. Reuben did the same to his own neck and hair. He had small blunt hands, but they moved—as he did—with a fine deliberation. Everything about the way he moved, in fact, suggested someone conserving himself in the face of an impending battle, an illness that he knew he could not beat, or an unbearable feeling that he knew he would simply and finally have to feel. For the first time since she had met Reuben, she offered a smile and he returned it with a slow solemn nod before resuming the lead.

What possible motive, she had to wonder, could this stranger have for treating her with such unearned and mannerly respect?

Behind her she could hear Harry humming something; he had such a reassuring voice, not especially strong but clear and valorous as rushing water. When the humming stopped she glanced back and saw that he was reading from another of his guidebooks, the one on native trees and plants. It was knowledge that bore no interest for her except in so far as having it might help her acquire some of his power. Harry was a great conqueror of things. When he took on a subject, he took it over entire, not obsessively but with a sanguine thoroughness that sometimes made her nervous, as if, once he had delved her through and through, he would leave her behind just as thoroughly. Charlotte did not want to be another topic on which one day he had finally sated himself. Even if there were not other reasons to hold some of herself back, this was reason enough.

And could he ever forgive her for this new knowledge she had not wanted, for what she had learned about men? A sudden raw shame came into her stomach. She was no longer innocent. She knew things, had done things. All of the shine of being Harry's girl, Harry's *trinket*, had been rubbed off. A dirty, needing, wanting world had simultaneously converted and convicted her: she was an adult. Adults did not need protection. And the very last thing she could stand to lose was Harry's protection.

A polite distance had opened between Abra and Reuben's old stallion. She watched the muscles of his rump flex, alternating with each step, left, right, left, right, unhurried and obedient, and felt herself settling into a dozy comfort. Between the Indian and Harry she felt safe; they were keeping her safe, these two men each with his own fields of knowledge, each a conquering hero. For now, she was safe.

And in that safety something terrible stole to the surface: They would not be looking for someone who stopped for hitchhikers; they would be looking for a man with a different approach, more aggressive, more obvious. And there might be another girl out there like Charlotte, just trying it out, hitchhiking for the first time, who maybe was mad about something, in that sort of mood, *the devil take it all*. There was something real and tangible at stake here—another life, another satchel of innocence someone had managed to carry away from the kingdom of childhood with its unsleeping monsters and its daily traumas disguised as lessons, all of them coming thick and fast as locusts in a private and inescapable parable of biblical proportions. Family bibles, she thought, each one personalized with barren dreams and born crosses, suppers trailing betrayals, doubtful redemptions.

Parables…people either broke down or went off, leaving you alone…that was what her life had taught her. That was the moral of her story. Relentless contingency.

But there was another life, anonymous but real.

She had missed the bus because she and Harry had had a bit of a row. About a woman who was going to be a doctor too—one of his classmates. Alex was her name. Charlotte didn't even have a major yet, and was in fact consider-ing dropping out, now that she'd met and married Harry. What more could she want, after all? After Harry.

Alex, she thought, staring into the melancholy depth of the forest whose tree trunks and branches scratched out the distance and held her to the nar-row viewless path. Alex was probably Harry's equal in ways that Charlotte could never dream of being or achieving. Even her name suggested equality, male but not male. Charlotte had not understood that Harry's friend was a woman. Alex this, Alex that. She pictured them side by side, peering into the half-dissected vitals of a bird or a rat, poking about with cold steel tools and making cold steely notations in journals, cracking jokes only an insider could get. Making eye contact.

The bus was gone and there she stood on the curb. Harry was back in the Faculty of Medicine building, and Alex somewhere in there too, and Charlotte was needing to file some kind of cosmic complaint, not exactly for his having Alex, or an Alex, but for occupying a world to which Charlotte would have only peripheral access, wifely access…social events or professional functions or per-haps during staff vacations, she might fill in as the receptionist. She might even help with accounting. She'd always been handy with numbers. Having children would increase the stakes, but just about the time they went off to live their lives, her female charms would begin their inevitable slump and slide. She might take up volunteer work, join a book club, take a last-ditch lover, have a small-scale breakdown. But it would all be part and parcel of the inequality for which she had gladly signed on. She hadn't driven much of a bargain, had she? And here it was, the seventies. From the very beginning she had been dazzled by Harry. She hadn't given herself much of a chance or even tried to be a person yet, she'd been so busy setting herself up as Harry's protectorate.

They camped late along Hat Creek. Using grasshoppers, Reuben and Harry caught a string of rainbows, no more than what they could eat that night, and Charlotte boiled rice, and then there were two cans of Le Sueur peas upon which she had stubbornly insisted. No matter the healthy attributes of frozen vegetables, Charlotte would never give up canned Le Sueur peas. Reu-ben had gone away and come back fifteen minutes later with a bright orange mushroom, chicken-of-the-woods, which they fried up with the fish. After dinner, after scrubbing the tin plates with gravel and creek water and spacing them out on a downed tree to dry, Charlotte took her towel and wandered downstream until she found a deep enough pool to bathe in. Washing had become especially important, all parts of her body but some more than others. The men had been reminiscing about Harry's father, and Harry's voice had gone wobbly. It had been a long day. Everyone was tired. She did not want to hear Harry's voice with so much feeling in it, not now, not this week. It had the effect of unstitching some of the day's seams enough to send her back to the tent and into her sleeping bag before any more came loose.

Within minutes, a car pulled to the curb, a turquoise VW beetle, maybe ten years old, judging by the thin chrome bumper and the seat configuration. A cheap car, repainted, balding tires. A student car. Clean—she had noticed that. It had made some kind of skewy difference as she leaned down to look through the passenger door glass. She can't now remember what he said. What she said. What she remembers: nice-enough looking guy, brown hair cut short but not so short that it said something else, something you wouldn't want to know. A man who was too fastidious could not be trusted with the accidents of being human. Small brown eyes, round as beads, olive skin, like her own; a checked shirt on a slim torso; flashing smile, bored, or hurried—one or the other—that tells her he might be doing her a favor, that he probably is doing her a favor. So she gets in. Because that's all she wants right now, a favor from a stranger. Maybe he looks a little like Ricky Nelson, or some other teenage star. She's not sure. She's not sure now and doesn't really want to know, because then she won't breathe so well.

He has his left hand on the steering wheel and it looks like it's trying to be casual, that hand with the fingers draped over the top, tapping, though the radio isn't on so there's no beat to follow. It's the other hand that isn't quite right but she can't say how. Not when it's shifting. When it's shifting it looks fine, but in the space between shifting it seems to scurry back toward his body, or the seat...she's not sure. There is a smell...vegetables...broccoli, it's in the top of a paper bag, back seat—he's been to market. Heading home. His window is half down. Hers is all the way up. The smell of the broccoli is making the car feel smaller than it already is. When she tries to find the window lever he says it's broken, but it's actually simply gone. Maybe that's the first sign. They're on the Lions Gate Bridge and it's not so far from Lynn Valley, from the neat middleclass neighborhood she lives in with Harry Fairbanks in their rented bungalow, and so she just wants to get over the bridge and figure out the rest of the way some other way. Walk. That'd be fine with her now. There's a lot of traffic that is helping her feel all right about this in a roundabout way. Commuters. Commuters seem to make everything feel normal, crankiness and petty aggressions, tailgating. She's never before hitchhiked, and she decides she's just nervous. Her mother used to say dramatic. That Charlotte should grow up to be an actress. Her backpack is propped in the gap between the driver and passenger sides, and she rests her hand on it, as if it's her dog watching out for her. Some of her friends hitchhike regularly. She ought to be able to do it too, though Harry's always telling her she looks too innocent for ice cream practically. It is something he seems to like about her, so she doesn't tell him otherwise. It is part of the part of her that isn't quarantined, her presumed innocence.

He's telling her that he goes to college too, not University but one of the city colleges. Money, he says, apologizing. It feels like a line he's used to advantage. Struggling, hard-working fellow cheerfully accepting his lot, making the best of things, philosophical about it, not jealous—that line. Some part of her decides to buy this line. And why not? Half of who anybody was was who he pretended to be, or wanted to be, or had to be just to get along. Then he's talking about girls he's dated and how difficult they are, making him quit smoking before they'll kiss him. University girls, not the ones at the city college—most of them smoke, he says. Now she remembers that he's chewing gum. He keeps his mouth closed. Someone has taught him manners along the way, but he has a slight under-bite and it doesn't look all that easy. She would rather not hear about girls and how difficult they are. She's wondering why he was driving around UBC when he attends one of the city colleges. "I quit smoking 2.6 weeks ago," he's telling her, and she makes herself mentally deliberate the .6, whether it means 6 out of 7 days or six-tenths of a week, because he's still saying things—about mood swings and lack of sleep and periods of random aggression. He says the word "gum," as if he's saying "uncle" and surrendering, then gestures at his mouth and smiles without parting his lips. It's not really a smile, it's a flinch. She wants to get out of the VW now. A dumb word enters her mind—shenanigans—one of her mother's. "What sort of shenanigans have you been up to?" Charlotte needs to laugh...shenanigans, shenanigans, shenanigans, she repeats to herself, trying to shrink what's happening down to a prank.

At the end of the bridge they drop into West Van and she suggests that he

let her off at the next corner. "Right here is fine," she says lightly, trying to sound
unfussy, trying not to officially recognize what might be happening, giving him
a chance, an out, a merciful lie, and stifling the panic that takes up her chest
like a ballooning explosion.

He doesn't even slow down.

By late morning on the third day they made it well into the lake region.
Crossing the Bonaparte River at Scottie Creek, following it east, then turning
north before reaching the Deadman River, they simply began to wander. Each
lake they passed sat quietly hopeless below them, passive and bound up in
woods. It was a cloudless day, the sun bleak and ubiquitous. Most of the bodies
of water—lakes, ponds, reservoirs, big and small—were named, but the one
the Indian finally led them to had no name, or no name that he knew of, and he
knew that country better than any, the outfitter had assured her.

"It is called No-name," he told them, which made it worse. Saddened her.
It seemed to render the lake vulnerable, unqualified for protection, the for-
malized namelessness of it. And it was embarrassing too, that it had not even
merited a name or inspired a friendly idea, a moment of vanity or possession
among early visitors—Bonnie's Lake, Heartwell Pond, Loon Lake. Here they
would find Dolly Varden, fish with a proper name, and yet they too would be
violated. The named and the un-named. Sooner or later, everything was violated, driven down to the knees of anonymity. Who were we, she wondered, if
we were just like everyone else, dirty and wanting and needing, anonymous as
we wheeled toward death in our passing cars?

They had arrived late. Reuben grained the horses and the mule, then she
helped him stake the animals in a sunny glen near the campsite where there
was a variety of wild grasses growing—wheatgrass, wildrye, bluegrass,
needlegrass. The needlegrass sewed itself into her socks as she led Abra and
Harry's big chestnut into the glen, the chestnut steadying Abra down to a tentative walk, the trust between them still cautious. For a while Charlotte sat in
the shade, picking out the needles, trying not to think. Harry strolled down to
the water to make a few casts at the place where a stream left the lake. Every
now and then the light touched his fair hair, marking where he stood and ac-
quitting her of thought. So long as Harry Fairbanks was there, believing she
was still who she was, she did not have to think too much.

Soon, two Dolly Varden, not like the sleek silvery Rainbows of the night

before but fat with a blue blush of color banding their sides and brilliant red
spots, swung from a length of cedar that bowed from their weight. Reuben ran
switches through them, mouth to tail fin, and they were cooked whole over
a fire until their flat glassy eyes hardened, and went as white and opaque as
dried beans. Kype-jawed, she had to notice, because it reminded her of the man
in the VW with his underslung mouth.

The no-name lake and the cloudless sky and the primeval emptiness were
conjuring a desolation all their own, as if bad things had once happened in the
place. Even the blue smoke, whorling and quixotic through the trees, seemed
baffled. It was too quiet. A breeze that they could not feel up on the slope under
the trees was chaffing the surface of the lake, portending trouble they were too
ignorant to detect.

After supper, the Indian threw his bag on a tarp down by the water and
in the late light stretched out with a book—poems, of all things. She'd seen
him with it the night before, and it tended to complicate him in ways she didn't
know how to resolve.

Harry was already in their tent, which from the outset had been a concession to his notion that women needed privacy. Harry could be counted on to
give up things for her, and though she did seem to need a great deal of privacy
right now, his thoughtfulness was galling. Needing it, she felt ashamed. "I
would like to hold you, Charlotte, if you will have that," he said in a voice so
gravely formal that she felt sorry for him, as if what had happened had forced
him back to an era when courtships were endless and women chaste as fresh
cream.

Out of the question, she heard herself think. What she said while she
sorted through some gentler surrogate words was his name, "Harry," and he
took that for assent. Maybe it was—just a little. She kept her back to him
though, where the muscles were bigger and blunter and there were fewer nerve
endings. Why, you could practically run a needle through them and expect
nothing worse than a distant ping of alert, the brain hardly bothering to acknowledge pain so inconsequential, so far away. It seemed a good way to be,
distant and removed from injury. You could get on with things that way, keep
running, keep keeping on. That was what was expected. But why did people
expect such grand things of someone they didn't know? To keep living, to keep
caring? There was a certain brand of universal importunity obtaining, a kind

of species-wide peer pressure to buy the line, all the clever lines, and stay alive no matter what. Life is grand, isn't it? Yes, of course it is. Life is so grand.

Lying there with Harry's breath on her neck, the bunched sleeping bags generous and soft fortification between them, she thought about the eyes of the Dolly Varden, white and impassive in their deaths. It was how she felt now, if it could be called feeling—sightless and impassive.

"Tell me something good," he whispered.

"I can't think of anything good."

"Then tell me a good lie."

She said, "I love you."

Harry gave a laugh that was really just his breath leaving him. "Is that the lie?"

"Water," she said. "I like water."

Glad, it seemed, to have found something that might distract her, he asked her what about water.

"The way it feels around my skin, the way it holds everything in place, the pressure of it, like borrowed skin, except I can still move. I can still get away."

She was no longer sure that she loved Harry Fairbanks, because she was no longer sure who she was, or who the *she* was who had once upon a time loved him. But one thing she *was* sure of was that it didn't matter either way. Nothing mattered. If she could have she would have erased her name to end once and for all, all mattering.

How would it be when they made love again? When she lost herself in touch entirely, which was what happened more often than not? Harry said that she was a sensualist. No more than the next girl, she thought to herself, though she couldn't help feeling a little ashamed. It was only that she knew how to shut off her mind and for a while live through touch. How would it be if she found herself doing something new? Would he look at her as if he didn't know her? Would he say something awful...*do I owe this to him?* "Don't be insulting, Harry," she might say. More likely, shame would exile her to the land of silence.

They met on a University-sponsored ski trip to Whistler, Harry one of two leaders commissioned to teach a group of sophomores Nordic skiing. Late one afternoon she had taken off her skis to climb up a tumble of boulders for the view, and one foot had gone out from under her, disappeared down a crevice and wedged. For a slip of girl lacking muscle in her arms, it was all she could do to hang there on winged elbows and bent knee, jackknifed for dear life. Several of her girlfriends skied by but dismissed her calls for help as fraudulent. And it may be that they were, that if she had tried harder she might have been able to extract herself. Out there in the meadow with the others, teaching them telemark turns, was Harry, a marvelous skier, and she knew that sooner or later he would come. His irritation with the others for ignoring her seemed to codify the incident and purify her motivations. The sun perched high behind him, the snow was blinding, the air aglitter with icy crystalline flecks, and she could not see his face as he hooked his arms beneath hers and pulled her from the crevice, suspending her for the longest time so that she might work her boot free from the crack. She'd been up there more than an hour, and her hands had gone white. What he did was to lift his parka, his turtleneck, and press her hands in the warm hollows of his underarms. "No," she said, "they're too cold." They *were* too cold. But he only gazed at her, into her eyes, with the intensity of someone sure of himself, of all the right things that there were to do in the world if only you'd had a good solid life, one that let you believe in things. Harry was happiest when he was helping someone. On her warmed hands his scent, with its salty tang of authority and exertion, suggested all she needed to know about him as a man. His upper lip quirked into an unexpected and unabashed show of passion. Instantly, as if some ancient cog had ground round at last to catch up another cog long ago meant to have been caught, the machinery moving now and something back there in the crowded cluttered clanking works beginning to sing, their meeting animated a classical dynamic: distress and rescue, innocence and protection.

Now Charlotte wondered how much she had not seen gazing up at Harry in that dazzling white light. How much she had tricked him into imagining about her.

Sleep was a valuable enterprise. She was not sleeping so well. Night terrors; gory images; weird sex. How was it that these terrible things were inside her? Where did they come from?

Human beings were horrible, one way or another. *God curse us, everyone.*

She reaches for the door handle, ready to jump out as soon as he has to brake at a light or a stop sign, to jump out no matter the stopping, the going, but the door doesn't open because the door's locked and at the base of the window the up-down button is missing. He says something, something that goes with another flinching smile. Charlotte can't remember that part, what it is that he says at the very moment she understands with every cell in her body that she's no longer a part of the world out there, the one washing by her window; she belongs to this world inside the VW, and the other world, her world, is past and gone now, zooming out and away like the expanding shock waves of an explosion.

He takes her into the neighborhood where she lives with Harry. The man doesn't know it and she decides not to tell him. Maybe she is protecting it, her home. Or maybe it is as if she has already said goodbye. Has already entered this new order. They roll by the house; she can see the lawnmower where Harry left it by the side gate, and the three pots of herbs on the front stoop. She is supposed to water them when she gets home. It is the only moment that opens a thin crack, a welling of tears. Time is stopped, or ripping past, or launching her into fright—it has so completely lost its measured and faithful validity.

He is holding himself. He may have been holding himself for a while, maybe six or eight turns, one quotidian block devolving into another, all the houses with trimmed lawns and topiaried hedges gazing sightlessly on her and her captor as they pass by in the slowed motion of nightmares and car accidents and suicide jumps from window ledges. She never learns his name. No-name. He takes her just four streets away, to a cul-de-sac formed by the western edge of Lynn Canyon, and turns off the engine.

"You don't need to do this," she says.

"Now, why is that?" he asks.

She can't really hear him; she seems to see the words in her mind, minus whatever personality inhabits his voice.

"You're a perfectly nice looking fellow." Having just seen her home with all its now bygone promise and possibility has imparted some strange state of calmness, as if just seeing it must mean she will see it again. At the same time it is as if she was viewing old photographs in the album of a lost life. "You can ask girls out. You could ask me out," she adds, trading in a concept that belongs entirely to this new order. The one that is telling her that she must survive.

The knife has been there all along—she realizes that. It must have lain alongside her backpack, slightly hidden, occupying his right hand whenever he wasn't shifting. A long steel blade like the kind her father uses to carve meat.

When he isn't touching the knife, he's holding himself. There is a lot of flesh rising between them, flesh and steel.

"I would go out with you. If you asked me out properly, I would accept. You're a nice looking fellow. You don't need to do this."

"Describe it," he tells her.

It takes her a little too long to understand what he wants, and he has to say it again.

She does what she is told to do. That and the other things. He wants her underwear; she removes them, he puts them in the bag with the broccoli while she pulls her pants back up. So far he has not touched her, and she takes this as a good sign. She has been instructed to touch him, but he has not actually touched her. Maybe, after all, he's just a piss-ant, a coward. She begins to feel sorry for him, to need this badly, to take these actions; she is, in fact, embarrassed for him. Her own base instincts, like that one at the very bottom, the one that is telling her to stay alive, she is still reticent to expose. Exposing her own needs would put her at his mercy. Right now she still owns some of the action, some of what will end up being deeds.

She talks about school, about her life, peppering the surface of this new world with casual chatter, as if they are indeed on a date. She never mentions Harry. She says again, "Why don't we go out for a regular date? We could do that, we could just go out on a date. I would like that."

It may be that he did touch her. But she just can't remember that part.

They have entered a place that is a time without name. It is all action, with deed as the outcome of that action, the past tense of action. Or maybe the past tense of action was regret. Time and space are one in such scenes. And she is trapped in such a scene before it must be condemned to deed.

That night, Reuben told her, she went down to the lake, walking into the black water with great quietude and courage, as if there was someone out there she was scheduled to save. She was wearing one of Harry's white undershirts, and so was visible even in the snuffed light of the new moon and the hard little stars pinned into the night sky. Thirty or forty yards out, she stopped and floated on her back. Then she began to swim toward shore. He could see the white of the undershirt and hear the movement of the water, and he knew—he told her—that she was at home in water, and so he was not yet concerned. It wasn't until she reached the shallows and the sloping bank touched her feet that she awakened. And then immediately he entered the water to catch her, her breath coming sharp and fast.

"You were asleep," he said.

She stared at him. He still had his short strong arms around her rib cage. He was not an attractive human being, his face too broad and his skin damaged, but he had the sweetest eyes she'd ever seen. She started to cry then, crumpling against him.

"To see in this darkness what you don't know..." he settled her on her feet before him and opened his palms to the hard little stars, and nodded, "that is something. But to see what you don't want to see..."

Once, when her father had gone off to a conference in Toronto for four days, her mother had all the stone in the house painted white. One coat for every day that he was absent, so that by the time he returned, the glossy paint was so thick, and still not quite cured, that you could press tiny frowns into it with your thumb nail. Her father had loved that stone wall surrounding the hearth; had laid it himself; had run his hands across its rough surface in thought, in boredom, in appreciation of its tactile proximity to earth.

She had every tree on the place cut down, too, even the Mountain Ash he had nursed from a seedling.

She slashed a giant X into the mattress and packed the wound with rotted apples from the neighbor's orchard. Then she used the knife to carve words into her arm, not so deep to kill, but still legible: a pity about the nights in bed.

So. So...her father had seen what he had not wanted to see.

They have been parked on an ordinary neighborhood street, houses facing other houses and at the end, a guardrail that keeps cars from plunging over the bank and down into Lynn Canyon. They are stopped parallel to the guardrail. It is not yet the time when families have all arrived home from work or school, and the street is quiet, though she is hopeful that inside one or more of the houses there are people beginning to wonder about the turquoise VW parked on their street. He tells her—and once again, she can't really hear his voice, can only see the words scurrying across her mind like terrible rats in the Devil's own penny arcade—that they, meaning he and she (they are a couple, it seems, in this new order), they are going to go down into the canyon together. He doesn't pretend to anything ordinary, like a nature hike or even a fete of groping and drinking that young people enjoy under trees and beside bodies of water. He says: "We are going to go down there now."

"Why?" she asks. The fear that she has held back suddenly dissolves into some kind of icy liquid metal veining through her body.

"I'm taking you down there now."

"Why can't we just have a date, a real date? You don't have to do this."

He says things… about how she looks and that he's sorry she had to be so pretty.

Had.

"I'll come around to the door and let you out," he says finally.

"You don't need to do that. I can let myself out. It will look funny, if you come round to let me out. People might notice. And anyway, you can trust me now, can't you, to let myself out? Here we've been sitting and talking about everything under the sun, and a date, a real date, and surely you can trust me now to let myself out of the car." In truth, it is only she who has been talking.

"A date," he says, flinching up his smile, emitting a huff.

"Sure."

He studies his reflection in the knife blade. "I don't believe you."

"Look, I'll give you my number…" she fumbles in her backpack for a pencil, a piece of paper, adding cheerfully, "Friday's best for me. Only one class, early. You can pick me up in the same place."

Somehow, it is this flurry of routine date-making details that causes him to hesitate. Looking not quite confused and not exactly off balance, maybe wobbled, maybe even the slightest bit pleased, he accepts the piece of paper she extends, her number and address—both false—scrawled on it. For a half a second he seems to belong to, or to recognize, the old world, the real world, not the one he has been busy creating inside the VW. Then he reaches in his breast pocket and extracts the up-down button for the door lock and simply hands it to her. He zips himself up. If they go down there she figures that he will have to kill her. In every terrible chaos of action and details, there is usually one point of exit best recognized by someone down there in the cellar where good and bad, black and white, freely consort. This is her point of exit. At the same time, she has accepted this new world so wholly, and acted so well across its stage, that she is actually worrying about hurting his feelings even as she casually, casually, screws the button back in place, opens the door, and runs.

He starts the engine and as he spins the car away he throws her backpack out the still-open passenger door.

No backpack, no identification, no name, no blame.

So, after all, he is a piss-ant, a coward.

The door is open at the first house she comes to, the screen door in place. A man is sitting on a couch in a dimly lit family room, watching the television. She cries through the screen door, "Help me, please, he tried to rape me, I need help! I need a phone…police…"

The man says, "I don't want to get involved," and rises to shut the door.

Next door, a woman in a kitchen, her husband approaching behind her. Charlotte says the words again. The woman picks up the phone. Her husband leads Charlotte into a living room, a cozy quiet sanctuary where good lives have gone on, and offers her a place on the couch. When the RCMP arrive, the couple hover in the doorway, looking worried about Charlotte, looking beautifully wonderfully human.

The kindness of strangers.

The owl woke her up. Harry was already gone. It was sitting in the Doug fir that towered over the tent, looking for the world like a small amputated human being, all torso. Heart's home. Somewhere not so far away that she couldn't tell its northerly direction, was another Great Horned Owl responding to hers, questioning her identity. *Who, who, who.* She did not feel so bad, or not as bad as she thought she would after the sleepwalking.

They were probably fishing. It was early, only five, and they had to have gone down to the lake to cast when the fish would be feeding.

Comfortably abandoned, she squizzled back into her sleeping bag, glad for the time alone and sad for it, as well. All the mornings of her world with Harry would be spent like this, with him gone off to work and the silence of the house and a day, already fractured, that she must learn to piece together. But how? She hadn't given herself much of a chance, had she? She'd stuck out her foot and tripped herself at every turn, hoping for someone to pick her up, someone who might restore what had been taken a very long time ago.

Overhead, the owl *who-who-ed* again.

And if she didn't know who she was, how could Harry? If she had to conceal so much of herself, lie about the unsavory bits, or maybe it was mostly the unlucky bits, to hold him, then she could not finally keep him. To have and hold him, she had to consent to letting him go. The idea of leaving him felt brave and cleansing. Even noble.

Anyway, she couldn't have told him everything, how people survived one blow or another, that sort of thing. Mothers who had gone round the twist, piss-ants who would as soon kill you as date you. It was no one's business how one survived; survival was a private matter, and the capacity to inhabit other worlds, however temporary, to understand a murderer's heart, for instance, or the strange everywhereness of knives and fear, was no one else's concern. Harry Fairbanks had never *had* anything, really, to survive. It was Harry who was the innocent.

Finding in this realization a hard satisfaction, something she might feel, like a flat stone in her pocket, as she walked away, Charlotte tried to smile, tightening the sleeping bag around her shoulders. A fine mist of condensation had formed on the ceiling of the tent, evidence of breath and warm-bloodedness, and she reached up to run a finger through it...*Charlotte*, she wrote, the name disappearing even as it took shape.

In memory what was a life anyway but a series of *tableaux vivants* that you visited now and then, like any tourist? Harry, her fellow tourist, appreciative, eager to believe, had thought that she was actually living when what she'd been up to was arranging things for his, and perhaps everyone else's, approval. What was left now to believe in? What was real?

Briefly, she thought of the Indian's solemn expectant face, the way little girls' faces were....

But people do survive, she thought again. Somehow people survive, though the means are not always salubrious. Of course, it may have been better not to have survived. At the very least, there would have been some clarity in that. Things would have made better sense, responsibilities assigned, punishments meted out, rewards awarded. Her mother had not survived, not intact. Her father was in Ottawa, making an ad-hoc go of things. Their little family had been cut down back in Penticton, right along with all those trees. But Harry's parents...even dying, they had survived together. What a marvelous legacy.

The owl overhead had been silent for a while.

She would have to tell Harry that she had been hitchhiking, or tell the authorities—someone who might keep it from happening again to someone else.

She felt strong and somehow better—briefly—than the human that she suspected she might be.

Harry. Thinking his name, she wanted to cry. *Beautiful man.*

Harry was the sort of person you became if you'd had a normal life.

Harry was also the nicest thing that had ever happened to her, rendering him wholly unbelievable.

It was best, really, to remove herself from his life. She simply didn't deserve him. He would argue with her, but it was not an argument he could win. He had never been much good at the mazy logic of emotions.

An exciting and headlong uncertainty rushed over her. She could do anything she wanted, wreck anything she felt like wrecking. No one would care. She might even secretly survive, which would make for a different sort of wreckage. Live a solid, solitary life, independent of anyone, needing no one. She could be a gardener, a landscape architect, as they called them now, helping things to grow and thrive. People might even admire her solitariness, her way with plants; might wonder among themselves about Charlotte as she aged away from the possibilities that radiated like rolling green fields around youth.

A sound suddenly, then in the next moment a shadow spreading over the tent, followed by the laborious *whoop-whoop* of the owl's wings lifting him heavily away. Everything fell before it could rise. Even great owls.

With the owl's departure, Charlotte decided to pay a visit to Abra, say hello. The long grass was soft and dewy up to her knees, and she was glad to be barefoot in the cool morning, glad that Harry was gone and that she had had the owl to herself, glad to have Abra to visit. Dropping over the rise and down toward the glen, she saw that all three horses were gone; Reuben too she discovered gone. Only the mule remained to eye her dolefully and waggle its halter, asking for grain and attention. What every creature needed and sometimes deserved.

Rushing back to the camp, she found everything eerily in place—grub boxes, tackle, the fishing rods secured against a tree, last night's plates stacked on a log. The lid to the coffee pot was off and the pot itself filled with water and sitting on the grate, but no one had started the breakfast fire. A loaf of bread sat on a board, one piece sliced, the knife half embedded in the loaf for another piece. Off to the side Reuben's tarp lay neatly folded with a stone on top to hold it down. His book of poems too, and the cottonwood root he'd been carving. She picked it up. It was Abra, her angular face and in-pointing ears. Had he carved it for her? Harry's can of peanuts was just over there in the pine duff, exactly where he had left it when they'd been drinking whisky the night before, waiting for supper.

Why had they left her? Where? Why hadn't they waked her? How could they have left without her? Something terrible had happened and they had simply left her. Or something wonderful, and they had ridden off to see it and had forgotten her. Or she was too small, too weak, too much trouble, not worth it... She glanced over at the tent, the Doug fir towering over it, the owl gone. The air, the trees, the water, all perfectly still, the absence of sound frightening, as if the world had sucked back into itself and left her utterly alone to fend for herself.

Abruptly it seemed important to be dressed, to have some protective coating, to be ready. In the tent she pulled on her boots and a wool sweater. Still cold, she dragged the sleeping bag with her to the stump she had occupied the afternoon before, and sat to wait. Her legs felt leaden, her hands were shaking. They had taken her horse, too. They had taken her way to get away. The mule was no good. You couldn't escape on a mule inured to pack. And anyway, where to go? How to go? And what if it wasn't Harry who came back, or Reuben? What if it was someone else who found her there alone, who might take advantage, who might hurt her? Nothing was as it once was; everything felt empty and alien and hollowed out with menace. The world was no place to be.

If she hadn't reason enough to leave Harry Fairbanks before, she did now. He would pay for this. If he came back, he would pay.

She had never been that important to Harry, *never*—she realized that now. Perhaps she had known all along. It was his work, his colleagues, like Alex, who really mattered. Who held his interest. He had a whole life, rich and rewarding, and she was just...just a girl. Or another one of the subjects he had swiftly dispatched.

For the first time in her life, she hadn't the faintest idea what she would do. As if to sort it out somehow, to stumble upon the thing she must do, she got up and walked down to the lake, looked at the water, flat and impervious, knelt to feel the temperature—a swimmer's habit—without really noticing it once she had. She went and looked at the mule again, who this time ignored her. She stared at the impressions left in the long grass where the other three animals had stood and stamped for oats. No good at making fires or at cooking over one, and not even remotely hungry, she nevertheless picked up Harry's tin of peanuts and rattled it gently, carefully replacing it within its perfect circle in the duff. As afterthought, she kicked it away, finally surrendering to tears and the increasingly familiar chaos of fear.

If Harry returned she would not submit to him, to his reliable kindness, his love, his male assuredness, his categorized food. Whoever she was or might become, it was equal to Harry Fairbanks—different, but equal.

God, she hoped he would come back to her! Then she might properly leave him—on her watch. But just to see him again, coming toward her....

It was two hours before they returned, trailing Abra, lathered and wild-eyed.

She threw her head back and released a sound that might have been a word, or a hundred words.

"We almost lost her," Harry called to her with a big smile. His face was red, his eyes brightly popped with that incurable enthusiasm of his, and he looked for the first time not so perfect.

Charlotte was already up from the stump, taking Abra's halter, touching her neck. "You okay, girl?"

"She made it all the way to the other side of the lake, she was tearing up to the plateau like the world was on fire."

"Well, it was," Charlotte said, "in her mind." She pressed her face into the crease behind the Arabian's soft ears. "Abracadabra," she whispered. Then she turned to Reuben, not yet ready to look at Harry. "There was an owl right over the tent."

"An honor."

"Yes, I know," she said without really knowing why or how she knew, without caring about her tears.

Harry was beside her, one hand squeezing her shoulder and the other on the chestnut's bridle.

"I don't ride well," she said to him coolly.

"Who *could* ride this screwy mare?"

"Don't be so tolerant, Harry. It's rather mean, when you think about it. And no, I don't ride *any* horse very well. Never have."

She looked up at him then, feeling ready finally for something unnamable but essential. "And don't do that again. Go off without waking me, without telling me something."

He tipped his head and removed the hand that had rested so comfortably on her shoulder, and shoved it into his pocket. "All right, Charlotte."

Charlotte, not Char, she noticed. He was looking at her differently, as if she had changed her hair or something, but not without a curious bit of appreciation. "I guess I'm still getting used to being two."

"Yes," she said, "well, I suppose we all are."

Biographies:

Steven J. Cahill lives in the Northeast Kingdom of Vermont where his creative nonfiction and memoir pieces have been published in *Vermont Magazine, North Country Journal,* and *Good Living Review*. His prize winning fiction appearing in *Gemini Magazine* was nominated for a Pushcart Prize and the Dzanc Book Award, and three of his short stories were chosen for New Hampshire fiction anthologies. His work is also included in a Hurricane Press collection and the Catamount Arts poetry anthology.

Daniel Degnan is a recipient of the Maureen Egen Writers Exchange Award from *Poets & Writers*. His work has been published in the anthology, *2Do Before I Die,* and online by *Opium Magazine* and *Poets & Writers*. He was a Sarah Lawrence submission to *Best New American Voices* and a finalist in *Opium Magazine's* 500-word memoir contest. In addition to writing, he is CFO of Winston Preparatory School, a school for learning disabled students with campuses in New York, NY and Norwalk, CT. He holds a BS in Art and Design from MIT and an MFA in Creative Writing from Sarah Lawrence. He lives in River Vale, NJ, with his wife, Dao, and his son, Daniel.

Kristin FitzPatrick is the author of *My Pulse is an Earthquake,* a short story collection (West Virginia University Press, 2015), which was a semi-finalist for the 2014 Mary McCarthy Prize in Short Fiction. FitzPatrick's work has appeared in journals such as *Colorado Review, The Southeast Review,* and *Epiphany*. Her writing has also been chosen for the Thomas Wolfe Fiction Prize, *The New Short Fiction Series,* and *Stories on Stage*. She is the recipient of fellowships from the Jentel Artist Residency Program and The Seven Hills School. Originally from the Midwest, she now lives and writes in southern California.

Perry Glasser author of *Metamemoirs* (Outpost19, 2013) has also written four other books of prize-winning prose. *Riverton Noir* was recipient of the 2012 Gival Press Novel Award; *Dangerous Places* (BkMk Press, 2009), a short fiction collection that received the 2008 G.S. Sharat Chandra Prize; *Singing on the Titanic* (The University of Illinois Press, 1987), a book recorded by the Library of Congress for the blind, and *Suspicious Origins (New Rivers Press, 1984),* short fiction, winner of the Minnesota Voices Competition. In 2012 he was named a Fellow of The Massachusetts Cultural Council for Creative Nonfiction/Memoir. He has been in residence at The Norman Mailer House, The Virginia Center for the Creative Arts, Yaddo, and Ucross, earned his MFA in Fiction at the University of Arizona, and teaches professional writing at Salem State University.

Marie Holmes was raised in various places, but mostly in Portland, Oregon. She lives in New York and earned an MFA at Sarah Lawrence College. Her stories have appeared in the *Coe Review* and *Blithe House Quarterly,* and *Teacher's Voice.* She teaches Spanish in New York City.

Tim Mullaney is a 2005 recipient of the Asian American Writers' Workshop's Van Lier Fellowship. His shorty story *Beanstalk* was published in *Washington Square.* His play *What to Say* was given a reading by TOSOSII Theater as part of the Robert Chesley/Jane Chambers Playwrights Project and his short play *Close Your Eyes* was workshopped at the StageLeft Theatre in Chicago. Mullaney is a graduate of the Creative Writing for the Media Program at Northwestern University, where he received the 2001 T. Stephen May Award for Excellence in Scriptwriting. As an actor, he has appeared in various productions, notably the Goodman Theatre's world premiere of the Philip Glass opera *Galileo Galilei,* directed by Mary Zimmerman.

Tim Johnston is the author of the novel *Descent* (Algonquin Books, 2015), the story collection *Irish Girl,* and the Young Adult novel *Never So Green.* Published in 2009, the stories of *Irish Girl* won an O. Henry Prize, the New Letters Award for Writers, and the Gival Press Short Story Award, while the collection itself won the 2009 Katherine Anne Porter Prize in Short Fiction. Johnston's stories have also appeared in *New England Review, New Letters, The Iowa Review, The Missouri Review, Double Take, Best Life Magazine,* and *Narrative Magazine,* among others. He holds degrees from the University of Iowa and the University of Massachusetts, Amherst. In 2011-12 he was the Jenny McKean Moore Writer-in-Washington Fellow at The George Washington University, and he teaches in the Creative Writing Program at the University of Memphis.

Karenmary Penn who lived in Bermuda for several years now lives in southern California with her husband, Kevin, and her daughter, Chloe. She earned her MFA in Creative Writing at the University of Arizona. She was a Schaeffer fellow at the University of Nevada in Las Vegas. She has published stories in *Indiana Review, Red Cedar Review, Willow Springs, Gulf Coast, Pittsburgh Quarterly, Glimmer Train,* and the Chicago Tribune. She has received a Henfield fellowship, a Nelson Algren Award, and an artist fellowship grant from the Nevada Arts Council.

Iqbal Pittalwala received his M.F.A. in Creative Writing from the University of Iowa in 1995. His stories have appeared in the *Seattle Review, Confrontation, Blue Mesa Review, the Harrington Gay Men's Fiction Quarterly, Trikone Magazine,* and others. His collection of short stories *Dear Paramount Pictures: Stories* was published in 2002 by SMU Press. He lives in Southern California, where he teaches fiction writing at UC Riverside Extension, the continuing education branch of the University of California, Riverside.

Lynn Stegner is the author of five works of fiction, three of them novels—*Because a Fire Was in My Head* (which won the Faulkner Award for Best Novel and was a Literary Ventures Selection, a Book Sense Pick, and a *New York Times* Editors' Choice), *Undertow,* and *Fata Morgana*—and the novella triptych *Pipers at the Gates of Dawn* (Faulkner Society Gold Medal in the novella category). She has also written an extended critical introduction to an assembly of her father-in-law's short fiction, the *Collected Stories of Wallace Stegner,* as well as editing and writing the foreword to a Penguin edition entitled *Wallace Stegner: On Teaching and Writing Fiction*. She also has taught writing at the University of California, Santa Cruz, the University of Vermont, the National University of Ireland, Galway, the Santa Fe Writers' Workshop, and Stanford University where she is currently teaching in the Continuing Studies Program. Among other honors, she has been the recipient of a Western States Arts Council fellowship, a National Endowment for the Arts fellowship, a Fulbright Scholarship to Ireland, the Bridport Prize, and a Raymond Carver Short Story Award. The anthology, *West of 98: Living and Writing the New American West*, which she co-edited and introduced, was published in September of 2011, and her volume of stories titled *For All the Obvious Reasons* is forthcoming. She divides her time between San Francisco, California and Greensboro, Vermont.

Mark Wisniewski's novel *Watch Me Go* (Penguin Putnam) was released this year. His other novels include *Show Up, Look Good* (Gival Press, 2011) and *Confessions of a Polish Used Car Salesman*, as well as the collection of short stories *All Weekend with the Lights On* and the book of narrative poems *One of Us One Night*. His fiction has appeared in magazines such as *The Southern Review, Antioch Review, New England Review, Virginia Quarterly Review, The Yale Review, Boulevard, The Sun*, and The Georgia Review, and has been anthologized in *Pushcart Prize* and *Best American Short Stories*. His narrative poems have appeared in such venues as *The Iowa Review, Prairie Schooner, Poetry International, Ecotone, The Hollins Critic*, and *Poetry*. He's been awarded two University of California Regents' Fellowships in Fiction, an Isherwood Fellowship in Fiction, and first place in competitions for the Kay Cattarula Award for Best Short Story, and the Tobias Wolff Award. In addition, his stories have won a Pushcart Prize. He lives with his wife on a lake in upstate New York.

Books from Gival Press—Fiction & Nonfiction

The Spanish Teacher by Barbara de la Cuesta
That Demon Life by Lowell Mick White
Tina Springs into Summer / Tina se lanza al verano by Teresa Bevin
The Tomb on the Periphery by John Domini
Twelve Rivers of the Body by Elizabeth Oness

For a complete list of Gival Press titles, visit: *www.givalpress.com*.

Books are available from Ingram, Follett, Brodart, your favorite bookstore, the Internet, or from Gival Press.

Gival Press, LLC
PO Box 3812
Arlington, VA 22203

givalpress@yahoo.com
703.351.0079